Praise for David S. Pederson

Murder at Union Station

"The story is full of engaging, lively characters…I also enjoyed the diversity in the novel, which one doesn't always find in historical fiction. It was a lot of fun to unravel the mystery of what happened…well-written, suspenseful, and smoothly plotted, and it kept me guessing until the big denouement at the end. It's a fast, enjoyable cozy mystery that I enjoyed."
—*Roger Hyttinen (Roger's Reads)*

"Where this story really works is in the 1946 setting…I thoroughly enjoyed this mystery and look forward to the next one."—*Sinfully Good Gay Books Reviews*

"A Clever Murder Mystery. David always delivers an exciting story, always cleverly put together so I can never figure out 'who done it' until it is all pieced together by the detective…There is always an elegance and charm to the stories David writes, which makes them stand out."—*LESBIreviewed*

Murder on Monte Vista

"A great new mystery!…[T]he way everything is described really puts me in the moment. You feel a part of the story, and the way it is written, even though you know Mason is talking to another character, it's as if he is talking to you personally too, so it is so easy to become immersed in the story and really be a part of it. Most enjoyable, super exciting, and a series I cannot wait for more of! What a fantastic mystery!"—*LESBIreviewed*

Death's Prelude

"I highly recommend this story, introducing Heath and giving more insight to his past, as well as setting up the series nicely. The most fabulous thing though was seeing Heath blossom into the detective I met in *Death Overdue*, and I can't wait to read the next mystery he has to solve."—*LESBIreviewed*

Death Overdue

"Deftly drawn characters, brisk pacing, and an easy charm distinguish Pederson's winning follow-up to 2019's *Death Takes a Bow*. Pederson successfully evokes and shrewdly capitalizes upon the time in which his mystery takes place, using the era's prejudices and politics to heighten the story's stakes and more thoroughly invest readers in its outcome. Plausible suspects, persuasive red herrings, and cleverly placed clues keep the pages frantically flipping until the book's gratifying close."—*Mystery Scene*

"David S. Pederson never disappoints when it comes to twisted and suspenseful mysteries...I highly recommend the Detective Heath Barrington mystery series, and *Death Overdue* in particular is suspenseful and an absolute page-turner."—*QueeRomance Ink*

Lambda Literary Award Finalist
Death Takes a Bow

"[T]here's also a lovely scene near the end of the book that puts into words the feelings that Alan and Heath share for one another, but can't openly share because of the time they live in and their jobs in law enforcement. All in all, an interesting murder/mystery and an apt depiction of the times."—*Gay Book Reviews*

"This is a mystery in its purest form...If you like murder mysteries and are particularly interested in the old-school type, you'll love this book!"—*Kinzie Things*

Lambda Literary Award Finalist
Death Checks In

"David Pederson does a great job with this classic murder mystery set in 1947 and the attention to its details…"—*The Novel Approach*

"This noir whodunit is a worthwhile getaway with that old-black-and-white-movie feel that you know you love, and it's sweetly chaste, in a late-1940s way…"—*Outsmart Magazine*

"This is a classic murder mystery; an old-fashioned style mystery à la Agatha Christie…"—*Reviews by Amos Lassen*

Death Goes Overboard

"[A]uthor David S. Pederson has packed a lot in this novel. You don't normally find a soft-sided, poetry-writing mobster in a noir mystery, for instance, but he's here…this novel is both predictable and not, making it a nice diversion for a weekend or vacation."—*Washington Blade*

"Pederson takes a lot of the tropes of mysteries and utilizes them to the fullest, giving the story a knowable form. However, the unique characters and accurate portrayal of the struggles of gay relationships in 1940s America make this an enjoyable, thought-provoking read."—*Gay, Lesbian, Bisexual, and Transgender Round Table of the American Library Association*

"You've got mobsters, a fedora-wearing detective in a pinstriped suit, seemingly prim matrons, and man-hungry blondes eager for marriage. It's like an old black-and-white movie in book form…"—*Windy City Times*

Death Comes Darkly

"Agatha Christie…if Miss Marple were a gay police detective in post–WWII Milwaukee."—*PrideSource: Between the Lines*

"The mystery is one that isn't easily solved. It's a cozy mystery unraveled in the drawing room type of story, but well worked out."—*Bookwinked*

"If you LOVE Agatha Christie, you shouldn't miss this one. The writing is very pleasant, the mystery is old-fashioned, but in a good meaning, intriguing plot, well developed characters. I'd like to read more of Heath Barrington and Alan Keyes in the future. This couple has a big potential."—*Gay Book Reviews*

"[A] thoroughly entertaining read from beginning to end. A detective story in the best Agatha Christie tradition with all the trimmings."—*Sinfully Gay Romance Book Review*

By the Author

Heath Barrington Mysteries

Death Comes Darkly

Death Goes Overboard

Death Checks In

Death Takes A Bow

Death Overdue

Death's Prelude

Death Foretold

Mason Adler Mysteries

Murder on Monte Vista

Murder at Union Station

Murder at the Oasis

Puzzles Can Be Deadly

PUZZLES
CAN BE DEADLY

by

David S. Pederson

2024

PUZZLES CAN BE DEADLY

ISBN 13: 978-1-63679-615-4

This Trade Paperback Original Is Published By
Bold Strokes Books, Inc.
P.O. Box 249
Valley Falls, NY 12185

First Edition: May 2024

CREDITS
Editors: Jerry L. Wheeler and Stacia Seaman
Production Design: Stacia Seaman
Cover Design by Inkspiral Design

Acknowledgments

Special thanks to Mike Macione, Margot Beckerman, and Erin Kreger for their invaluable assistance and contributions on Ann Arbor, Michigan, and its history.

And huge thanks to Jerry Wheeler and Stacia Seaman, my editors with the most-est, as well as everyone at Bold Strokes Books who have helped me so much, especially Radclyffe, Sandy, Cindy, Ruth, and Sheri.

To all my family and my terrific friends, who are my chosen family, and of course my wonderful mom, Vondell. In memory of my dad, Manford.

And to my wonderful husband, Alan, who is always supportive and encouraging.

Finally, to all my readers. I thank you from the bottom of my heart.

CHAPTER ONE

Wednesday afternoon, October 4, 1950
Skip Valentine's apartment in Chicago

"What's a six-letter word for 'fatal,' Purrvis?" Skip said. The tabby looked over from his perch on the window sill, blinked slowly, and meowed. "'Murder'! Of course you're right. And today's a perfect day for a murder, I'd say. Weather-wise, anyway." Skip hurriedly scribbled the final letters into the squares of the newspaper puzzle and checked the small table clock, smiling broadly. He marked his time on a little pad beneath his previous entries, then set it and the newspaper aside, glancing back at his feline friend once more as he did so. "Now what shall we do?" Skip said, but Purrvis ignored him this time, his attentions focused on a little brown sparrow perched on a tree branch outside, its feathers blowing and ruffling in the harsh wind and rain. Skip sighed, got to his feet, peered out the window at the sparrow, gave Purrvis a scratch, paced about, and sat down again.

Skip was easily bored. He'd taken a bath, washed his ginger-red hair, done a load of laundry, had lunch, and finished his latest book. *Arthur Godfrey and His Friends*, a favorite program, didn't start for another two hours, and it was too early for dinner and too miserable outside to go for a walk. Absentmindedly, he picked up a *Life* magazine and flipped through it as he wondered what Henry was doing that afternoon. Almost as if on cue, the phone on the side table began to ring. He could reach it from where he sat, so he picked it up quickly.

"Hello?" he said. Skip enjoyed phone calls. They were always a mystery until the answer to that first hello, and he was glad for someone to talk to right now, no matter who it was.

"Hello, Skip, it's Henry." A rich, deep male voice resonated through the line and receiver into his left ear.

"Well, hello," he said. Mystery solved. "How are you?"

"Fine. I'm not interrupting, am I?" Henry said.

"No, not at all. I was just thinking of you, as a matter of fact, and you have perfect timing. I finished the crossword puzzle in the paper, and I broke my old record."

"As I recall, your old record was nine minutes and something."

"Nine minutes and thirty-two seconds, to be precise."

"So, what was your time today?"

"Nine minutes, twenty-nine seconds," Skip said proudly.

Henry whistled. "You are one smart cookie, Valentine."

"Thanks, but it's not so hard once you get the hang of them. I'm good at puzzles."

"Not me. I think I spent the better part of an entire afternoon on one of those crossword things once. For me, puzzles can be deadly."

Skip laughed. "Maybe we can do one together sometime."

"Sure, that could be fun. But say, I've got some news for you about this weekend."

Skip twirled the phone cord around his fingers, noting his nails needed trimming. "I've been anxious to find out what your big surprise is. I just can't imagine. All you've told me so far is that we're going somewhere. So mysterious."

"Well, I know you like a good mystery, but don't get too excited, it's not a trip to Paris or New York. How do you feel about a weekend in Ann Arbor?"

"A weekend in Ann Arbor? I'll say it's alliterative." Skip tried to keep the disappointment out of his voice. "Why do you want to go to Michigan?"

"Well, it's complicated."

"Go on," Skip said, getting to his feet. He had a feeling this would be a lengthy conversation, and the phone cord would just reach the bathroom, so he retrieved his fingernail clippers, nail file, and buffer along with a towel and returned to his place on the davenport in the living room.

"My Uncle Ambrose, Ambrose Booth Rutherford, lives in Ann

Arbor with his elderly mother. He's not technically my uncle, and I haven't seen him since way before the war. He's my mother's second cousin."

"I always get confused by first cousins once removed, second cousins, and whatnot," Skip said, spreading out the towel on top of the coffee table. "What is this Ambrose fellow to you?"

"Well, um, I'm not sure, exactly. I've always just called him Uncle Ambrose, though he's only about seventeen or eighteen years older than me. I guess technically he might be my second cousin once removed, or something like that, anyway."

"All right. But I still don't understand why you want to visit him all of a sudden," Skip said with a light chuckle, taking the clippers in his left hand as he cradled the phone receiver between his left ear and shoulder. He started on his right pinkie finger, making sure the clippings landed on the towel.

"It all boils down to money, to be honest. The Rutherford money."

"Oh? Do tell. I wasn't aware there *was* Rutherford money, or Rutherfords, before just now. Your last name is Finch."

"Yes, as I said, he's related on my mother's side. I was only vaguely aware of the money myself, being distant relations and all. I mean, we've always known that side of the family was well off, but it wasn't discussed."

"Good breeding, I suppose," Skip said. "One never talks about how much money one has."

"Or doesn't have, which in my case would be practically none," Henry said. "But anyway, two weeks ago my mother got another letter from Lillian Peacock Waters, she's the older sister of Ambrose's mother, and she lives in Traverse City, Michigan. She and my mother correspond fairly regularly, and Mom always keeps me up to date on family doings."

"Gossip by post," Skip said, finishing with his right pinkie.

"Exactly. Where else can you get all the news that's fit to print on two pages for the price of a three-cent stamp?"

"Have these Rutherfords always had money?"

"Ambrose's father Giles made a fortune in lumber at the turn of the century, but then he died from tuberculosis when Ambrose was only a year old or so and his brother Arthur was just five, leaving Arthur as the heir."

"Okay."

"But then a year or so later, Arthur died of pneumonia."

"How sad," Skip said. "And that left Ambrose as the heir."

"Yes, with a caveat that as long as his mother is alive, she has equal control of the finances. Giles wanted to make sure she was taken care of and not abandoned. My mom never met the older child, doesn't remember him since he died at the age of five, and doesn't know Ambrose all that well. He used to come down to Chicago fairly regularly, but it's been some time. I've never been to Ann Arbor and have never met his mother."

"This is all rather interesting, Henry, but I still don't see why you want to spend a weekend with these people. It sounds like you hardly know them."

"I suppose it does seem odd. But it all comes back to the most recent letter my Great-Aunt Lillian Waters sent. In it, she told my mother that Gabria, Ambrose's mother, is in poor health and declining rapidly. When she passes, the estate will go to Ambrose. Since he has never married and has no male children, if he remains single and childless when he dies, it goes to the next oldest male relative. Believe it or not, that's me. Our family tree is pretty tight."

"It would have to be a male relative," Skip said as he finished his right hand. "All that patriarchal nonsense."

"Well, in this case, it benefits me since I'm a male, so I'm not going to argue."

"A homosexual male, to be precise. I take it they don't know?"

"They *definitely* don't know. I think if they did, they'd find an excuse to overlook me as the heir."

"Our little secret, then," Skip said. "And knock me over with a feather. I'm dating an heir and I didn't know it." He switched the receiver to his right ear and cradled it on his shoulder once more as he started on his left.

"Uncle Ambrose is only in his early forties and apparently in good health, so I wouldn't get too excited. Still, Great-Aunt Lillian said I should plan a trip to Ann Arbor and sign some papers at Mrs. Rutherford's lawyer's office sooner rather than later, just as a formality. The rest of the family has already signed."

"What kind of papers? I mean, if you're the heir, why do you have to sign anything? Wouldn't it just all be in the will of your uncle's mother, or his?"

"I don't know. Legal stuff. They probably have certain terms I have to agree to in order to get the money when and if the time comes."

"Well, don't sign anything you haven't read and understood."

"I won't, don't worry. Anyway, I figured this might be a good time to head up there and take care of it since I'm in between jobs for a few days, and you already told me you have some time off from the library."

"Right, I work tomorrow, but then I don't have to be back until Tuesday. They're having the whole place fumigated for bookworms."

Henry laughed again. "I don't know why, but I find that funny."

"Bookworm is a generic term applied to silverfish, spider beetles, paper worms, and more. Since they all feed on paper and thus books, a bookworm is considered someone who likes to read."

"I didn't know that was where the term came from. I can tell you've been spending time on the research desk at work."

"One of my favorite places to be. You know, I'm surprised your Uncle Ambrose never married. Is he that awful?"

"On the contrary, I remember him as being attractive and bright. I guess he never found the right girl."

"Or perhaps the right fellow," Skip said.

"Maybe. Maybe it runs in the family. Or perhaps he's heterosexual and he'll still find his mate. It only takes one, but you have to find him or her, and you never know where or when that will happen," Henry said. "I found mine in the middle of a crosstown bus on Valentine's Day when he knocked me in the head with a baton."

"It was standing room only, and my baton was under my arm. *You* were lucky enough to have a seat. My baton barely touched you as the bus took a sharp turn."

"It knocked my hat off."

"And I picked it up for you, gentleman that I am. *And* apologized profusely."

"And then I asked you why on earth you were carrying a baton on a bus in the first place."

"Because I was on my way home from marching band practice, of course."

"So you said."

"It was true. And you got off at my stop and followed me home."

"I didn't follow you home, I walked with you."

"And when we reached the front door of my apartment building you asked me to dinner that very night."

Henry chuckled. "And you said yes, though I found out later you'd just finished an early supper after practice."

Skip laughed, too. "I was so full, but you were so charming, my proverbial tall, dark, and handsome man, that I couldn't say no."

"I'm glad you didn't."

"Thanks, me too—though I could barely eat a bite."

"I thought you were such a light eater and a cheap date. You only ordered a salad and no dessert."

"Well, I've made up for it since then. By the way, how did you know I was a fellow homosexual? You never did say."

"I didn't know for sure, but you *were* carrying a baton. And you're a bit of a dandy. I think you were the only man on the bus in a bowler hat, a full three-piece suit with a gold watch in your vest pocket, handkerchief in your suit pocket, cufflinks, spit-shined oxfords, and two rings on each hand, carrying a Louis Vuitton satchel and a baton. Do you always dress like that for marching band practice?"

"Don't be silly. We practiced in the gymnasium, and I changed in the locker room before and after."

"Sure, but you have to admit you were a tad overdressed for the crosstown bus. I had on a simple suit and tie, like most of the other men."

"And you looked extremely handsome in it, I'll never forget. But getting back to your uncle."

"What about him?"

"I can't help but think that an attractive, rather bright, wealthy man would be in high demand. And if he's in his early forties, he's still fairly young."

"He *was* serious about one woman, I guess. His mother wrote my mother a letter a year or so ago telling her all about it, speaking of gossip."

"Oh?"

"Yeah. She was an actress. I can still remember her name, Marjorie Banning. Same name as my old English teacher in high school."

"What happened to her?"

"Gosh, Mrs. Banning must be in her eighties by now, if she's still alive. I'm sure she retired from teaching long ago."

"Henry Finch, you know full well I meant the actress."

Henry chuckled once more. "Sorry, I couldn't resist. According to my mom, Mrs. Rutherford took tremendous pride in running Miss Banning off. She felt an actress was beneath her son, which is funny considering she wanted to be an actress as a young girl, I'm told."

"Hypocritical," Skip said.

"Definitely. And Ambrose hasn't cut the apron strings yet. He's over forty and still lives with her, so there you go."

"Mrs. Rutherford sounds like a tough cookie."

"Yes. But if Miss Banning was truly a love interest, that would be the answer to which way my uncle swings, so to speak."

"Not necessarily. She could have been a smoke screen."

"That's possible, I suppose. I've heard of men doing that."

"So have I, and with a mother like that I'd say it's very possible. So, you want to go to Ann Arbor to sign those papers this weekend, is that it?"

"Well, yes. I sent Uncle Ambrose a letter a week ago, asking if it would be all right if we stayed at the house, but Mrs. Rutherford is the one who responded and said we were welcome to visit. Frankly, I was surprised."

"If she's in as bad a shape as this Mrs. Waters says she is, perhaps she wants to finally meet you before she dies," Skip said. "Maybe she wants to critique the second in line to the Rutherford money and see if she approves." Two nails on the left hand done.

"I hadn't thought of that, but you could be right. Hopefully, I'll measure up."

"You'll measure up and then some, but are you sure you want me along?"

"Of course. Having you by my side will only add to my confidence. You're charming, handsome, and smart. With you there, how could I lose?"

"You do know how to sell me on a trip to Ann Arbor, but won't they wonder who I am and why I'm there?"

"I already told them in my letter that you're a friend, a buddy, and that you would be coming with me. We'll be in separate rooms, I'm sure, just two young bachelors."

"That doesn't sound like much fun." Three nails on the left hand done.

"Plenty of time for fun when we get back. Who knows, maybe we can sneak in a rendezvous late at night while we're there."

"Now, that sounds better," Skip said. "You're hard to resist, you know. It would be challenging behaving myself all weekend."

"Sweet talker. What I still can't figure out is, what does a guy like you see in a crazy old man like me?"

"What are you talking about? You're bright, funny, and dangerously gorgeous. And you're not old. You're only twenty-five."

"Thanks for that, and you're only twenty-two. Your whole future ahead of you."

"You have your whole future ahead of you, too."

Henry paused and let out a long, slow breath. "Some future. I was discharged from the Army three years ago, and now with the war in Korea I may end up being recalled."

"And *I* may get drafted. Maybe we could go together."

"You're exempt from military service because you have flat feet."

"What's that got to do with anything?" Skip said.

"I did some checking because I was worried about you. They say anyone diagnosed with flat feet is not suited to marching and could sustain spinal injuries and is therefore exempt. And your feet, as cute as they are, are as flat as Donald Duck's."

"Gee, thanks. Well, maybe you won't get recalled to active duty."

"Maybe. I could even end up stateside with the Army National Guard, but hard to say. If it happens, at least I'll have a steady income and three squares a day again. I gotta tell you, Skip, being an heir to the Rutherford fortune sounds pretty swell, but in the here and now I'm not much of a catch. I'm dead broke, living in a one-room apartment on Sheridan Road, no job…"

"You *do* have a job," Skip said. Only the left thumb to go.

"Yeah, fry cook at Daley's on Cottage Grove Avenue. You must be so proud. I start next Wednesday."

"There's nothing wrong with being a fry cook, Henry. Besides, it's only until you can find something else."

"What I need to do is finish school, but money is in short supply right now. To be honest, when I wrote Uncle Ambrose, I also asked him for a loan, just temporarily, until I can get on my feet and go back to college. I'm laying out my heart and soul to you, Skip. I'm not proud to have to ask for a loan, but the way I see it, it's my money, too, since I'm a member of the family."

"Asking for a loan is nothing to be ashamed of, Henry. But *I* have money. My folks, as much as I miss them, left me pretty well off. Very well off, as a matter of fact. It's the least they could have done after naming me Horace Quintus Valentine."

"That is quite a mouthful."

"No kidding. They named me after Quintus Horatius Flaccus, better known as Horace, a Roman poet during the time of Augustus."

"Yikes, I guess it's a good thing they didn't go with Horatius Flaccus Valentine. Either way, Skip fits you better."

"I think so, too. My uncle gave me the nickname Skipper when I was five, and it eventually became just Skip. He was a sailor."

"In the Navy?"

"In the yacht club. Anyway, I'd be happy to loan you some money."

"Absolutely not, out of the question."

"Why?"

"Because family is one thing. We've only known each other a few months."

"Eight months as of the fourteenth. And you, mister, are a stubborn man."

"It's one of my best qualities," Henry said.

"I can think of other qualities of yours I like better, but have it your way. So, what did your uncle or whatever he is say about the loan?"

"He didn't say anything, because it was his mother that wrote me back, remember? Boy, does she have bad penmanship. She didn't mention the money or the loan, but she did say we're more than welcome for the weekend. I thought perhaps if we went, I could talk to Ambrose about it in person, maybe be more persuasive."

"You *can* be persuasive. I know that firsthand."

"Thanks. I'm hoping my uncle will be as appreciative of my talents and take pity on me."

"So, we're off to Ann Arbor, then." Left hand done also, he set the nail clippers on the side table and picked up the nail file, smoothing out any rough edges.

"Right, if that's okay. Do you mind?"

"I guess not. I've never been to Ann Arbor, and it might be fun."

"Splendid. I'm not sure about fun, but with you along it will be more tolerable, anyway. And my mom will be happy you're coming with me, too. She seems to like you, not that I'm surprised."

"And I like your mother. She's a peach."

"Funny you should say that. She told me she's going to make a peach cobbler for us to take. It's a Finch family tradition. Anyone we go to visit overnight gets a peach cobbler, like it or not."

"In my family, it's a buttermilk pie. Maybe I'll make one for you sometime."

"I'd like that. My mouth is watering already."

"Good. So, a trip to Ann Arbor. Well, I'm on board if you are."

"Thanks, Skip. That means a lot to me."

"Of course. *You* mean a lot to me. Are we taking the train?"

"No. I looked at the schedules, and the times aren't that appealing. We'll drive."

And driving is less expensive, Skip thought. "All right, good. I prefer driving anyway. But what are we driving in? Neither of us has a car."

"Not to worry. My friend Bernie said I could borrow his '39 Ford Coupe."

"Oh, okay. When do we leave? When are they expecting you?"

"I said we would get there sometime Friday afternoon. How about I pick you up early, say six thirty? It's about a five-hour trip, so we'll arrive close to lunch."

"Will they be okay with that? It seems rude to show up hungry and at meal time."

"Hmm, perhaps you're right. How about I pick you up at ten, then?"

"That sounds much more civilized. Besides, it takes me a while to get ready, you know. I don't do well with early mornings."

"I remember. I'll pick you up at ten, and we can stop at a diner in Kalamazoo, which is about the halfway point."

"Okay. What should I pack?"

"Mrs. Rutherford told me dinner is served at seven. And she said they don't dress for it."

"Oh my, that must make for an interesting evening. Hopefully they don't serve hot soup."

"Skip..."

"I'm just kidding, Henry. Honestly, that makes it easier, not dressing."

"For me, too. My one and only tuxedo has been in mothballs since before the war. It would need days to air out."

They heard a distinct click on the line.

"Hello?" Henry said.

"This is Mrs. Granger. I need the phone, please," an elderly voice said.

"Sorry, Mrs. Granger. We're almost through," Henry said.

"Thank you." The line clicked again as she disconnected.

"Party lines, ugh. I suppose we'd better hang up."

"Yeah, I suppose so. I'll see you Friday at ten, and we'll head back Sunday morning after breakfast. I'm assuming you're okay with missing church."

"Wouldn't be the first time. Just because my father was a church usher and my mother the organist and member of the choir doesn't mean I inherited their pious ways."

Henry laughed again. "You most certainly didn't. I'd say about the only thing religious you inherited is the ability to be on your knees for a lengthy time."

"Flatterer. I'll see you Friday morning, Finch."

"See you then, Valentine."

Skip hung up the receiver and rolled his head about, cracking his neck. "Well, Purrvis," he said, carefully picking up the towel from the coffee table, "looks like I'll have to find someone to watch you for the weekend, and I'll have to figure out what one packs for a weekend in Ann Arbor."

CHAPTER TWO

Friday morning, October 6, 1950
Skip Valentine's apartment in Chicago

Skip stepped out of the shower and dried off with a fluffy white bath towel before walking into the bedroom, where Purrvis had taken up a spot on the bed, licking himself clean. Skip gave him a scratch on top of the head, to which he responded with a noisy purr. He had one of the loudest purrs Skip had ever heard, which was why he named him Purrvis when he found him in the street, flea-bitten, skinny, and forlorn. "Mrs. Notley from down the hall will look in on you while I'm gone, my friend. Be kind to her. No scratching and no biting."

Purrvis purred louder, still licking himself.

"That's right, get yourself nice and clean, dear boy, like I just did. Now I have to get dressed, though. Sometimes I envy you not having to deal with clothes."

Skip walked over to the closet and the dresser and extracted various garments, laying them out on the bed next to his already-packed suitcases. Purrvis watched, suspending his self-cleaning temporarily, as Skip put on white cotton briefs and a crewneck T-shirt, followed by a white dress shirt with silver cufflinks and new green pleated trousers. Green and white argyle socks were next, followed by black wingtips, a black leather belt, green tie, and a black single-button sport coat with a white pocket square. He put his gold pocket watch and fob in his pocket and picked up his black Hamburg and gave it a quick brush, setting it jauntily atop his head. Finished, he admired himself in the full-length mirror, then twirled around, making sure the back was all right, too. "Well, Purrvis, what do you think?"

"Meow," he answered loudly.

Skip smiled. "Thanks, buddy. You look good, too. Very handsome indeed, and divinely clean." He carried his suitcases out to the hall, then went back for his raincoat and umbrella, giving Purrvis a final kiss and a scratch behind the ears. He locked the door of his apartment and walked down to 212, where he gave a spare key to Mrs. Notley, with last-minute instructions on the cat's care and feeding. Assured all would be well, Skip put on his raincoat and carried his bags and umbrella down to the sidewalk, pacing back and forth in the morning fog waiting for Henry. The weather was dirty, damp, and dreary, not much improved from the last two days. He tugged his raincoat close about him as he continued to pace, careful to avoid puddles. To pass the time he practiced his twirling, using his umbrella as a baton, throwing it up in the air, spinning it about, and catching it behind his back, much to the bewilderment of one of his neighbors, watching from a window.

Finally, at one minute to eleven, just as Skip executed a perfect backhanded catch, Henry drove around the corner, ground the gears of his friend's cherry red 1939 Ford De Luxe coupe, and stopped close to the curb. He grinned as he hopped out and zipped around the front of the car to where Skip was standing, looking him up and down.

"Well, as I live and breathe, Valentine, you look smashing."

"How can you tell? I'm covered practically head to toe in my raincoat."

"Yeah, but it's a divine raincoat."

Skip laughed, taking in Henry's blue and white houndstooth coat, white shirt, navy blue trousers, and tie. His short, dark brown hair was parted on the side, slicked down, and swept back. "Not so bad yourself, Finch, quite fetching."

"Thanks, I manage to dress myself okay sometimes. All done playing with your umbrella?"

Skip frowned. "I wasn't playing, I was practicing, I'll have you know, in place of my baton."

"I thought you were going to quit the marching band."

"I'm only going to participate in parades and such, but I still need to practice."

"You're the only fellow I know who knows how to twirl a baton."

"Believe me, I got ribbed about it all through high school, but I stuck with it."

"Good for you, and I admire your gumption and coordination." He glanced down at Skip's bags. "Jeepers, two suitcases? We're only going for the weekend."

"You, Mr. Finch, don't understand what all goes into looking like a dandy, as you say. Besides, one never knows about the weather."

"Aw, it will clear up soon, I can feel it." He opened the trunk of his car and squeezed the two cases in next to his banged-up old suitcase, the spare tire, and a tool kit. A rusty metal box was wedged in along the side. "There we go, all set. You can stick your baton, uh, umbrella, I mean, behind the seat."

"Very funny. What's that, by the way?" Skip asked, pointing to the rusty gray metal container.

"Oh, my tackle box, of course. My fishing pole is on the floor of the car. I had to angle it to get it in. I bet there's some good fishing in the Huron River."

"Fishing? You never said anything about going fishing this weekend, Henry."

He looked abashed. "Oh, didn't I? Well, only if we have time and opportunity, of course. And if you want to, naturally."

"Isn't it a little out of season?"

"Nah, you can fish for trout well into the middle of October. Do you like fishing, Skip? I guess we never talked about it before."

Skip tried to look cross, but couldn't. Instead, he laughed. "I'm no good at it, but sure, I like to fish, I suppose. I've only tried it once or twice. Did you bring more than one pole?"

"Er, no, but I'm sure we can borrow one."

"Uh-huh, if there's time for it."

Then they both laughed, and Henry slammed the trunk shut as Skip opened the passenger door and climbed in. "Careful of the peach cobbler. I thought maybe it would be safer on the floor up here with us rather than in the trunk," Henry said.

"I'll keep an eye on it, but don't blame me if there's a piece or two missing by the time we get there," Skip said with a mischievous smile.

Henry smiled back at him and then went around to the driver's side, climbed in behind the wheel, and they took off.

Chapter Three

Midday Friday, October 6, 1950
En route to Ann Arbor

"What's our route?" Skip said as Henry steered the car south through the fog on Federal Street toward West Van Buren on their way out of Chicago.

"I marked it in pencil on the maps in the glove box I got from the gas station. You can be my navigator, if you don't mind."

"Sure. I'm good at reading maps *and* I can fold them back up again."

Henry smiled. "As I said, you're a smart cookie, Valentine. A man of many talents."

Skip smiled back as he opened the glove box and unfolded the maps of Illinois and Michigan, noting the heavy pencil lines Henry had drawn from Chicago to Ann Arbor. "Looks pretty straightforward."

"Seems to be, 41 to Highway 12. Even if we stop in Kalamazoo for lunch, we should get to my uncle's place around three or so."

"Sounds good to me," Skip said.

They drove north, listening to music on WLS 890 AM out of Chicago until they lost the signal, then Skip fiddled with the dial until they picked up a South Bend, Indiana, station. That lasted to Kalamazoo, where they stopped for lunch. Henry pulled into the Brook Meadow Diner right off the highway, the weather much improved. The sign on the roof of the diner proudly proclaimed it had twenty-four-hour service and featured the Big Chief Indian burger with cheese.

"Those poor people," Skip said, getting out of the car and glancing up at the sign once more. He slipped off his raincoat and left it on the seat.

"Who?" Henry said.

"The natives, of course. I don't think it's very dignified to name a hamburger after them. Did you know in 1833 they were cheated out of five million acres of their land for $40,000 in trinkets and trappings? And in 1840, they were forced to relocate across the Mississippi River."

"Well look at you, all interested in history," Henry said as they walked toward the doors of the diner.

"History is fascinating, I think. When you said we were stopping in Kalamazoo on the phone the other day, I decided to read up on its history at the library yesterday. And on Ann Arbor, too, among other things. I found out that Ann Arbor was founded in 1824. It's the county seat and home to the University of Michigan. It was also home to the Potawatomi, until white settlers who were after lumber and land forced them out."

"Men like Ambrose's father, I suppose. It's sad what happened to the natives."

"I think so, Henry. I wish more people did. They were here first."

"Yes, this country belongs to them. You have a big heart, Skip."

"Thanks, but so do you."

"Well, right now my stomach is feeling big *and* empty. Come on, let's get something to eat."

They declined the Big Chief burger, both deciding instead on the grilled cheese sandwich with a tomato slice and a pickle for forty-five cents, along with two large Cokes. While they waited for their food, seated across from each other in a red vinyl booth, Skip filled Henry in on more of the history of Oshkosh and Ann Arbor.

When they had finished eating, the bill was paid, and they were back in the car, Henry turned the wheel out onto Highway 12 again, stopping only briefly for gas just up the road. With the tank full, the windows washed, and the oil checked, they started once more, listening to the Perry Como hour on the radio as they chatted back and forth about the news of the day, roadside attractions they passed, and who they thought was going to win the World Series.

After about two hours, they crossed into the city limits of Ann Arbor, ending up on Huron Street.

"Your pencil line ends here," Skip said. "What's the address of your uncle's house?"

"It's 1117 Woodlawn. Check the Ann Arbor map. It should be in the glove box, too."

Skip found it beneath a battered old flashlight and a pair of blue woolen mittens with holes in them. "Okay, got it." He scanned it, using the river to orient himself. "Keep going on Huron to State Street. Then take that to Packard, then turn left on Woodlawn Avenue."

"Perfect, thanks," Henry said.

They drove slowly through the neighborhoods, arriving in front of a faded beauty of an era not so long ago, badly in need of a paint job and repairs. A porch ran across the center third of the house, with four large marble columns supporting an ornate balustraded balcony. Four sets of windows, two up and two down, stood on either side of the center portion.

"This must be it," Henry said, turning off the ignition and setting the brake. "Quite a place."

"Big, if a bit run down," Skip said. "What exactly does Ambrose Booth Rutherford do, anyway? I don't think you ever said."

"Do?"

"For a living. You mentioned his father was a lumber baron, but what does he do?"

"Oh, well, I don't think he does much of anything. He lives on his investments and a fat bank account, I guess."

"Gee, doesn't that get boring?"

Henry laughed. "I'd like to be bored like that."

"You know what I mean. How does he pass the time, day in and day out?"

"I know he likes to golf and play tennis. He's a premier member of the Barton Hills Country Club. I'm sure he'll be happy to tell you about it."

"I'm sure we can find other things to discuss," Skip said. "Like why doesn't he fix the place up a little if he has so much money?"

"It does look like it could use a little tender loving care."

Skip gazed out the car window. "Yes. And it looks like there was a fire in that outbuilding."

Henry saw an old two-story carriage house set back from the street, now probably used as a garage. The left side had been burned and the walls charred and blackened, like scars and bruises on a boxer's face. "Good thing it didn't spread to the main house. And speaking of, I suppose we should go in."

"Yes, I suppose so. Glum-looking place, though."

"Maybe it's cheerier on the inside," Henry said as they got out. Skip stepped onto the boulevard, his raincoat over his arm and his umbrella under it, and took another look at the house. From behind a pink lace drapery in one of the second-story windows, he glimpsed a wisp of a woman staring down at them. Skip gave a little wave to her, as it seemed the polite thing to do, but the old lady retreated hastily behind the curtain.

"Did you see that woman in the upstairs window?" Skip asked as Henry wrestled the suitcases out of the trunk of the Ford coupe.

"What woman?" Henry said, slamming the trunk down and catching the edge of his thumb. "Son of a motherless goat," he said, his face contorted in a combination of anger and pain.

Skip stifled a laugh. "Ouch, are you hurt?"

He stuck his thumb in his mouth, looking for all the world like a wounded little boy. "I'm fine," he mumbled, removing his thumb and shaking his hand back and forth.

"Nothing broken? Not bleeding?"

"No and no. I'm fine."

"Good. If we weren't in public, I'd kiss it to make it all better."

"That would definitely make it all better. Thanks, Valentine."

"Don't mention it, Finch," Skip said as he picked up one of his suitcases.

"So, what were you saying about a woman?" Henry said, still nursing his thumb.

Skip looked up again, but the windows were now all empty as they stared back at him like soulless eyes. "An old lady was watching us from that upstairs window on the right. I waved to her, and she vanished."

"Probably Uncle Ambrose's mother. Or maybe a ghost. Who knows?" Henry said. "It looks like an ancient house, probably a few people have died here. Anyway, I think I can manage mine and one of your two suitcases, plus my tackle box," he said, "if you can carry the peach cobbler and your other case."

"Why don't you leave the tackle box in the car?"

"There are valuable supplies in there, Skip. Lures I hand tied, lead sinkers, all kinds of stuff. You clearly don't understand the art of fishing."

Skip sighed but didn't respond as he retrieved the tin from the floor of the car and carried the peach cobbler and his suitcase across the wide, sagging porch, Henry trailing behind.

Skip pressed the doorbell, and they waited. Presently the resplendently carved wooden door creaked open, and they were face-to-face with a slender woman wearing a black skirt, white blouse, and a green cardigan sweater. She wore her curly, light blond hair, kissed ever so slightly with silver, fairly short. Just a hint of lipstick on her lips, nothing else in the way of makeup, and she didn't need it, Skip thought.

"May I help you?" the woman said flatly.

Henry set the bags down on the porch. "Good day. I'm Mr. Finch, and this is my friend, Mr. Valentine. We're here from Chicago. Are you Mrs. Rutherford?"

The woman looked them up and down, one to the other. "No, I am not. Mrs. Rutherford is over twice my age and in ill health. I'm Jane Grant, the housekeeper."

"Oh," Henry said. "My apologies, of course. How stupid of me. How do you do? I mean, er, what should we call you? I'm afraid I don't have much experience with domestics. I thought they wore uniforms, or at least an apron."

The woman drew her sweater closed and stared at him scornfully. "Miss Grant will do. I don't see the need for a uniform. I wear what I want, and the Rutherfords are fine with it." She frowned ever so slightly. "A bit of work getting ready for you, and not much time to do it. I wasn't exactly sure what time today you'd be arriving."

"Oh, I'm so sorry," Henry said.

"Last-minute house guests are difficult. I had to get your rooms prepared and aired out, menus planned, groceries bought, linens washed, mattresses flipped and turned, and a cake baked. You've no idea."

"I do apologize, but we were under the impression you were expecting us. I sent a letter and Mrs. Rutherford responded over a week ago," Henry said.

"Mrs. Rutherford," the housekeeper said, clicking her tongue. "That's the crux of the problem right there. Come inside."

The two of them stepped into the entryway, which was dark and dull, much like the outside of the house. In the center of the back wall, opposite the front door, was a set of double doors with stained glass windows set into the upper halves. Beneath their feet, the tile inlay was chipped and worn.

"This way," Miss Grant said, pushing open the stained glass doors and leading them into the formidable main hall. The floor was dark walnut, worn down and rutted in spots from years of footsteps. Above their heads, a heavy old glass and iron chandelier hugged the fourteen-foot-high plaster ceiling. At the far end of the hall, a wide staircase rose gracefully up to a landing, turned left, and climbed to another landing before continuing a short distance toward the front of the house. Three matching stained glass windows, centered on the back wall, filtered in the murky light. So much for being cheerier on the inside, Skip thought.

"The necessary room and door to the backyard and basement are through that door under the landing. The kitchen is just beyond, not that you'll need to go in there. Should you require anything, you've only to ring," Miss Grant said. "Did you want to freshen up after your drive?"

"I'm fine for now. We stopped for lunch, and I used the men's room at the restaurant. Henry?"

"I'm fine, too, thanks for asking."

"It's my job. Set your bags by the doors. Jake will take them up to your rooms. Put yours on the right, Mr. Valentine, and yours on the left, Mr. Finch, so I can tell him whose is whose," she said.

"Yes, ma'am," Henry said. "I'll leave my tackle box here, too, if that's all right."

"Your what?"

"My tackle box. I brought it in case there was any time to do some fishing."

"I see. Yes, of course, put it with the other bags. Mr. Valentine, you can leave your raincoat and umbrella as well. What's that?" Miss Grant said, pointing toward the tin container Skip held.

"A peach cobbler from Mrs. Finch, for Mr. and Mrs. Rutherford," Skip said.

"I'll take it to the kitchen," she said, reaching for it.

"No, thank you. We'll give it to them ourselves," Henry said. "My mother insisted."

Jane stared at Henry for just a moment before withdrawing her outstretched hands. "Very well, this way." She walked to an oversized door on the left side of the hall, stepped inside, and held it open for Henry and Skip. "Wait here in the blue drawing room. I'll let Mr. Rutherford and the sister know you've arrived." She turned and left without another word, closing the door behind her.

"Jeepers," Skip said.

"Yeah, she sure is something."

"Who's this sister?"

"I'm not sure. As far as I know, Uncle Ambrose didn't have a sister. I guess we'll find out. Seems kind of dark in here—oppressive."

"I noticed that." Skip, still carrying the peach cobbler, walked over to one of the windows facing Woodlawn Street and peered out. "I don't think these have been washed, inside or out, in years. There's a film over them, and it's filtering the light. Gloomy."

"Miss Grant's not doing her job," Henry said.

"Don't let her hear you say that."

"She probably does have good ears. Those types usually do."

"Yes," Skip said. "She called this the blue drawing room, and I can see why. Blue wallpaper, blue furnishings, blue rug, yet it's all dull and flat."

"Yes, the woodwork has a gray cast to it, darkened by years of coal fires and gas lights before electricity came to Ann Arbor, I suspect. It's an old house."

Skip sniffed the stale air. "It smells old. I imagine that scent is embedded deep into the brick and mortar." He surveyed the rest of the room. The back wall held a fireplace similar to one that was in the hall. To the right of it stood a forlorn upright piano, and to the left a solid-looking door. "I wonder where that goes."

Almost as if in answer, a woman emerged. She wore a long-sleeved black tunic that kissed the floor and hid her feet, with a white apron over that in the front and back. She swayed from side to side when she walked, giving her the appearance of a penguin, which Henry found amusing. The tunic was secured about her waist by a woolen belt, from which hung a set of rosary beads. Upon her head and shoulders was a plain white wimple that exposed only her pale face, with a black veil at the back that flowed down to her shoulders. Her complexion was smooth and pale, free of makeup, and her eyes, set behind a pair of thick horn-rimmed glasses, were a brilliant blue beneath bushy eyebrows. She wore no jewelry except for a heavy gold cross about her neck and a small, simple silver band on the ring finger of her left hand.

"You're Mr. Valentine and Mr. Finch," she said. Her voice was strong, but her words were slightly garbled as if she had marbles in her mouth.

"Yes, that's right," Skip said. "I'm Skip Valentine. And you are?"

The nun peered at them over the top of her glasses. "I'm Sister Barnabas. Jane told me and Mr. Rutherford that you'd arrived. I was in the dining room having tea. You shouldn't have come."

"I beg your pardon?" Henry said.

"This is not a good time for a visit. We're caring for Mrs. Rutherford. I'm a nurse. She told us only yesterday that you were coming as if she'd just remembered. She's forgetful lately," the sister said. Her teeth, Skip thought, seemed too big for her mouth. "Mrs. Rutherford is not well. She hasn't been for many months. You shouldn't have come without speaking to her son first."

"I'm terribly sorry. We don't mean to impose. I did write my uncle a letter asking if it would be all right to visit, but his mother is the one who replied and said it would be okay. I suppose I should have telephoned to confirm, but it's long-distance, and I'm a bit short of funds at the moment. I didn't want to reverse the charges."

"I see. Well, you're here now. Mr. Rutherford would say it's God's will."

"What would you say, Sister?" Skip said. He was annoyed at being told once more they weren't welcome in this dreary, ancient, soulless house.

The nun looked at him. "I would say God works in mysterious ways. He'll be down shortly."

"God will be down shortly?" Skip said.

"Don't be cheeky, Mr. Valentine. It's not becoming a gentleman. Mr. Rutherford will be down shortly. Good day." The nun turned and left through the same door, closing it firmly behind her.

Skip looked at Henry, who was standing next to him, mouth agape. "Close your mouth, Henry."

"What was that all about?"

Skip shrugged. "I've no idea. But I'm sure we'll find out."

"I'm not certain I want to find out."

"I know exactly what you mean. This house, these people. It's rather unsettling and not very welcoming."

"And a talking penguin. Granted, one with some kind of a speech impediment, but nonetheless…"

"Henry Finch, that's not polite."

"Sorry."

"It's all right. I guess I wasn't expecting a royal welcome, but I wasn't exactly expecting this, either."

"Nor me."

"Do you think we should leave?"

Henry shrugged. "I don't know. Let's wait and see what Uncle Ambrose has to say first. I certainly don't want to intrude if this is a bad time."

"I agree. At least we now know who the sister was that Miss Grant referred to."

"Right," Henry said.

The door from the hall opened and a gentleman stepped in, closing the door behind him. He was in his middle or early forties, dressed in a double-breasted navy suit with a red tie and white pocket square. He had a kind face, with a deep crease across his forehead, his brownish blond hair receding and thin. When he smiled at them, it seemed as though his entire face smiled. He strode toward Henry and Skip with an easy gait, hand outstretched. Henry grasped it firmly.

"Henry, how delightful to see you. My goodness, it's been years. You're looking well," the man said and then looked over to Skip.

"And you're Mr. Valentine, I presume. Such a pleasure to meet you." He shook Skip's hand also before turning back to Henry. "I'm so glad you both decided to visit."

"Thank you, Uncle Ambrose," Henry said. "It's good of you to put us up for the weekend. However, the sister was just in here, and she mentioned this may not be an opportune time for a visit. We can certainly come back another weekend."

"Nonsense, I wouldn't think of it. You came all that way from

Chicago. Don't listen to Sister Barnabas. Your visit just caught us by surprise, that's all. You see, my mother intercepted your letter and responded to it without consulting me. We were only made aware of your impending arrival late yesterday when Mother made an offhand remark. We weren't entirely sure we believed you were coming until I telephoned your mother this morning. I tried to reach you, but you'd left already."

"I'm so sorry about that, Uncle. I assumed you were expecting us."

Ambrose held up a hand. "Think nothing of it, please. All's well that ends well. Jane has prepared the two guest rooms for you, so everything's in order."

"Thank you, you're too kind. Speaking of my mother, your aunt sent her a letter not long ago. She mentioned your mother not being well, and Sister Barnabas brought it up too, just now," Henry said.

Ambrose's expression turned softer, almost melancholy. "Dear Aunt Lillian. Always sticking her nose in where it doesn't belong. It's a wonder she has a nose left. She's also coming sometime this weekend, God help us all. Her plan is to move Mother into a nursing home first thing Monday morning."

"Well, er, yes, I didn't know that, but she did mention I should sign some papers at the lawyer's office while I'm here."

"Collier, Cole, and Karbouski."

"Sorry?"

"The family lawyers. No doubt Aunt Lillian wants you to sign some letter of intent or some other legal nonsense since you're my heir."

"She did mention something along those lines."

"Well, don't get too excited, my good boy. I don't plan on going anywhere for some time."

"Oh no, I didn't mean to imply—"

Mr. Rutherford held up a hand again and smiled. "It's all right. I'm only joshing with you. Their office is nearby on the corner of Wells and Packard." He consulted his watch. "You may wish to go this afternoon. They're closed on the weekend."

"I will. Anyway, I was sorry to hear about your mother."

"Thank you. She hasn't been well for several months. She has moments of lucidity, of course, but then there are times…well, you'll meet her. I think she'll like you both. It may do her some good to have some new people about. She hasn't left the house in weeks."

"If you're certain we're not imposing, Mr. Rutherford," Skip said.

He smiled once more, and his brown eyes sparkled. "Not at all, Mr. Valentine. If two young men like yourselves would be considered an imposition, I should want to be imposed upon every day."

Perhaps this weekend will be okay after all, Skip thought.

"Why don't we all sit down and visit for a bit? We have so much to catch up on," Mr. Rutherford said. "I can have Jane bring us some refreshments."

"We'd like that, Uncle, but it's been a long drive, and I think Skip and I would like to get settled first. And I suppose I should get to the lawyers' office."

"Oh, of course, forgive me. Certainly, certainly. It's an easy walk, but I suppose to save time you should drive," Mr. Rutherford said. "Their office is only open until four thirty or five, I believe. When you get back, park in the drive on the left. That side isn't used much since the accident."

"Yes, we noticed there had been a fire," Skip said.

"Horrible, dreadful, a little over a month ago, the end of August," Mr. Rutherford said. "It killed our handyman. The smoke got to him, and he couldn't get out in time. The heat was intense, and the fire a ravenous snake. The ancient, dry wood of the old carriage house was like a plump, dead rat, offering no resistance to the hungry snake's jaws."

"Goodness, that's awful," Henry said.

"Yes, a tragedy. A faulty heater was the cause. It started in his quarters. He was an amateur photographer and had his darkroom there. According to the fire department, his developing fluids fed the flames, and it spread rapidly."

"It's a wonder the whole building didn't go up," Henry said.

"A credit to the Ann Arbor Fire Department, no doubt. The area that burned is where he lived, on the upper left-hand side. The upper right side is the old hayloft from when it used to be a carriage house. My car is parked below that. Fortunately, the building is still structurally sound, and the roof on the right is intact. I'm hoping to get the repairs done soon."

"Did the man have any family?" Skip said.

"A brother out in New York. We've sent word but haven't heard back from him yet. Apparently, they were estranged. Most of his belongings were lost. There's not much left, I'm afraid. His old dog died, too, right next to him."

Skip felt a lump in his throat. "I'm so sorry to hear all of this, Mr. Rutherford. Are you sure this weekend is a good time for a visit? To have houseguests?"

"Absolutely. The distraction will do me good, do all of us good. Please stay."

"All right, Uncle, thank you, but please let us know if we can do anything to help. Oh, and my mother sent along a peach cobbler." Henry took the tin from Skip and handed it to him.

Mr. Rutherford broke into a happy grin, clearly delighted. "Your mother's peach cobblers are a treasure. I haven't had one in years. Please thank her for us. We'll have it with dinner tonight, along with some vanilla ice cream." He strode across the room and yanked a bell cord near the fireplace. "Have you ever had one of his mother's peach cobblers, Mr. Valentine?"

"No, sir, not yet," he said.

"Then you're in for a treat, an absolute treat."

The door from the hall opened again and Miss Grant stood there, framed within it, looking stoic. "You rang, sir?"

"Mr. Finch's mother sent along a peach cobbler. Please take it to the kitchen and serve it tonight for dessert along with vanilla ice cream, Jane."

She stared at him a moment, ignoring Skip and Henry, a blank expression on her face. "Yes, I know about the cobbler. I tried to take it from them earlier, but they insisted on presenting it to you personally. I've already prepared a chocolate cake for dessert this evening."

"The cake can wait until tomorrow, can't it?" he said.

"It won't be as moist then, Mr. Rutherford. I can put the cobbler in the icebox. It will keep better than the cake would."

"All right, Jane, you know best. Do we have ice cream?"

"I can have Jake grind some in the morning."

"Excellent, thank you. You can leave the door open, we're just about to go up."

"Yes sir." She took the cobbler from him and left without another word.

"You'll like Jane's chocolate cake," Mr. Rutherford said. "And the peach cobbler tomorrow night will give us something delightful to look forward to."

"Of course, Uncle. I very much enjoy chocolate cake, and Skip does, too."

"Splendid. Well, let's go up so the two of you can get settled in your rooms and then you can go downtown, Henry. There will be time to visit later. We dine at seven, in the dining room right next door. Jane will be serving fish this evening since it's Friday."

"Okay," Henry said. "I like fish."

"Good. The sister and I often sit in the yellow drawing room before dinner, around six," he said as the three of them walked out of the blue drawing room. "Please join us this evening."

"We'd be happy to. And where is that, Uncle?"

"Oh, through that door on the right," he said, pointing across the spacious hall. "The door on the left, closest to the stairs, leads to the library. Feel free to explore the house as you wish. I'd stay out of the basement, though. Just a dirt floor down there, full of spiders and mice, and dark and dank. Anyway, I hope you'll enjoy your stay." He looked about wistfully. "She needs some repair and updating, but I'm sentimental about this place. I like her the way she is."

"That chandelier is sure something," Henry said, pointing up to the heavy iron and crystal fixture above the doors to the entranceway.

"Been hanging there since the house was built. It was originally gas, but we converted it to electric," Mr. Rutherford said.

"How on earth do you ever get up there to change the bulbs?" Henry said.

"That chain the chandelier is hanging from goes across the ceiling and down the wall to a gearbox. We keep the gear handle on top of the clock," Mr. Rutherford said, pointing to a large grandfather clock down the hall. "Once the handle is inserted into the gearbox, you remove the safety pin and crank it down, then back up again. It's only lowered when Miss Grant or Jake cleans it occasionally or when a bulb needs to be changed. Fortunately, the bulbs last a fair amount of time."

"Beats having to use a ladder, I suppose," Skip said.

"Absolutely. Shall we go upstairs?" Mr. Rutherford motioned them toward the staircase and they obliged, climbing slowly toward the first landing.

"Those are magnificent, Uncle," Henry said, pointing at the three stained glass windows that stood above the second riser of stairs.

"They're original to the house, like the chandelier. Most everything is original. We haven't changed much."

That, Skip thought to himself, was obvious. He didn't share Mr. Rutherford's enthusiasm for the house or its condition. The three of them paused at the top, looking about the hall, which like the one below was eighteen feet wide and over nine feet deep from the railing to the back wall.

"My room is to the left, over the library," Mr. Rutherford said. "Mother's room is in front. Sister Barnabas is staying in the room over the entry hall, the old nursery. You'll be there, Mr. Valentine, and Henry, you have the room just here."

"Where does that go?" Henry said, pointing to a door on the second landing they had passed.

"To a small hall where the bathroom is located. My mother and I have a connecting bath, but you two will have to share that one with Sister Barnabas, I'm afraid. Also off that hall is the hall to the servants' quarters above the kitchen wing. Best to stay out of there. Miss Grant is rather territorial."

"You just have the one servant, Mr. Rutherford?"

"Plus her nephew, Jake. He's this side of useless, I'm afraid. I haven't replaced the handyman position yet, so he fills in as best he can."

"Miss Grant mentioned Jake was going to bring our bags up," Skip said.

"Hopefully he got them in the right rooms. Please let me know if he didn't. I wouldn't suggest confronting him yourself. He's not all there mentally, you see, and every time I correct him, he gets upset. I don't think he cares for me much."

"Why is that?" Skip said. "Because you correct him when he makes a mistake?"

"No, not just that. He's been here since he was a small child. His mother used to be the cook here, Miss Grant's younger sister. For some reason, I think Jake blames me for his mother's death. She died in the doctor's office during a medical procedure for a female problem when he was only twelve, I believe."

"It must have been difficult for him to lose his mother at such a young age," Henry said.

"I suppose it was," Mr. Rutherford said. "Jake struggled in school and was often suspended and finally dropped out. Besides being slow, he's hot-tempered and easily frustrated."

"Poor fellow," Henry said.

"Yes. I do what I can for him. Anyway, I hope you like your rooms. They all connect, by the way. My room with my mother's, her room with the sister's, the sister's with yours, Mr. Valentine, and yours with Henry's, though that door is locked and the key for it was lost long ago, I'm afraid. Well, I have some work to do in the library, but I shall see you in the yellow drawing room an hour or so before dinner at seven. Remember, we don't dress."

Skip suppressed a giggle. "We'll be there, Mr. Rutherford, thank you."

"My pleasure. There's a call bell in each room near the fireplace should you need anything. Good day." He turned and retreated down the stairs to the second landing and then onto the main floor.

"What time is it, Skip?"

"Three thirty," he said, consulting his gold pocket watch.

"Okay, time enough to unpack, freshen up, and go see the lawyers. Want to come with?"

"No, thank you. We can explore Ann Arbor tomorrow. Right now, I want to get comfortable and have a little nap. Meet here in the upstairs hall at six?"

Henry grinned. "It's a date."

CHAPTER FOUR

Late Friday afternoon, October 6, 1950
The Rutherford house

Skip went into the room assigned to him, noting his two suitcases, umbrella, and raincoat had been placed upon the metal double bed. He set his hat down and ran a comb through his ginger hair as he kicked off his shoes. Back out the hall door, he descended the four steps to the second landing and went into the small, square hall to the bathroom. Hoping to find a glass for a drink of water, Skip tugged on the knob of the cabinet above the pedestal sink but found it locked. Puzzled, he used the toilet, washed his hands, and then retreated back to his bedroom. He walked over to the connecting door to Henry's room, knocking playfully on it three times. A response in the form of two knocks came rapidly, so Skip bent down and peeked through the keyhole. One of Henry's green eyes was staring back at him.

"Can you hear me?" Skip said.

"Yes, can you hear me?"

"Yes. How's your room? Everything okay?"

"Fine. Too bad this door is locked and doesn't have a key. I guess I won't be sneaking into your room after bedtime."

"Probably for the best. Don't forget Sister Barnabas is right next door to me. If we do anything, it should be in *your* room."

"Okay by me."

"But we'll still have to be quiet."

"I can be quiet when I need to be," Henry said.

"Uh-huh. The last time you stayed over at my place, my neighbor cornered me in the laundry room the next day and asked if I was okay. She thought maybe I was having some kind of an attack the night before because of all the grunts, groans, and moans."

"Don't worry, I'll use my sexy whispering library voice for my sexy librarian while we're here."

"Good. Don't make me shush you," Skip said, chuckling. "By the way, I was just in the bathroom and noticed the medicine cabinet was locked."

"How did you happen to just notice that?"

"I wasn't being nosy, honest. I was looking for a drinking glass."

"I'm sure you can get one from the kitchen."

"Yes, but don't you think it's odd the cabinet was locked? I mean, since that bathroom isn't used by your uncle or his mother, and I'm sure there's a separate servants' bath, it had to be Sister Barnabas, and what could a nun possibly have in there that she needs to keep locked up?"

"Beats me, but it's none of our business. Anyway, I need to get going before the lawyer's office closes."

"Okay, see you later," Skip said. He straightened himself back up, realizing he had better unpack. He had ample room in the closet and dresser drawers for all his things, almost nothing needed pressing, and his two suitcases fit under the bed. When he was finished, he closed the drapes and undressed down to his underwear before stretching out, anxious to close his eyes for ten or fifteen minutes, which turned into an hour and five minutes, and he awoke with a start at a quarter after five. Groggily, he got out of bed, slipped on a robe he'd found in the closet, and stumbled out the door to the bathroom to freshen up and brush his teeth. He got dressed, choosing a simple dress shirt, cardigan sweater, bow tie, and trousers, and stepped out into the hall, closing the door behind him as the clock below struck six. He walked the few steps to Henry's door and knocked three times. Henry answered almost immediately, a smile on his face, his cheeks rosy.

"Evening, Valentine."

"Good evening, Mr. Finch. Don't you look dapper?" Skip said, admiring Henry's green necktie, red vest, and brown checked coat.

"Why, thank you very much."

"I thought dinner was casual, though. You said they didn't dress."

"I think he meant no black tie or tuxedo."

"Oh. I can go back and put on a jacket, but I didn't bring much in the way of that type of clothes except for what I wore on the way here and what I plan to wear when we leave. I didn't want to overdress and stand out, so I focused more on sweaters, shirts, ties, nice shoes, scarves, and such. You know, fashionable, casual attire suitable for a visit to a small town in autumn."

Henry laughed. "And you still look far more dapper than me. Why do I get the feeling you researched what to wear in the library before we left?"

"I may have glanced through a few periodicals. Anyway, let me go put on a sport coat."

"No, you're fine. This is 1950. Times are changing. In fact," Henry said, slipping off his jacket and placing it back into his room, "I'll join you."

"Okay, if you're sure."

"I'm sure. Trying to eat while wearing a sport coat is uncomfortable, and I inevitably end up spilling something on it, anyway."

"Well, you look handsome with or without the jacket. Did you get everything straightened out with Collier, Cole, and Karbouski, by the way?"

"More or less. It was just going over the estate paperwork that the late Giles Rutherford had arranged. I signed a few documents, and even though I read them carefully, I'm still not sure what they all said or meant. Lawyers and their jargon, ugh."

"Well, I'm sure it's fine, and I'm glad you got it taken care of. Shall we go down?"

"We shall."

As they started to descend the stairs, the door from Mrs. Rutherford's room was flung open, revealing a wisp of an old woman wearing a blue flannel nightgown, her grizzled feet bare. She looked small and frail within the oversized doorway, like a shriveled-up little girl.

"You there, stop. Who are you?" she said. "What are you doing here?"

Henry and Skip turned toward her and climbed back up the two steps they'd descended. "I'm Henry Finch, and this is Skip Valentine, ma'am. You must be Mrs. Rutherford."

"You know who I am?" she said, cocking her head. Her thin, gray hair was long and hung loosely about her shoulders, some of it tangled like the strands of an old, dirty mop.

"Just by process of elimination, I suppose. I think we've met most of the rest of the household," Skip said.

"There aren't many, not anymore. You're a handsome man, Mr. Valentine. You're not bad either, Mr. Finch."

"Uh, thanks, Mrs. Rutherford," Skip said, embarrassed.

"The two of you are friends?"

"That's right, Mr. Valentine is a close, personal friend."

"I see. Ambrose had a friend like that. I didn't like him one bit. He was a pretty boy, stupid and needy. He only wanted to be friends with my son because of my money."

"What happened to him?" Henry said.

"I ran him off, that's what happened to him, and good riddance. Pretty boys are always stupid," she said, glaring at Skip.

"I disagree. Physical beauty is no way to judge someone's intelligence, Mrs. Rutherford," Henry said. "Or anything else."

"Oh, great googley moogley," she said, raising her voice as she wagged a finger in his face. "Don't disagree with me, young man. You're a guest in my house, aren't you?"

"I'm sorry. I didn't mean to upset you, ma'am," Henry said.

She jerked her head toward Skip then. "Your friend defends you." She thrust her left arm forward and back, awkwardly. "I used to be young and pretty once, you know. Do you have children?" she said, pointing a bony, crooked finger at Skip.

"No. No, I don't. Neither of us does. Neither of us is married."

"Don't. Children will ruin you, ruin your life. I'm glad you came. I saw you pull up. I watched you from my window. Are your rooms all right?"

"Uh, yes, fine, just fine," Henry said, looking confused. "Thank you."

"Good. I've not been well and haven't had much time to fix things up lately. So many things need doing, and Jane and her nephew Jake are worthless. The whole place needs a coat of paint, the carriage house needs repair, and the garden is a mess. Do you like ice cream?"

"Why yes, I do. Do you?" Skip said.

The old lady nodded, drool dripping from her gaping, toothless mouth. "Very much. But Ambrose commandeered my freezer for his nasty vodka. Now I can't have my ice cream."

"He took over your freezer?" Henry said.

"Yes, he did. It's a big one, a walk-in, in the basement. I bought it when they started rationing food during the war. Smart, yes? I could stock up, you see."

"Pretty clever, Mrs. Rutherford, a wise investment."

"And I kept ice cream there, so I could have it whenever I wanted. All kinds of flavors. But then Ambrose decided he wanted to be a vodka connoisseur because someone at his club said it was sophisticated. Well, la-di-da."

"He must enjoy vodka," Skip said.

She snorted. "He drinks too much. Not just vodka, but all kinds of booze. Even that nasty penguin drinks a sherry now and then. I don't think it's right. It says in the Bible, 'Do not get drunk on wine, it leads to debauchery.' I think that's right, anyway."

"By nasty penguin, you mean Sister Barnabas," Skip said.

"Sister Booger Snot I call her. I'm so cold." Mrs. Rutherford shivered, jerked left and right, then thrust her head back and forward, staring at them. "Come here, come closer. Let me look at you."

Henry and Skip dutifully walked over to her with some trepidation. Up close, she appeared older and frailer, her eyes a liquid green, with tremendous sags and folds of skin beneath them.

"My son Ambrose was born and raised here. Born in my bed. Both my children were. Arthur died, you know, when he was five. Died in this house."

"Yes," Henry said. "Your sister told my mother about it, and she told me. I'm so sorry."

"Terrible thing. I miss Arthur. He was a good boy."

"I can only imagine," Skip said. "But you do have Ambrose."

The old lady's body shook as if she was having a convulsion, and then she froze. "Ambrose is mean and rude. Arthur was kind, gentle, and handsome. You remind me of him."

"Ambrose seemed warm and pleasant to us, Mrs. Rutherford," Henry said.

"Good. You're our guests. I don't abide by rudeness, never have, and he knows that."

"He was very welcoming," Skip said.

Mrs. Rutherford stared up at him. "Do you know where my teeth are?" She took a step closer to him, and he noted her breath was foul, like rotting fish.

"Uh, um, no, I don't, ma'am."

"Hmph, most likely she took 'em. She claims I tried to bite her last night."

"Did you?" Henry said.

Mrs. Rutherford turned and stared at him, then threw her head back and laughed. "I not only tried, I did!"

"Oh my," Skip said.

Mrs. Rutherford laughed for nearly a minute, then she looked left and right, her mood turning somber. "Come in, I have something to show you," she said, motioning for them to enter her bedroom. Henry looked at Skip, but he walked inside, so Henry followed behind as Mrs. Rutherford closed the door. It was a large room, done in pink, with pink striped wallpaper and lots of lace, but it was a dingy pink and the lace was yellowed. Mrs. Rutherford went slowly to the bureau and opened the top drawer, extracting a tarnished silver box. She held it gingerly in both hands as she walked back to them, somewhat unsteadily. "This is a treasure," she said in a hoarse whisper. "I keep it hidden because Ambrose is a snoop, and I don't trust that Jane or Sister Booger Snot, either. Here, hold it," she said to Skip.

Skip took it in his hands as carefully as he could, finding it surprisingly light. Whatever treasure it held must not weigh much, he thought.

"*No!* Not that way, turn it around so I can open it," she snapped.

"Oh, I'm sorry," Skip said, turning it as instructed.

"That's better, now…" With her clawlike, crooked fingers, she slowly opened the box on its hinges and reached inside, withdrawing a lock of curly red hair. She held it up close to Skip's face and ran it across his left cheek. He recoiled involuntarily, shaking it off.

"Don't be afraid, my dear," she cooed. "Isn't it soft? It's a lock of Arthur's hair, taken from his little head after he died."

Skip shuddered.

"Arthur had wonderful naturally curly hair, such a pretty color, not like Ambrose. Ambrose's hair has always been coarse and straight. Could never do a thing with it. He's losing most of it now, going bald, like his father." She cackled at that and then gazed lovingly at her treasure. "I used to show this lock of hair to Ambrose when he was a little boy to encourage him to brush his hair and keep it clean, but I'd never let him touch this, oh no. It's too precious."

"Yes, I see, very precious," Henry said, with a disgusted look on his face. "You should put it back in its box for safekeeping. You never know who's about."

Mrs. Rutherford closed her withered hand around the lock of hair, her eyes now wide. "You're right! They all watch me; they're always watching me." She placed the hair delicately back inside, slammed the lid, and snatched it away from Skip, who was only too glad to let her have it. When she had deposited it safely into the bureau drawer once more, she returned to them, staring from one to the other, her eyes still large and wet but sunken into her face.

"You have pretty hair, Mr. Valentine. Red, like fresh blood, like Arthur's was."

"I think Skip's hair is more like cinnamon," Henry said.

"Oh, what do you know?" she snapped at him. Then she turned her attention back to Skip. "Blue eyes, too. I like blue eyes."

"Yours are green, Mrs. Rutherford, like Henry's," Skip said. "I love green eyes. They're unusual. It must be a family trait."

"Family trait? Oh, that's right, we're related, aren't we?" the old woman said, staring at Henry now.

"Yes, ma'am. Your son Ambrose is my mother's second cousin, so you're my first cousin twice removed, I think. It's a bit confusing."

"*You're* confusing. We were talking about my eyes. So many suitors used to comment on them. The suitors are all gone now, all gone. I'm all alone."

"I'm sorry to hear it, ma'am. Well," Henry said, shifting his weight from foot to foot, "I suppose we should be getting downstairs…"

Mrs. Rutherford shivered again, tugging her nightgown tight about her tiny body. "I'm so cold. I don't like the snow and ice. It's winter, isn't it?"

"Early October, but it is chilly tonight," Henry said.

"This old house is always cold and drafty. The wind moves right through it. It's haunted, you know."

"Haunted?" Skip said.

"Quite so," she said, nodding and bobbing her head. "Augusta Savage's friend held a séance here."

"Who's Augusta Savage?" Henry said.

"Don't you know? She's the woman that used to visit me. Through her friend, I found out Arthur still resides here, still bounces his ball, and still plays in the hall. I talked to him," she said wistfully. "He's happy in the afterlife, and I'm glad. But recently new spirits have come. They frighten me, and they probably frighten Arthur. The new ghosts are Bitters and his dog, I'm sure of it."

"Who?" Skip and Henry both said, almost in unison.

"The old handyman," the woman said, her voice dry and hoarse. "Joe Bitters. He lived above the carriage house with his old dog. They both died there one night, a little over a month ago, I think. You can still see the remains of the fire."

"Oh yes, I noticed it when we pulled up earlier," Skip said. "And we talked about it with Ambrose. He didn't mention the handyman's name, though."

"I've been after him to get the building repaired properly, among other things. He keeps putting it off. Perhaps once it's repaired, Bitters will stop his haunting and go back home."

"Why do you think he haunts this house?" Henry said.

"Because he's angry that his home was burned. I hear him pounding and his dog barking in the middle of the night sometimes. It goes along with something Mrs. Savage told me just after the fire."

"The one whose friend had the séance," Skip said.

Mrs. Rutherford stared at him, her mouth agape as more drool ran down her chin. "Yes, yes, that's right. Were you there?"

"Uh, no, you mentioned it earlier," Henry said.

"Did I? Hmm, I don't remember that. She came to call, you see, Augusta Savage, that is. She doesn't come around much anymore, though she lives just behind here. I think Ambrose keeps her away."

"What did Mrs. Savage tell you when she visited, Mrs. Rutherford?" Skip said.

The old woman stared at Skip, her liquid green eyes growing more wet. "You're a handsome fellow. A pretty boy. But your friend is right, I don't think you're stupid."

Skip blushed. "Uh, thank you, but what did the neighbor lady tell you about Bitters?"

Mrs. Rutherford took in big gulps of air through her gaping, toothless mouth and rolled her wet eyes about before speaking again, her voice low and gravelly. "I told her about the barking and the pounding I'd heard all of a sudden, and she said it must be the spirits of Bitters and his dog."

"Why would she think that?" Henry said.

"Because the noises started soon after the fire, you see. She said if they're haunting this house, he's angry his home was destroyed, and the pounding and barking means their deaths may not have been an accident."

"Not an accident?" Skip said.

"Mrs. Savage thinks they were intentionally locked in when the fire started. She believes he may have been pounding on the door to be let out while his dog barked, and so they continue it in the afterlife."

"But if that's the case, then it wasn't an accident. It was murder," Skip said, his eyes wide.

"Skip, it's all one woman's opinion based on someone knocking and a dog barking in the middle of the night," Henry said, looking at Mrs. Rutherford. "Did they find any evidence of the door being locked?"

"No, but that doesn't mean it wasn't. Why else would they haunt? They're not at peace, locked in, their home destroyed."

"Perhaps you were dreaming when you heard the noises," Henry said.

"No. I was awake. I couldn't sleep, so I was roaming about the hall. The neighbor lady, Mrs. Savage, Augusta Savage, have you met her? She lives in the house just behind. She said it must be the ghosts of Bitters and his dog. She's a gossip, you know. She used to call on me every week. Not so much anymore. I think Ambrose keeps her away. He doesn't like gossip and doesn't believe in spirits and séances."

"I see," Skip said. "So, what else did Mrs. Savage have to say?"

Mrs. Rutherford looked about the room as if to make sure no one else was there, then she lowered her voice more, so much so that Skip and Henry both had to take a step toward her to hear clearly. "She told me Bitters said he had a secret and would be coming into some money. That he found something important and valuable. That was right before the fire."

"Hmm, that does sound suspicious," Skip said.

"If it's true," Henry said.

"She also told me, Augusta did, that Bitters left a clue to his secret behind, in various notes that he'd written, just in case."

"Where?" Henry said.

"All he would tell her is something about how a sharp mind will find a clue, and pull, uh, something or other, and something about the location of the keys to find his notes."

"What notes? Where? And where would the keys be?" Skip said.

Mrs. Rutherford put her right hand to her forehead. She looked tired. "I don't know. No one knows. Probably they were burned up in the fire. Until the mystery is solved, however, and the carriage house repaired, I think Bitters and his dog will continue to haunt this house, pounding and howling and probably scaring poor Arthur's gentle spirit away."

"How often have you heard these spirits?" Henry said.

"A few times. Usually when I can't sleep and I wander the house alone," the woman said, her folds of loose skin bobbing up and down. "I used to have a dog, you know. Such a sweet boy, Gipper was his name. He liked doughnuts."

"What happened to him?" Skip said.

"He ran away. He was always by my side. He didn't much care for Ambrose, though he took to that idiot Jake a bit, which annoyed me. He seemed to dislike that nasty penguin, too. Can't say I like her either."

"Sister Barnabas, you mean," Henry said.

"No, Sister Booger Snot. Ambrose brought her here to take care of me because I was sick, or so he says. Do I look sick to you?" Mrs. Rutherford swayed back and forth, a bit of drool still in the corner of her mouth, her wet green eyes large and wild, like a stormy sea.

"Uh, I'm sure your son was only concerned about you," Henry said.

"Horse feathers. That bucket head doesn't care a thing about me. No one does, no one ever has, except Arthur and Gipper. Arthur's gone, dead, you know. And Gipper's gone, too. I was so surprised when he ran away. It's broken my heart. He was only a couple of years old."

"I'm sorry, Mrs. Rutherford. Maybe you can get another dog," Henry said.

She shook her head, and the drool dropped down onto her nightgown unnoticed. "Never another dog like Gipper. Never," she said softly. She was crying now, and she dabbed at her eyes with a dirty handkerchief she'd drawn out from one of her sleeves. When she was finished, she stuffed it back and gazed past Skip and Henry toward the other side of the room. Skip and Henry both turned and looked, but Mrs. Rutherford was staring at something they could not see.

"Ma'am…" Skip said quietly, turning back to her.

Mrs. Rutherford broke her gaze. "Do you boys know who I am?"

"Er, yes, you're Mrs. Rutherford," Henry said.

"No, I'm Gabria Peacock. You've seen me on the stage, haven't you? I'm a famous actress. You want my autograph, don't you? I'm so tired."

"Perhaps a nap," Skip said.

Mrs. Rutherford's head snapped up, her liquid eyes now blazing. "A nap? Do you think I need a nap? I'll decide when I nap and when I don't, young man, thank you very much. Don't look at me! Don't look at me! Go away, now, I'm tired. No autographs!"

They stared at her, Henry open-mouthed again.

She took a step toward them and raised a crooked fist. "Get out! How did you get into my dressing room in the first place? I'm not dressed, I'm not dressed. I shall call the police. Help!"

Henry and Skip hurried to the bedroom door and stepped out into the hall, turning back as Mrs. Rutherford slammed the door in their faces.

"Well," Henry said. "She certainly is something, and that breath could peel wallpaper."

Skip put his finger to his lips. "Shh, she may hear you."

"Bats in the belfry," Henry said, twirling his finger about his temple.

"Poor thing," Skip said. "But that fire…"

"What about it?"

"I remember your uncle saying it happened in August, and he also said it was most likely caused by a faulty heater. Why would anyone need a heater in August?"

"It can get cool in the evenings, even in July and August sometimes."

"Hmm. I suppose. But those notes this Bitters left behind. He told Mrs. Savage about them."

"Skip, your mind is whirling with information you obtained from a woman who's clearly not right in the head. Leave it be and let's go down, I'm getting hungry."

CHAPTER FIVE

Friday evening, October 6, 1950
The Rutherford house

The two of them turned and descended the staircase, then went past the library to the yellow drawing room. It was open, and Mr. Rutherford and Sister Barnabas were both inside, seated on worn chintz wing chairs on either side of the fireplace, which had a fire burning.

"Ah, there you two are. I was afraid you'd both fallen asleep," Mr. Rutherford said, glancing up at the mantel clock as he got to his feet. It was six twenty.

"Our apologies, Uncle. We were on our way down when your mother caught us in the upstairs hall. She wanted to chat."

Mr. Rutherford looked troubled. "Oh, I see. So, you've met Mother, then."

"Yes. She seemed pleasant but confused, at least toward the end of our conversation," Henry said.

"That, I'm afraid, is often the case," Mr. Rutherford said. "She has rapid mood swings sometimes and memory issues. And she's started making things up."

"What exactly is wrong with her?" Henry said.

"Senility. There's no cure, and it seems to be advancing rapidly. We've tried to make her as comfortable as possible at least," the sister said, once again peering at them over the top of her glasses.

"How dreadful for her," Skip said. "She mentioned something about a man called Joe Bitters and his dog."

"Bitters was our groundskeeper," Mr. Rutherford said. "He was our handyman, too, and good at fixing almost anything. Motor cars, electric lights, radios, you name it. Also a pretty decent photographer when he was sober. He had a drinking problem, you see."

"That's unfortunate," Henry said.

"Yes. He first came to work here seven or eight years ago. He was a veteran, in his fifties. His wife had left him, he'd spent some time in jail, and he'd been fired from his job at a repair shop downtown, and a couple of other places before that. My mother, against my better judgment, decided to give him a chance and hired him. That was before she got so ill, of course."

"That was generous and commendable of her," Skip said.

"I suppose so, though I think the real reason was that he came cheap and desperate, and he was talented at fixing things, as I said. He lived above the garage in the old chauffeur's quarters. As time went on, his drinking got worse and so did his demeanor. He and his dog both died in the fire. It was gruesome."

"I can't imagine. Mrs. Rutherford said a neighbor, Mrs. Savage, thinks he was locked in," Skip said, ignoring Henry's glare. "That he couldn't get out when the fire started."

"Yes, I know what Mrs. Savage thinks, but they found no evidence of that. Most likely, Joe was drunk and unconscious and just never woke up. It was the middle of the night, very early morning."

"Then why does this woman think he was purposefully locked inside?" Skip said.

"Because she has an active imagination. Mrs. Savage used to visit Mother every week, and she had her dotty old friend hold séances, too, getting her all worked up. The last time she was here, Mother was in a state, vexed, agitated, and angry. Fortunately, we haven't seen Mrs. Savage since. I think Mother scared her away."

"She said she thought *you* were keeping Mrs. Savage away," Henry said.

Mr. Rutherford rolled his eyes. "I would have if I could have."

"Your mother also said she thinks the house is haunted by Bitters's ghost, and the ghost of his dog," Skip said. "That their spirits aren't at peace because their home was destroyed and because of the way they died."

Mr. Rutherford laughed. "Forgive me, I don't mean to laugh at Mother's expense. It's just all so absurd. Again, more nonsense, encouraged by that Savage woman."

"I can only imagine, Uncle. This must all be so trying for you, and here we are in the way."

"Oh, on the contrary. Your presence here is a welcome relief and distraction from what I have to deal with on a daily basis. Did Mother also tell you that my dear, dead older brother's ghost still plays ball in the hall? That she hears the ball bouncing? That she supposedly talked to him during one of those séances Mrs. Savage's crazy friend held?"

"Yes, she did," Henry said.

"She's told all that to me, too," Sister Barnabas said, her teeth almost protruding from her mouth. "About Bitters and his dog, *and* little Arthur."

Mr. Rutherford put a hand to his forehead and closed his eyes momentarily. "Dear Arthur, the perfect child, Mother's favorite. I don't remember him, of course, as I was only about two years old when he died. I have no recollection, but as far back as I can remember, my mother always compared me to him. 'Why can't you be more like Arthur? Arthur would eat his peas. Arthur never cried, Arthur never broke things, Arthur always played quietly.' It's all I ever heard."

"That must have been difficult for you," Henry said.

"I often wonder what would have happened had he lived. I think she canonizes him in death." He sighed and rolled his shoulders as if feeling a tremendous weight upon his back. "But let's not talk about that. Come sit here by the fire and tell me all about what's been happening with your mother, your younger siblings, and the rest of the family, Henry, and about what's new in Chicago. I want to hear how you and Mr. Valentine became acquainted, also."

Mr. Rutherford took his seat in the wingback once more, and Skip and Henry sat on the sofa, facing him and the sister. Henry chatted for some time, telling stories and answering questions about his family, his experiences during the war, and his life in Chicago. It seemed Miss Grant was at the hall door all too soon, announcing dinner as the clock struck seven.

They all crossed the wide hall into the dining room. Mr. Rutherford sat at the head of the table and motioned for Skip to sit at his left, with Henry to Skip's left. Sister Barnabas sat across from Skip, to Mr. Rutherford's right.

"Is your mother not joining us?" Skip said.

"Jane takes a tray up to her around six thirty," Mr. Rutherford said. "I'm afraid Mother rarely ventures downstairs anymore."

A young man came in through the door from the butler's pantry, carrying a gray soup tureen decorated with gray roses, which he placed clumsily on the sideboard, the lid slipping sideways. He was large, solidly built, and thick. His dark, short hair lay on top of his head in clumps, sticking up this way and that, and his brown eyes seemed dull on either side of a large nose, which had clearly been broken once or twice. He wore a red bandana about his neck, and another protruded from his left back pocket.

Mr. Rutherford snapped at him. "Do be careful, Jake, for heaven's sake."

"I did the best I could," the man said sullenly as he glared at Mr. Rutherford and straightened the lid of the tureen. He hurried back through the swinging pantry door as Jane entered and began ladling out the soup into bowls and serving them.

"I was surprised to see Jake bring in the soup," Mr. Rutherford said.

"I'm sorry, sir, the tureen was rather heavy for me."

"I see. Well, never mind, it's fine."

"I'll make sure he stays in the kitchen the rest of the evening," she said, going back through the door into the pantry and the kitchen beyond.

"The soup smells delicious," Henry said, taking a spoonful.

"I hope you like it. Jane's a whiz in the kitchen."

"You said Jake is her nephew? There's not much of a family resemblance between him and Miss Grant," Skip said.

"He was her younger sister's son. Annabelle was different from Jane in every way. I think he takes after her."

"What does he do here, exactly?" Skip said.

"Odd jobs, mostly. When the old cook quit, Jane suggested we hire Annabelle, and she brought Jake with her. He was a boy then, and he's eighteen now."

"His mother died during a medical procedure?" Skip said.

"That's right, when Jake was twelve. Rather than hire a new cook after Annabelle passed away, Jane agreed to take on the cooking as well as the housekeeping duties, and she's done exceptionally well. She also raised Jake through a sense of obligation and duty. He had nowhere to go, and he was still a child."

"How sad," Skip said.

"Yes. Annabelle, Jake's mother, never married, so, of course, Jake wasn't planned. Unfortunately, my mother calls him Jake the mistake."

"That's cruel and rather harsh. Surely she doesn't call him that to his face," Skip said.

Mr. Rutherford took a spoonful of soup before replying. "Mother *can* be cruel and harsh, especially lately, and she lashes out at Jake anytime he does something stupid, which is often, I'm afraid. He's not too bright. A little touched in the head. Even the army wouldn't take him when he tried to enlist a few months ago. He failed his ASVAB."

"Armed services vocational aptitude battery," Henry said.

"That's right. I think his IQ is around seventy."

"Where does he sleep?" Skip said.

"In the attic."

"Oh? There are bedrooms up there?"

"An old storage room, but it works for him," Mr. Rutherford said, finishing the last of his soup. "There's an empty servant bedroom next to Jane's, his mother's old room, but he likes it up there in the attic for some reason."

"But where does he bathe? Where does he toilet?" Skip said.

"He shares the second-floor servants' bathroom with his aunt Jane."

The door from the hall opened abruptly, and they all stared as Mrs. Rutherford entered, dressed in a red and white chevron print skirt with a bright green flowered blouse, buttoned incorrectly and half untucked, a yellow scarf about her neck, her gray, stringy hair pulled back into a knot. Dirty gray house slippers adorned her gnarled feet. It was a colorful ensemble, and Skip gave her points for boldness, but he didn't think Christian Dior would approve. Mr. Rutherford, Skip, and Henry stood dutifully, Mr. Rutherford's napkin falling to the floor.

"Mother. What are you doing down here, dear? Hasn't Jane brought up your tray?"

She glared at him as she shuffled to her spot at the table, at the opposite end from Mr. Rutherford. "She did, and I sent it back down again. We have guests, Ambrose. It would be rude of me to dine in my room when we have guests."

"But are you feeling up to it? You're not well."

"Whoop-dee-do. So you keep telling me. I'm fine. Healthy as a horse. Tell Jane to set my place." She sat down with a flourish, and Mr. Rutherford, Skip, and Henry followed suit.

"Where did you get those clothes?" Mr. Rutherford said.

"From one of the bedrooms above the kitchen. Someone has stolen all of mine. I wasn't about to come to dinner in my nightgown."

"If I'm not mistaken, those clothes belong to Jane. You took them from her room, didn't you?"

"They belong to me! She took them from me and hid them in her room."

"Yes, Mother, whatever you say." The table fell silent as Mr. Rutherford rang for the housekeeper.

Presently the door from the butler's pantry swung open. To Jane's credit, she paused only momentarily at the sight of Mrs. Rutherford before going to Mr. Rutherford's side.

"I'm sorry, sir. She refused her tray. I wasn't aware she'd be coming down."

"It's all right, Jane. Mrs. Rutherford has decided to join us for dinner. Set her place at once and bring her soup course. Oh, and I'll need a fresh napkin," he said, handing her the one that had fallen to the floor. "I'll see that your clothing is returned to you promptly. If anything's damaged, I'll replace it."

"Thank you, sir."

"Oh, and I'd advise you to keep your bedroom door locked from now on."

"Yes sir, I will."

Jane left and returned promptly with a place setting for Mrs. Rutherford. She filled her soup bowl from the tureen, got her a glass of water, and then placed a fresh napkin on Mr. Rutherford's lap before going swiftly back to the kitchen.

Mrs. Rutherford took a spoonful from the bowl. "What type of soup is this?" Her voice was still hoarse and raspy.

"Tomato and eggplant, Mother," Mr. Rutherford said.

"Your brother liked tomato soup," she said. "And ice cream."

Mr. Rutherford looked pained. "Yes, I know. You constantly remind us of all of his favorite things."

"He always ate anything I gave him without argument. I will not allow Arthur to be forgotten, Ambrose. He was my son."

"I'm your son, too."

"Not like Arthur. Pass the bread."

Skip and Henry exchanged glances as Sister Barnabas passed her the bread. Mrs. Rutherford was certainly abrupt for someone not abiding rudeness.

The table fell mainly silent then as the soup course was followed by fried cod and green beans, with the chocolate cake for dessert. Skip noticed Mrs. Rutherford ate little of anything, content with mostly just pushing her food about her plate, sometimes with her fork, sometimes with her fingers.

When the cake was finished, Jane served coffee. Mrs. Rutherford finally seemed to take notice of Skip and Henry's presence. She looked down the table at them and cleared her throat, getting everyone's attention.

"Who are you two?"

"This is Henry Finch, and this is his friend, Mr. Valentine," Mr. Rutherford said. "The company you insisted on coming down to dinner for."

"Never saw them before," she said. "But it's delightful to have guests. I get so lonely."

"We met you upstairs, in the hall before dinner," Henry said.

Her head moved back and forth. "I don't think so. I would have remembered that. Though the one you call Valentine looks familiar. You're friends, you say?"

"Yes. We met each other earlier this year and seemed to hit it off."

"Hmph. Why are you here in my house? Why are you visiting?"

"Well, uh, I needed to sign some papers, and I wanted to stay over. You said it would be okay," Henry said.

"*I* said it was okay? Why would I do that? I don't know you."

"You responded to a letter I'd written to your son here, Ambrose."

"Oh yes, the letter. Why didn't you say so? I remember now. You're the fellows from Chicago. I carry the letter with me for safekeeping. They can't be trusted," Mrs. Rutherford said, looking about at the others. "None of them."

"Uh, well, yes, as I said, I wanted to visit, and I thought maybe Uncle Ambrose, Skip, and I could maybe do some fishing," Henry said.

She cocked her head. "Fishing? Good fishing here in the Huron River. My husband and I used to fish sometimes. You like to fish?"

"Yes, ma'am, I do. I brought my equipment."

"Tie your own lures?"

"Yes, ma'am, and pretty good ones, if I do say so myself. I have some in my tackle box along with a brand new spool of fishing line. I have my own pole, too."

"Do you have a big pole?" the old woman said.

"Average, I guess. About seven feet."

"That's a good size for bass fishing. Shorter rods are good for more accurate casts, though."

"I didn't realize you knew so much about fishing, Mother."

She stared at him. "You never asked me. You only care about your golf and tennis."

"But you never took me fishing as a boy."

"Because you were a nasty little child. And you're a nasty man. You keep me locked upstairs."

"Mother! I do not keep you locked upstairs. I'm trying everything I can to make you happy and comfortable."

"Oh, bull twinkies, Ambrose. What a load of malarkey." She turned her attention back to Henry abruptly. "You sent me a letter," she said, pointing a shaky finger at him that quickly pointed upward, then downward, before she retracted it.

"Yes, I did send a letter. I mentioned that before," Henry said. "I, uh, actually sent it to your son, Ambrose."

"No, you sent it to me," Mrs. Rutherford said. "I have it here," she said, withdrawing a soiled envelope from the sleeve of her blouse. "It was lying on the hall table a week or so ago, and I snatched it up. I've been keeping it, you see. I didn't tell them you were coming until just recently. They can't be trusted. I wrote you back and gave it to the postman myself."

"I never did see your actual letter, Henry, though she told us about it, finally. May I, Mother?"

She looked at her son doubtfully. "What's the magic word, Ambrose?"

"Please, Mother."

"Please, what?"

"May I please see the letter?" Ambrose said, gritting his teeth.

Mrs. Rutherford smiled, clearly happy with herself. "Arthur always had such good manners," she said. "He never forgot to say please." She handed the envelope to Henry, who passed it to Skip, who in turn handed it to Mr. Rutherford, who removed the letter from its envelope and read its brief contents silently to himself.

"So, you need a loan, Henry," he said, putting the letter in his breast pocket when he'd finished rather than return it to his mother. She seemed not to notice.

"Well, yes, if that's possible. Not all that much. Perhaps we could discuss it in private after dinner," Henry said.

"We certainly could," Mr. Rutherford said as he finished his coffee. "But I'm afraid there's nothing to discuss. My funds are tied up in investments, and I currently have very little cash flow. Ask me again next year."

"Oh, I see. I wasn't aware," Henry said.

"Don't be embarrassed, my boy. There's nothing wrong with asking. If you don't ask, the answer will always be no. I'm sorry to disappoint you."

"It's my money, Ambrose, not yours, not yet," his mother said tersely from her end of the table, her voice rougher, as if she'd just smoked a carton of cigarettes in one sitting.

Ambrose looked aghast. "Well, yes, of course, Mother. Our money."

"Not our money, *my* money. I'm not dead yet. It will be your money when I'm gone, but not until then. Giles made sure I would be taken care of, and I don't plan on going anywhere for a long time, despite what you may hope."

Mr. Rutherford looked shocked and pained. "Mother, that's a terrible thing to say. I would never hope for such a thing. We're giving you the best care we possibly can."

"Who, her? Sister Booger Snot?" Mrs. Rutherford now pointed a bony finger toward Sister Barnabas, who up to this point had been relatively silent.

"That's completely uncalled for, Mother, please apologize to her at once."

The sister appeared unfazed by the insult. "It's all right, Mr. Rutherford. She's not well, you must remember that."

"Sister Barnabas is a nurse," Mr. Rutherford said. "She agreed to come here and care for you at home so you wouldn't have to go to a hospital."

"Agreed my foot. You're paying her, aren't you?"

"We're paying her expenses, of course. Plus room and board."

"It's my duty to God to provide and care for you, Mrs. Rutherford," she said, rubbing her left temple as if she had a headache.

"Duty, schmooty," Mrs. Rutherford clucked. "I don't need a nurse." She jerked her head from side to side again, almost involuntarily. Then she pointed back to Ambrose.

"They're coming to take me away, aren't they? First thing Monday morning."

"Your sister Lillian feels that you need more care than we can provide, and perhaps she's right."

"Lillian is my older sister. She takes care of me."

"Of course she does. She loves you. We all love you and want what's best for you."

"I don't believe it." She stabbed a finger at Henry. "If this boy needs a loan, we should give it to him. He's family, isn't he? What's her name's son."

"Louise. Louise is my second cousin. She's Henry's mother."

"Louise, that's right. I remember her. Pretty girl, sweet and polite. Give the boy some money."

"There's no money to give Henry at the moment, Mother," Mr. Rutherford said. "Just as there's no money to repair the carriage house completely right now or paint the house. As I said, almost everything's tied up in investments, stocks, and bonds. And now with you needing additional care, that will use up a good portion of our liquid assets for the foreseeable future."

Mrs. Rutherford crossed her arms and pursed her lips angrily. "I don't need additional care, and who put you in charge of my money? I want more coffee."

"I'll ring for Jane, and Father did, in his will. As his son, I am the heir but obligated to care for you, of course."

"Is that what I am? An obligation?"

"No, of course not. I mean, yes, you are, but you're also my mother. I'd care for you regardless. But because of the way Father set things up, I can't do anything major without your consent, you know that."

"Pish posh, fish fosh. Money. I don't recall consenting to any of it. We have money for *her*." She glared at Sister Barnabas again. "Take it from her and give it to him."

"It's all right. I'll get by," Henry said. "The money would have helped, of course, but I'll manage."

Mr. Rutherford turned his attention to him. "Of course you will. You're a bright, ambitious young man."

"Lillian," Mrs. Rutherford said. "Where is my sister? I like her, she's nice to me. She was at our wedding."

"Lillian is coming sometime tomorrow, on the early afternoon train from Traverse City. She's going to help you get settled into your new place on Monday."

Jane came through the pantry door. "You rang?" she said.

"Pour my mother some more coffee, please, Jane, and you can clear the dessert plates, I think."

"Yes, sir," she said, stepping toward the sideboard and picking up the coffeepot.

"Lillian will know what to do," Mrs. Rutherford said. "She won't let you lock me away somewhere."

"It was her idea to move you to a nursing facility where you can get round-the-clock care."

"If anyone should be locked away, it's that idiot Jake. He's stupid and worthless. He needs to be in an institution," Mrs. Rutherford said.

Jane's hand shook as she poured the coffee and began picking up the plates.

"Stop it, Mother."

"It's true. You treat him better than you do me. Lillian will put a stop to that. You'll see when she gets here, she'll tell you. She knows about money, too."

"Money is the root of all evil," Sister Barnabas said to no one in particular.

Mrs. Rutherford glared at her. "Just try getting by without it, Sister. Vows of poverty, ha. You seem pretty comfortable in my house, sleeping in a cozy warm bed with a down comforter, eating my food, and drinking my wine. And you look like you could stand to lose a pound or two, so you're clearly not missing any meals."

"Mother, please."

"But you should get your teeth fixed so you can speak better, Sister Booger Snot. You sound like you have a mouthful of marbles. And you took my teeth, didn't you? Are you wearing my teeth? Are you?"

"Of course not, Mrs. Rutherford. We took your teeth because you bit me, and quite hard."

Mrs. Rutherford laughed at that, drool running down the sides of her mouth, her eyes merry. Then she became somber and angry again. "Why are you here, anyway?"

"We've been over this many times," Mr. Rutherford said. "Just a few moments ago, as a matter of fact. The Convent of the Immaculate Heart of Mary sent her here to take care of you. Sister Barnabas is a trained nurse; she comes highly recommended."

"I'll be leaving Monday afternoon, Mrs. Rutherford, once you're on your way to your new place."

"Good, go, skedaddle, but *I'm* not going *anywhere* except to my room. Send Jake the Mistake in my place." She stood up abruptly, upsetting her full coffee cup. Henry, Skip, and Mr. Rutherford got to their feet, too, as she left the dining room without another word, her body jerking awkwardly.

Mr. Rutherford looked embarrassed as they all sat back down. "I'm so sorry, Sister," he said.

"Think nothing of it. I understand. It's perfectly natural in her condition," she said, though she looked shaken. "Shall I go up and attend to her?"

"No, probably best to leave her be. Hopefully, she'll settle down and go to bed. You can retrieve Jane's clothes from her later."

"All right."

"She can keep them," Jane said. "I don't want them back."

"As you wish," Mr. Rutherford said. "I'll reimburse you for them, of course. Please clean up the spilled coffee and clear the rest."

"Yes, sir."

Mr. Rutherford glanced about the table. "Well, on a lighter note, why don't we retire back to the yellow drawing room and leave Jane to her work? I could use a distraction right now. I haven't purchased a television set yet, but is anyone up for a game of cribbage? You two against the sister and I."

"I'm game," Henry said, "No pun intended."

"I think that pun was very intended," Skip said. "But I'm game, too."

"Count me in," the sister said. "Perhaps it will help my headache."

"You've another?" Mr. Rutherford said.

"Yes, I've had so many of them lately."

"Perhaps a sherry will help," he said.

Chapter Six

After dinner Friday evening, October 6, 1950
The Rutherford house

The four of them returned to the yellow drawing room and took their places at a small table near the front windows while Mr. Rutherford extracted a deck of cards and a cribbage board from a drawer and lit up a cigarette.

"Henry, pour us some brandy, won't you? It's there on the sideboard. And some sherry for the sister. Bring over an ashtray, too. There's one on the mantel."

Henry got the ashtray and then poured three glasses of brandy and one of sherry. Mr. Rutherford dealt six cards to each person and then placed the deck off to the side, awaiting a cut. "Give me a good crib," he said to each of them, taking a sip of brandy followed by a puff on his cigarette.

The first game went by quickly, with Skip and Henry winning easily. The second took a little longer, but Ambrose and the sister were eventually victorious. They decided a final game must be played to determine the victors of the night, so Skip dealt out the cards. When that game had ended and Skip and Henry were once more the winners, Mr. Rutherford leaned back in his chair and finished his third drink. "Well, I'm done in. That's sixteen cents we owe you two. Remind me to pay my half of it to you tomorrow."

"Where is Lillian?" a raspy voice called out abruptly from the doorway to the hall. All of them turned to look at Mrs. Rutherford, dressed once more in her blue flannel nightgown, but wearing black rubber galoshes upon her feet this time.

"Mother, what are you doing downstairs again?"

She took a few tentative steps toward the card table, the galoshes squeaking on the parquet floor, and looked at each of them in turn. She coughed, not covering her mouth, and put her right hand to her chest. She was apparently having trouble breathing. "I can't sleep, not tired."

Mr. Rutherford looked at Sister Barnabas, and then at his mother again. "It's late, Mother."

"Late?" she said, swaying from side to side. "Time waits for no one. Where is Arthur?"

Mr. Rutherford stubbed out his cigarette in the ashtray, put the cards and cribbage board away in the drawer from which they'd come, and stood up, Henry and Skip following suit.

"Arthur isn't here anymore, you know that." His words and tone were gentle, as if speaking to a child.

"Why not?" Mrs. Rutherford snapped. "I want Arthur, I miss my son."

"I'm your son, too."

"A sorry excuse for one." She spat out the words, gasping for each breath, still clutching her chest.

The words must have pained Mr. Rutherford, but perhaps he'd heard them so often they no longer hurt that much. "You don't look well, my dear. Let Sister Barnabas take you back up to bed."

The sister cautiously took a few steps toward her, as if approaching a wild animal, but Mrs. Rutherford didn't appear to be in the mood for a squabble anymore tonight.

"All right. I suppose that would be okay," she said quietly.

"That's right. We'll all go up to bed," Mr. Rutherford said.

"Yes, I'm rather tired, too," Sister Barnabas said. "I'm going to put you to bed, Mrs. Rutherford, and in just a few minutes you'll be in dreamland, sound asleep, all right?"

Mrs. Rutherford looked at the nun and held out her left hand, her right still clutching her chest. Sister Barnabas took the hand in hers and led her out the doorway and up the stairs. When they had gone, Mr. Rutherford looked back at Skip and Henry.

"I'm sorry about Mother."

"No need to apologize. We understand," Henry said.

"Thank you, truly. In some respects, I feel as if I've already lost her. Only every day I lose a little more."

"I can't imagine how difficult this all must be for you," Skip said, still nursing his drink.

"No, I suppose you can't. I think I'll have another brandy. Henry?"

"Just a short one," Henry said. "Your mother mentioned earlier you were a bit of a vodka connoisseur. I'm surprised you're not having that."

"I do like a good vodka, properly chilled, but I find it's more of a summer drink. Now then, I have some cigars in the library, let's sit in there for a bit." Mr. Rutherford poured the drinks and the three of them moved into the library, where Mr. Rutherford extracted a Cuban cigar from a humidor on the desk. "Care for a smoke, gentlemen?"

"Uh, no thank you, sir," Skip said.

"Not for me, either, Uncle, but thanks."

"Suit yourselves," he said, striking a match and lighting the tip of the cigar. "Please sit." Mr. Rutherford made himself comfortable in the overstuffed chair, and Skip and Henry took chairs opposite him. "I like this time of night. Everything's quiet, no one telephones or comes to call, dinner is finished, the servants have gone up, and Mother is usually asleep. Sometimes I sit here by myself, smoking and drinking, until I nearly nod off."

Henry took a sip of his brandy. "Are you usually the last to go up?"

"Yes. I'm always the first to come down and the last to go up. I turn out the lights and lock the front door, then I go to bed." Mr. Rutherford took a deep, long swallow and then set the glass down, rubbing his eyes. "It's a nice respite from my mother."

"I can understand that. Dealing with her on a daily basis must be trying," Henry said.

"It has its challenges. As you're aware, my aunt Lillian is coming here tomorrow to assist with transferring Mother to a nursing home this Monday, which, I must admit, will be helpful to us both."

"I think that's a good idea," Henry said. "I'm sure Sister Barnabas is capable, but she'll have round-the-clock care."

"Yes, of course, I can't argue with that. By the way, Henry, I'm sorry again about the loan. It's just not a good time."

"Of course," Henry said, downing the last of his drink perhaps a bit too fast. "I understand. Well, if you'll excuse me, I'm afraid I'm rather tired." He got to his feet, leaving his glass on the table between the chairs.

Skip looked at him, surprised. "You're usually more of a night owl."

He returned Skip's gaze. "Yes, but I had a long day of driving, and I didn't have time to nap after settling in as you did. I'll see you all in the morning. Good night."

"Good night," Skip and Mr. Rutherford both said.

"Are you sure you don't want another brandy, Mr. Valentine?" Mr. Rutherford said after Henry had gone.

"No thank you, I'm not much of a brandy drinker."

"Oh? What's your preferred poison?"

"Gee, I don't know. I like wine, and a cranberry and soda is always good."

"Why am I not surprised?"

"What do you mean?"

"Just that you didn't seem to have enjoyed your brandy. There's still a swallow or two in your glass."

"Oh, yes," Skip said, polishing it off with a slight grimace. "Anyway, I should be going up soon, too. Henry and I want to do some exploring around the town tomorrow."

"All right," Mr. Rutherford said, getting up and turning out some of the lights in the library. "By the way, I understand you two met earlier this year?"

"That's right, on a crosstown bus, believe it or not."

"How unusual. No girlfriends?"

"Er, not at the moment, no. I'm only twenty-two and Henry's twenty-five," Skip said, getting to his feet.

"That's not that young. Most young men your ages are married with families of their own."

"Times are changing. Who knows? We may both decide to never marry and have children. Who needs that responsibility?"

"Ah, I see, modern men," Mr. Rutherford said, turning out the rest of the lights in the room except for the one overhead, and placing Henry's dirty glass on the sideboard for Jane to clear in the morning. He studied Skip. "You're not funny, are you?"

Skip bristled. "Some people think I'm hilarious."

"You know what I mean, Mr. Valentine, I'm sure. A handsome young man, fond of cranberry and soda, a snappy dresser, and no girlfriend, not married…"

"I certainly don't believe marriage is required of everyone when they reach a certain age, nor should it be expected, sir."

"I disagree. Marriage is an institution."

"So is a psychiatric hospital, but I don't want to spend any time in one."

"Then you'd best be careful about your behavior."

"What's that supposed to mean?"

"I'm just inferring. Perhaps I'm wrong, I hope I am."

"You're inferring I'm funny because I don't have a girlfriend? Because I'm single and don't fancy brandy straight up?"

"In part, yes."

"What about Henry? Do you think he's funny, too?"

Mr. Rutherford stared at him. "No, I don't, but I think I shall have to discuss your friendship with him," he said, lighting a fresh cigarette. "It's my impression that he's easily influenced, that he's innocent and impressionable. I saw the way you looked at him during dinner and over cribbage, your hands almost touching at times, and how you hung on his every word and laughed at his jokes."

"He's my friend, why wouldn't I laugh at his jokes?"

"Someone has to carry on the Rutherford name, you know. He needs to get married."

Skip walked closer to him, annoyed and irritated. "His last name is Finch, not Rutherford."

"That can be changed. And what's important is the bloodline, anyway."

"Why? What does it matter? And why do you care that Henry and I are friends, funny or not?"

"I'm not sure I like your defensive tone. You're a guest in my house, remember."

Skip paused, then dropped his voice. "I'm sorry, I shouldn't have been argumentative. Don't take out your feelings for me on him. Henry's honest, dependable, and hardworking. What he needs right now is money."

"So he's said. I wish I could help him." He ground out his cigar and took out his cigarette pack, staring into it before shoving it back into his pocket. "Goodness, I'm almost out of smokes."

"Isn't there any way you could loan him something, Mr. Rutherford? Even if it's just a little bit? He doesn't need much, just enough to help him get back on his feet. He's trying to support his mother and siblings, too, you know, and he wants to go back to school."

Mr. Rutherford raised his eyebrows. "Ah, now I see. No wonder Henry went to bed early."

"What are you implying?"

"He asked you to speak on his behalf, didn't he?"

Skip felt his face flush, and anger quickly rose within him. "No, he most certainly did not. He'd be furious with me if he knew I'd mentioned it. Henry is far too proud."

"Not too proud to ask for money from a relative he barely knows and only sees occasionally," Mr. Rutherford said.

"He is the heir, *your* heir, as you pointed out, so it's his money, too, in a way."

Mr. Rutherford laughed. "I don't plan on going anywhere anytime soon, so I think he'd better find himself a job."

"He has a job. And he'll find another, better one soon. And he wasn't asking for a handout, only a simple loan. I'm sorry I brought this whole thing up. Good night." He turned and walked swiftly out into the hall. Mr. Rutherford followed suit as he switched off the overhead light.

"Good night, Mr. Valentine," he said curtly, closing the door behind him.

Skip climbed up the stairs, fuming. He'd just reached his bedroom door when he heard a thunderous crash that sent a shiver through the very floorboards he was standing on and shook the whole house. He turned as quickly as he could and went back down the stairs to the front hall, which was much darker and eerily silent. Only the sconces along the wall now shone, barely illuminating the scene by the doors to the entrance hall, which was in shadow. Mr. Rutherford was lying prostrate on the floor, seemingly unconscious, an arm of the chandelier across his legs, surrounded by broken glass. The heavy fixture had apparently come crashing down upon him as he made his way toward the front door to lock it for the night.

The door from the blue drawing room opened and Sister Barnabas raced to Mr. Rutherford, checking for a pulse. She looked up at Skip, who had come closer. "He's alive. Help me get this off him."

Henry appeared, too, followed by Miss Grant in her robe and nightgown, and Jake, who was still fully dressed, down to the red bandanas protruding from his back pocket and around his neck. They all cleared away some of the debris, and then Henry helped Mr. Rutherford, who had regained consciousness but seemed stunned, to the sofa in the yellow drawing room.

"Get a cold washcloth, Jane," the sister barked. "And Jake, clean up that mess in the hall. Mr. Finch, get him a brandy." She knelt by Mr. Rutherford, who looked pale and shaken.

"What happened?" he said, his voice weak and cracking.

"The hall chandelier fell, came loose most likely, and struck you. You're lucky it wasn't a direct blow, or you would have been killed," she said.

"How strange," he said weakly.

"What were you doing in the blue drawing room, Sister? I thought you'd gone up," Skip said.

The nun looked at him over the top of her glasses. "I did go up, but just to put Mrs. Rutherford to bed with a sleeping draught. Then I took some aspirin and came back down. Since you were still with Mr. Rutherford, I went across the hall."

"You didn't want to join us?"

"Your conversation appeared, shall we say, rather heated and private."

Skip flushed again, remembering how angry he'd been and the things that had been said.

"I see." He turned his attention back to Mr. Rutherford, who was lying now on the sofa, his head propped up with a pillow. "Well, I'm glad you're all right, sir. Can you stand on your own?" Skip said.

"Yes, I think so. I'm fine. Thankfully I don't think there's anything broken. I just feel a trifle woozy." He took the brandy Henry brought him and lay back down as Jane entered with the wet washcloth, handing it to Sister Barnabas.

"Hold this cloth to your head, Mr. Rutherford. I think we should have a doctor examine you just in case. You may have a concussion," the sister said.

Mr. Rutherford shook his head, causing the washcloth to slip, water from it dripping onto his shirt. "No, no need for a doctor, I'm fine. I just want to go to bed." He managed to drink most of the brandy, spilling only a little down the side of his face onto the sofa.

"As you wish, sir," Sister Barnabas said. "Jane, you may go for now. I think Mr. Finch and Mr. Valentine can get him upstairs to his bedroom."

"All right," Jane said. She looked doubtful and concerned but retreated and left nevertheless.

"Oh, I'm afraid I never did get the front door locked. Mr. Valentine, would you mind?" Mr. Rutherford said, now sitting up on the sofa again, holding the washcloth to his forehead rather sloppily. "Henry, another brandy, please, no ice this time."

"Yes sir," Henry said, going to the sideboard once more, his uncle's empty glass in hand.

"I'll be happy to," Skip said, glad of an excuse to get away. He went back out in the hall to the entry, and then on to the front door, which he dutifully locked before examining the latch that held the chandelier chain in place. He was careful not to get in the way of Jake, who was sweeping up the broken glass, having moved most of the metal pieces out of the way already. Henry came out of the drawing room.

"I thought I'd come to check on you," Henry said. "You okay?"

"A little shaken up, but not as much as your uncle. You?"

"Likewise. Get the front door locked?"

"Yes, all done. I also had a look at the chandelier latch here," he said, pointing to the contraption on the wall, his voice low and quiet.

"Oh?"

"I don't see how it could have accidentally come undone. If I'm looking at this right, and if I remember what your uncle told us, to lower it you have to insert the crank and then remove the safety pin, holding on to the crank. Only then can anyone wind it down."

"That sounds right. So, what happened?"

"If you ask me, somebody inserted the crank, removed the safety pin, and then let go, letting it spin wildly down on top of Mr. Rutherford."

"You mean on purpose?"

"That's the way I see it, Henry. The crank is clearly in the gear hole, and remember he told us they keep it on top of the clock?"

"Maybe Miss Grant or Jake forgot to put it back the last time it was cleaned, and the safety pin slipped."

"At exactly the moment Mr. Rutherford was nearly beneath it? I think we should call the police."

"But why would anyone want to hurt him?"

Skip stared at him but didn't reply right away, fighting something inside him. Finally, he took a deep breath. "I don't know. By the way, I noticed you were already downstairs when it happened. I thought you'd gone up to bed."

"I did. Or at least I was upstairs. I heard the crash and rushed down. You had your back to me, focusing on what had happened, so I guess you didn't see me."

"But you're still fully dressed."

"I was using the bathroom before going to my room, brushing my teeth and all. I'd just finished when the accident happened."

"All right," Skip said. "Let's go talk to your uncle before he goes upstairs."

Together they walked back to the yellow drawing room, where the sister and Mr. Rutherford were conversing. Briefly, Skip filled him in on what he had found, but his reaction was almost identical to Henry's.

"I appreciate your concern, Mr. Valentine, but it was simply an unfortunate accident. The police would come to the same conclusion."

"But they could take fingerprints on the crank, question the suspects…"

"What suspects? The members of this household? Let's not add insult to injury."

"There is Jake…" Sister Barnabas said quietly.

"I don't want to think about it," Mr. Rutherford said. "Not now. I think right now we should all go to bed. I'm feeling much better."

"But the boy has anger issues, he's lashed out at you before."

"I know. I've spoken to Jane about it, but let's not talk of it tonight." He turned to Skip and Henry. "Remember, breakfast is served in the dining room, à la carte, between seven and nine. Come down as you wish. I'm always the first one up, a morning bird, I am. I usually wake with the dawn. Sister likes to sleep in when she can, and Jane usually takes a breakfast tray up to Mother around seven thirty or eight."

"Perhaps Mr. Finch or Mr. Valentine can assist you in getting up the stairs and into your room, Mr. Rutherford," the sister said.

"Good grief, I'm fine. Leave me be. I can manage on my own. Go on now, go, all of you," Mr. Rutherford said, a hint of irritation in his voice.

Skip opened his mouth to speak but couldn't think of anything else to say, so he followed Henry out and they went upstairs to their rooms, Sister Barnabas staying behind just in case.

When Skip had brushed his teeth, undressed, and put on his pajamas, he knocked three times on the connecting door. Henry answered with two raps of his own. "What's up?" Henry said in a low whisper.

"I can't help feeling the chandelier falling wasn't an accident."

"But if anyone was standing at the lever, crank in hand, Mr. Rutherford would have easily seen them, Skip."

"That's true, but the lever is just outside the door to the blue drawing room. Someone could have reached out, inserted the crank, and let it go when they saw him coming. And I saw Sister Barnabas coming out of the blue drawing room."

"I suppose that's a possibility, but she has no motive. If anyone did it, and I don't think that's the case, my money would be on Jake. As Uncle Ambrose and Sister Barnabas said, he has anger issues. And did you notice he was fully dressed?" Henry said.

"Yes, I did, but so were you."

"What's that supposed to mean? I told you I was using the bathroom before going to my room to get ready for bed."

"I know, sorry. But Jake couldn't have been hiding in the blue drawing room, or the sister would have seen him."

"He may have been in the hall, in the shadows, or in one of the deep doorways. And Jake knows how to operate the crank."

"Yes, you're right. Ugh, it's all enough to make my head hurt."

"Mine, too. But I still think it was just an unfortunate accident. Let's try to get some sleep, okay? I'm exhausted."

"Okay, Finch, night. Meet in the hall at seven?"

"Sure. Night, Valentine."

Skip was asleep as soon as his head met the pillow, but he slept fitfully, tossing and turning. He had a dream where Miss Grant, Sister Barnabas, and Mrs. Rutherford were putting together a jigsaw puzzle with him, but none of the pieces fit. Mrs. Rutherford got angry and upset the table. And then he was in his bed, and Sister Barnabas was trying to put him to sleep, all the while talking softly and sweetly, but he couldn't understand her because her mouth was full of marbles, which kept dropping out and hitting him in the face. And Jake kept banging and breaking things, but nobody but Skip seemed to notice. And the worst of it, Jake morphed into Henry, only he was naked except for a red bandanna, and he was laughing maniacally while pounding on Skip's door as a mutt barked in the distance.

Abruptly Skip awoke, confused and sweating, but the noises continued. His mind went immediately to the ghosts of Bitters and his dog. He threw back the covers and swung his legs over, his feet landing on the soft area rug to the side of the bed. The room was dark, and the noises stopped as quickly as they had started—or did they? No, it was just Skip's heart pounding loudly, his breathing heavy. He switched on the bedside lamp and stood, not sure what to do. Had he imagined it? Had he dreamt it? Needing validation, Skip walked over to the connecting door to Henry's room and softly rapped three times upon it once more. Almost immediately two knocks came back in response.

"You heard it, too?" Henry said. "The pounding and the barking?"

"Yes, it woke me up. Where was it coming from?"

"I don't know, but it sounded like it was inside the house, yet far away, distant, if that makes any sense."

"Like ghosts," Skip said.

"Maybe. I'm going to have a look in the hall."

"Meet you there."

Skip went out as quietly as he could. Henry was already there, wearing striped pajamas that almost glowed in the darkness. They stood there listening, staring at each other dimly, but the house was silent. The clock in the hall downstairs struck three, and they both jumped, then laughed nervously.

"Doesn't seem like anyone else in the house appears to have heard the noises," Skip said.

"They must all be sound sleepers. I'm surprised it didn't rouse Mrs. Rutherford, though. She said she'd heard it before, remember?"

"Yes, but the sister said she'd given her a sleeping draught, so I suppose she slept through it."

"True. Let's try to get some more sleep. We can investigate in the morning."

"I hate to break it to you, Finch, but it is morning," Skip said, yawning.

"Ugh, you're right. See you in a few hours." Henry leaned over and kissed him in the dark, and Skip felt it go down to his bare toes.

"May I say you look pretty attractive in those pajamas, Mr. Finch?"

Henry wrapped his arms crisscrossed over his chest. "Thanks, but it's so dark you can barely see me. And it feels weird wearing pajamas. At home, I sleep naked."

"I know, same here."

"Just the way I like it. Ugh, I'm cold. This house is awfully drafty."

"Want me to keep you warm for a while?" Skip said, moving close and speaking low.

"I thought you'd never ask," Henry whispered. He took Skip's hand, and the two of them disappeared quietly into Henry's room and shut the door.

CHAPTER SEVEN

Early Saturday morning, October 7, 1950
The Rutherford house

Skip snuck happily back to his own bed after an hour or so, but awoke again at six fifteen and figured he might as well get up and get dressed. He was putting on his saddle shoes when he heard a man's voice cry out, and several thumps, bumps, groans, and moans. "Now what?" Skip said to himself as he ran out of his bedroom. The hall, however, was surprisingly empty and no one seemed about.

He peered over the railing, the east-facing stained glass windows filling the landing and stairs with filtered, multicolored morning light. At the bottom he could just see Mr. Rutherford, his left ankle twisted oddly, looking up at Skip.

"I'm afraid the noise you heard was me falling down the stairs, Mr. Valentine."

"Yikes." Skip started down, but when he reached the top landing, Mr. Rutherford called up again.

Be careful. I tripped over something, I'm not sure what."

Skip proceeded cautiously but could see nothing on the stairs. The hall clock was striking seven. The remains of the chandelier, Skip noticed, had been cleared away, leaving nothing but the wire and chain hanging from the ceiling.

"Are you all right?" Skip said.

"My ankle's a bit turned, but I don't think anything's broken. Can't imagine what I tripped on."

"What happened?" Henry said, coming through the door under the landing. "I heard a lot of thumping."

"I tripped on the stairs, but I'm okay," Mr. Rutherford said.

"Where were you, Henry?" Skip said.

"Hmm? Oh, well, I slept quite soundly after we, uh, I mean, after I, uh, finally fell asleep. I woke up and thought I'd come down to the kitchen for a glass of milk. After I finished, I used the powder room under the stairs, which is when I heard all the noises."

"You came down in your robe and pajamas?" Skip said.

"Sure. I didn't want to get dressed just yet, and I figured everyone else was still asleep. I thought I'd go up to shave and wash before putting on what I planned to wear today."

"I see. Well, get your uncle to his feet and into a comfortable chair, maybe get him some water. May I borrow your handkerchief, Mr. Rutherford?" Skip said, holding out his hand. "I want to check the stairs."

"My handkerchief? Certainly," he said, extracting it from his pocket. "Here you are, but what are you hoping to find?"

"Maybe whatever tripped you." Skip took the handkerchief and climbed back up the first flight of stairs, scanning each riser carefully. Something caught his eye near the top. In the molding to the right was a tiny bit of fishing line. Just above it, a small screw protruded from the wood. Using the handkerchief like a glove, Skip carefully undid the screw and deposited it in the pocket of his trousers. He went back down and into the library, where Henry had helped Mr. Rutherford into an overstuffed chair and propped his leg up on the matching ottoman.

"Better ring for some ice for his ankle, Henry," Skip said.

"Right," Henry said, tugging on the bell cord by the fireplace.

"Did you find anything on the stairs, Mr. Valentine?" Mr. Rutherford said.

"As a matter of fact, sir, I did. A tiny screw in the molding, nearly invisible. Didn't you say you're always the first one up in the house? The first one downstairs?"

Mr. Rutherford nodded thoughtfully as he bent to massage his ankle. "Yes, always. They call me the early bird, and the early bird catches the worm, you know. But what does that have to do with anything?"

"Someone may have rigged a trip wire knowing you would be the first one down, so to speak. You could have broken your neck," Skip said.

"A trip wire? That's absurd."

"I don't think so. It would be a fairly simple matter to put a screw into the wood, attach a wire or string, and run it across the step and down the stair wall. Then all someone would have to do is wait for you to start to descend, give it a good tug, and trip you up. The wire probably wasn't attached tightly to the screw, so when your foot hit it, it came loose. Whoever pulled it wound it back up and disappeared before you saw them."

"Disappeared to where?" Mr. Rutherford said.

Skip walked back out into the hall and then returned. "They were probably standing next to the door under the landing, below where I found the screw, and then went through the door after you'd fallen," he said. "Did you see anyone, Henry?"

"No, but I was in the toilet. The hall through that door also goes to the kitchen, basement, and yard."

"I guess it could have been anyone," Skip said, but he was looking at Henry.

"Or no one," Mr. Rutherford said. "I don't know about any screw in the wood, but most likely I tripped over my own feet, not paying attention. You have an active imagination."

Skip looked doubtful. "I don't know. The chandelier last night, and now this? It's too much of a coincidence, in my opinion."

"Well, a trip wire could hardly be considered an accident. But who in this household would seriously want to harm me, unless..."

"Unless?"

"It came to me last night after I'd gone to bed that I thought I saw Jake lurking in the shadows in the hall. I didn't think much about it then because he's always skulking silently about, but now, well, I don't know what to think. Still, I'm surprised I didn't notice a wire running across the steps. I have fairly keen eyesight."

"It may not have been a wire. I found a small piece of what appears to be fishing line on the stairs, too, which is nearly invisible." Skip's mind went immediately to Henry again and his tackle box, as much as he didn't want it to. "Did you lock your bedroom door last night, Henry, after I left?" Skip said.

"After you left, Mr. Valentine?" Mr. Rutherford said, raising an eyebrow. "What were you doing in Henry's room?"

Skip felt his cheeks flush. "Oh, well, I went in briefly to borrow something, that's all. So did you lock it?"

"My door? No, why?" Henry said, also embarrassed.

"Just a thought. By the way, Mr. Rutherford, did you hear anything around three this morning?"

He shook his head slowly. "No, nothing. I woke up at six, my usual time. I think I slept well considering all that happened earlier. Sister Barnabas gave me a sleeping draught, too. Why do you ask?"

"Because Henry and I both heard a dog barking and someone pounding."

"At three in the morning?" Mr. Rutherford said, raising his eyebrows.

"That's right. It woke us both up. I mean, it woke me up, and I got up to find that it had woken Henry up in his own room. We weren't together, of course," Skip said, his cheeks blushing once more as he remembered Mr. Rutherford's earlier comments and accusations.

"It sounded as if the noises were coming from inside the house," Henry said.

"Nonsense. You each had a bad dream. I'm afraid my mother's put notions into both your heads is all. All that talk of Bitters and his dog haunting the house. Utterly ridiculous."

"But it's all so strange, Mr. Rutherford. And what are the chances of the chandelier falling just as you walked beneath it? And the trip wire at the top of the stairs?" Skip said.

"Most likely accidents, and I don't believe in ghosts," Ambrose said. "That screw may have been there for years, left over from when we had a runner on the stairs, perhaps."

Henry and Skip both looked at each other as Miss Grant entered. "You rang, sir?"

"Mr. Finch did," Skip said. "Mr. Rutherford's had a bad spill down the stairs. I'm surprised you didn't hear it."

"I've been in the kitchen, starting breakfast." She walked over to Mr. Rutherford. "Are you all right, sir?" she said.

"I'm fine. Just a bit of a swollen ankle, nothing broken. Would you be so kind as to bring me some ice for it?"

"Of course," she said. "Perhaps you *should* have had a doctor look after you last night. You may have a concussion after all. You might have gotten dizzy, causing you to lose your footing."

"I didn't get dizzy or lose my footing. I tripped, Jane. Something or someone tripped me."

"It does appear that way," Skip said. "By the way, Miss Grant, did you happen to hear anything during the night? Around three this morning?"

She looked at Skip. "Why, no, I didn't. I'm a sound sleeper, nothing wakes me except the dawn."

"What about Jake?" Skip said. "Did he hear anything?"

"I don't believe so, no. He didn't say anything to me about any noises or barking. If he'd heard anything, he would have said something when I saw him this morning," Miss Grant said.

"What time did you come down to start breakfast?" Skip said.

"I get up at five thirty and come down to the kitchen at six or six fifteen. Breakfast is ready by seven, sometimes a little earlier."

"I suppose you use the back stairs," Skip said.

"Of course," she said. "Was there anything else you needed?"

"No, Jane, thank you," Mr. Rutherford said.

"All right. As soon as I get that ice, I'll finish setting everything up in the dining room."

"Good. Oh, and Jane, tell Jake I wish to see him."

"He's started making the ice cream for tonight's dinner, sir."

"That can wait. I wish to see him immediately."

Miss Grant looked troubled and upset. "Yes sir. Excuse me."

"Mr. Rutherford, I think you should telephone the police and have them investigate this," Skip said.

He held up his hand. "Absolutely not, I'd be a laughingstock. There's no evidence."

"I have the screw I extracted from the molding. It may have someone's fingerprint on it," Skip said, taking it out and holding it in the handkerchief for him to see.

Mr. Rutherford looked at it closely. "As I said, who knows how long it's been there? And it's so small I doubt there would be any prints, but *if* I decide to phone the police after I speak with Jake, I'll bring it to their attention."

"Do you think that's wise, questioning him yourself?" Skip said. "Wouldn't it be better to let the police do it?"

"*If* there actually was a trip wire, as you seem to think, and *if* Jake was involved, it may have been his idea of a practical joke, that's all. Not a funny one, I must admit, but just a joke. I don't want to get the authorities involved unless absolutely necessary, for his sake and Jane's."

"You could have been killed," Skip said.

"I highly doubt it. The chandelier almost completely missed me. And the little fall down the stairs? As you can see, I'm none the worse for wear except for a sprained ankle. I'll be right as rain tomorrow. Now don't give it another thought, please. Besides, we have a nurse in the house, remember? I'll be well taken care of."

"I still think it should be reported, but that's up to you, of course."

"Indeed it is." He nodded toward Henry. "You should get dressed before Sister Barnabas sees you cavorting about the house in your robe and pajamas."

"Oh, yes, I will. Time got away from me. It's getting late."

"I'll say it is," Skip said. "We were supposed to meet in the upstairs hall at seven, and here it is a quarter past, and you're not dressed."

"As I said, time got away from me."

"I'm sure," Skip said, turning to Mr. Rutherford once more. "Where is Sister Barnabas, by the way?"

"Probably giving my mother her morning sponge bath. She'll be down later."

"Most likely she hasn't heard all this commotion, then. Let's go back up to your room, Henry. I want to check something, and then you can finally get dressed. We'll be down later for breakfast, Mr. Rutherford."

"Certainly, take your time. I'm not going anywhere," he said.

"Let us know if you need anything, Uncle."

"I will. Now run along and get dressed. I need to speak with Jake."

Skip and Henry went up to Henry's bedroom, leaving Mr. Rutherford in his chair, his leg still elevated upon the ottoman.

"Where's your tackle box?" Skip said as they entered Henry's bedroom.

"Right here by the door," he said, pointing down to the rusty gray box sitting next to the dresser.

"Hmm, convenient for someone to slip in during the night or early morning hours and take a piece of your fishing line to use as a trip wire," Skip said. "Who knew you had it?"

Henry scratched his head. "Well, Miss Grant and Jake, of course, from when we arrived, and everybody else, too, I guess. I mentioned it at dinner, remember?"

"Right. Hmm. Take a look inside. Does it look like anything's been disturbed?"

Henry bent down and examined the contents. "It's hard to tell," Henry said, closing the lid. "I am afraid I'm not as fastidious as I should be when it comes to my fishing equipment, and I doubt I'd miss a little fishing line. The new spool hasn't been touched, but I have a partial one in there, too. Someone may have snipped some off."

"Okay. By the way, did you notice what Miss Grant said when I asked if she'd heard anything during the night?"

"Sure, she said she hadn't heard anything and that she was a sound sleeper. Only the dawn wakes her."

"Exactly," Skip said. "But what *didn't* she say?"

"Huh?"

"I mean, she didn't ask why I was wondering that or what, if anything, I had heard."

"Gee, you're right. And when you asked if Jake had heard anything, she mentioned the barking. How would she know if she hadn't heard it? I admit that's a bit odd," Henry said.

"She's a bit odd."

"I'm beginning to think so, too."

"Also, did you notice how upset she seemed when your uncle said he wished to see Jake right away?"

"Yeah, do you think she thinks Jake had something to do with the accidents?"

"Possibly. Maybe he did. And why would Miss Grant lie about hearing the pounding and barking?"

"I don't know, but we should steer clear of this Jake character. He sounds like trouble."

"I agree, but we don't know all the goings-on of this house and the relationships within it yet."

"And I don't think it's our business to find out, Skip," Henry said.

"Mr. Rutherford should have at least reported it to the police."

"But maybe he did trip over his own feet, as he said."

"You think it was an accident, too?"

"I'm not sure. I mean, it's possible the screw could have been there for a while. And it's possible the chandelier just fell. We don't know. At least he wasn't badly injured, and he seems to want to handle it himself with Jake, so I think we should forget about it."

"What about that tiny piece of what appeared to be fishing line?"

"If that's what it was, it could have been stuck in the lid of my tackle box and dropped off when Jake carried it upstairs, or it could have been lying there for years. Remember, Mrs. Rutherford and her husband used to fish. Anyway, I suppose I'd better get dressed. I'm peckish."

"Okay. Say, after we eat, why don't we take a stroll and explore the neighborhood? It looks like a lovely morning."

"Sure, that sounds good," Henry said. "I'll meet you in the dining room for breakfast as soon as I'm ready."

"Okay. By the way, do you happen to have a nail file and a paper clip?"

"Huh? What for?"

"Never mind. Do you?"

"Well sure, I have a nail file in my shaving kit, and there's a paper clip on those papers the attorneys gave me for my records," Henry said.

"Good. Let me have them, please."

Henry got the items and handed them to Skip. "Here you go. Part of me wants to know why you want them and another part definitely doesn't. I'm surprised you don't have a nail file of your own."

"I do, but I broke it earlier last night. See you in the dining room. Careful on the stairs," Skip said with a smile as he put the paper clip and file in his trousers pocket and exited Henry's bedroom. He went down, holding carefully to the banister and watching for anything else out of the ordinary on the steps.

Chapter Eight

Breakfast, Saturday, October 7, 1950
The Rutherford house

Henry made it to the dining room by seven forty-five, freshly shaved and dressed.

"Something smells wonderful," he said as he entered.

"Looks like Miss Grant is a good cook," Skip said. "Eggs, bacon, hash browns, orange juice, coffee, coffee cake, strudel, and more all on the sideboard. I was tempted to start without you. Your uncle decided to eat in the library because of his ankle and have a tray brought in, and apparently, Miss Grant will take a tray up to his mother's room per usual."

"I see. What about Sister Barnabas?" Henry said.

"I haven't seen or heard from her yet."

"Well, no sense in waiting any longer. Let's eat."

"Sounds good to me, mister."

Each of them filled a large plate, and Henry put bread in the toaster for them. When it was done, he extracted it carefully using the silver tongs provided and brought it to the table, where homemade jam and butter awaited. When they'd nearly finished eating, Sister Barnabas came in from the hall, moving slowly along from side to side, as usual. Henry and Skip got to their feet. "Good morning, Sister."

"Good morning, gentlemen, I trust you both slept well," she said, looking at them over the top of her glasses once more.

"Yes, thank you, more or less, and you?" Henry said.

"I did, I usually do. Please sit, I can serve myself," she said, moving over to the sideboard as Skip and Henry sat back down.

"Nothing disturbed you, Sister? Say around three in the morning?"

She turned slightly to look at Skip. "Disturbed me? No, nothing. I slept soundly. Why?"

"Mr. Finch and I were both woken up by a strange noise," Skip said, watching her face.

"What kind of a noise?"

"A dog barking and someone pounding."

The nun moved back to the buffet. "How odd. There are no dogs in the neighborhood that I'm aware of, none close by anyway, and I can't imagine why anyone would be pounding so early in the morning. My, the bacon looks delicious, nice and crisp."

"Did you hear about Mr. Rutherford's accident?" Henry said. "The one on the stairs this morning?"

She kept her back to them as she placed various food items onto her plate. "Miss Grant informed me when I'd finished bathing Mrs. Rutherford. How unfortunate. Though two accidents so close together does make one wonder. I'm glad once again he wasn't badly injured."

"Yes, he was lucky," Skip said. "What does it make you wonder, Sister?"

"About what God is thinking, of course."

Skip leaned back in his chair. "Not exactly what I was wondering. May I pour you some coffee?"

The sister turned around, a full plate in hand, and sat at the table. "Yes, thank you. Black."

Skip poured a cup and handed it to her.

"Thank you," she said, glancing at Skip and Henry's plates. "It appears as though you two are all finished eating."

"Yes, but we don't mind keeping you company," Henry said.

"Oh, how nice."

"But, uh, we need to get going, Henry. We've lots to do."

"We do?"

"Yes," Skip said firmly.

"Don't worry about me," Sister Barnabas said. "Go and do what you need to do. I'll be fine."

"All right, we'll see you at lunch, Sister," Henry said, rising to his feet, with Skip following suit.

"Miss Grant is serving meatloaf, I believe," she said, taking a sip of her coffee and a forkful of scrambled eggs. "Not one of her better dishes, but I'm sure it will be fine. Enjoy your morning."

"And you as well," Skip said as he and Henry exited the dining room.

"What are all these things we need to do, Skip?"

"A nice, long walk, for one, but I need to get my hat first. Let's go back upstairs."

"I'll wait here. My hat's still hanging by the front door in the entryway."

Skip frowned. "I'd appreciate it if you'd accompany me upstairs."

Henry looked at him curiously but didn't argue. "Okay, let's go."

At the top of the stairs, Skip paused. "Wait right here, Henry, okay? I need to use the bathroom first."

"All right, but hurry up," Henry said. Skip went back down the four steps to the landing and proceeded through the small hall into the bathroom, locking the door and turning on the overhead light. The cabinet above the sink was still locked. It was the old-fashioned kind, mounted to the wall and painted white. Skip tried the nail file first, but its end was too big for the keyhole. The paper clip was just the right size but hard to maneuver, and the angle wasn't the best. At last, he hitched up his trousers and sat on the sink, finding that to be much better. In three clicks, the cabinet swung open, revealing an assortment of bottles and thingamabobs, as well as a toothbrush, toothpowder in a tin, lipstick, a compact, nail polish, and some rouge. There was a bottle of hair dye, too, but what caught his attention the most was a clear glass bottle with a metal screw cap, its label missing. Inside was a silvery liquid that shimmied around when he shook it. He placed everything back where he found it and closed the cabinet door. Skip wiggled the paper clip back and forth, up and down, and back and forth again until finally, he heard a click. Sliding off the sink onto the floor, he gave the knob a gentle tug, and it didn't budge. Satisfied, he gave the toilet a flush, ran the water in the sink, stepped out the door, and went back up the four steps to the hall.

"All set?" Henry said.

"Yes."

"Good, then get your hat, and let's go."

The two of them walked to Skip's door.

"If you see or hear anyone coming while I'm in there, knock three times. Our signal, remember?" Skip said.

"Huh? Why?" Henry said, puzzled.

"Because I need a lookout, silly."

"To get your hat?"

"Because I want to have a peek about in Sister Barnabas's bedroom."

"What for?"

"If I knew, I wouldn't have to look. But there's something odd about her. I dreamed of her last night. Plus, she was conveniently in the blue drawing room right before the chandelier incident, remember?"

"Skip, you're going to get us both in trouble. Nuns aren't creepy, they're well-mannered and helpful, and pure and kind."

"Clearly you didn't go to a Catholic school," Skip said.

"Chicago public schools, all the way."

"And you probably got a much better education."

"You can't go snooping about her room. It's not right."

"If she's what she says she is, she has nothing to hide. Did you notice anything odd about her at the breakfast table?"

Henry thought a moment. "No, why? What did you notice?"

"For one thing, I don't like the way she's always staring at us over the top of her glasses. And for another, she didn't say grace, genuflect, or pray before starting to eat. Doesn't that strike you as unusual?"

"Maybe she just forgot, or did it silently because we were there."

Skip rolled his eyes. "Oh, for heaven's sake, just wait out here in the hall. If anyone comes, *especially* her, knock three times on my door. Got it?"

"Got it. Oh, bother. Hurry up and don't be long."

"I won't, I promise."

Skip glanced about to make sure no one was in sight, then gave Henry a peck on the cheek before disappearing into his bedroom. He extracted the paper clip and nail file from his pocket once more and picked the lock to Sister Barnabas's room fairly easily. The room was almost square in shape, with the door to the hall on the back wall, three windows overlooking the balcony, and a single door on the opposite wall in the front corner. Skip walked over to that door as quietly as he could, cringing every time the wood floor creaked. It was unlocked and he opened it slowly, cautiously peering in at what he discovered was Mrs. Rutherford's room. Fortunately, she wasn't visible. Skip closed the door again as quietly as he could and moved to one on the opposite side of the room, but this one *was* locked. The nail file did the job this time, and it soon swung open silently. Skip found himself staring at an assortment of colorful dresses, blouses, skirts, and other fashion apparel. On the floor were several pairs of stylish shoes. He turned around and inspected the rest of the room carefully, but found nothing else out of the ordinary.

❖

Meanwhile, Henry was pacing back and forth in the hallway when he saw a shadow over the railing on the stairs. It was Sister Barnabas. Quickly he knocked and pounded three times upon Skip's bedroom door. Hoping he'd heard him, he looked back at the stairs as she reached the first landing, carrying her glasses in her hand.

"Sister," he called down to her loudly, "finished with your breakfast so soon?"

"I wasn't as hungry as I thought, Mr. Finch," she said, as she started slowly up the second run of stairs toward him, grasping the handrail and using it to haul herself up. "And I'm afraid I have another headache. They've become frequent and bothersome lately. It might be these glasses," she said, putting them back on.

"I'm sorry to hear that. Perhaps some fresh air or a morning stroll," he said.

"No, just a cool compress, some aspirin, and a lie-down with my glasses off will help. Are you waiting for Mr. Valentine?"

"What? Er, yes, he had to get his hat. He should be out soon. We're going to go for a walk and explore the neighborhood."

"I heard there's a football game today. Best to avoid downtown or the stadium area."

"Good to know, thanks." He turned and pounded three more times.

"Why are you knocking so hard? You'll disturb Mrs. Rutherford, and you're making my headache worse," she scolded. She was on the second landing now, breathing heavily.

"Sorry. Going to your room, then, Sister?" Henry said as loudly as he could.

"Yes, I find that's a good place to lie down. As soon as I get some aspirin from the bathroom. And I'm not deaf, Mr. Finch, though perhaps you should have your hearing checked."

"Yes, perhaps so. Hearing loss seems to run in my family, you know," Henry said, almost shouting. "It comes and goes." He was stalling for time as best he could and hoping Skip could hear him.

❖

Skip had heard the pounding the first time, and the second time wasn't helping his nerves. He had scurried back into his room, but it dawned on him he had left the closet door unlocked. Quickly he ducked back inside and over to the closet, closing the door as quietly as possible and once more using the nail file to relock the lock. Then he dashed back into his room, securing the connecting door just as he heard the hall door to Sister Barnabas's room open and close.

When he stepped out into the hall a minute later, straw hat in hand, Henry breathed a sigh of relief and wiped a bead of sweat off his brow with his handkerchief. Sister Barnabas was nowhere to be seen. "You practically gave me a heart attack, Valentine," he said, much softer now. "She got her aspirin and went back to her room. What were you doing in there for so long?"

"I'll tell you all about it on our walk."

"All right, let's go," Henry said.

Sister Barnabas opened her bedroom door and peeked out at them over the top of her glasses. "Excuse me, gentlemen, but if you two are going for a walk, I wonder if you'd be so kind as to pick up some cigarettes for Mr. Rutherford? I told him I would get them for him, but I'm afraid I'm not feeling up to it now that I have this headache again."

"Certainly, we'd be glad to," Henry said.

"Thank you. Mr. Rutherford will reimburse you. He smokes Lucky Strikes. You are going out, then, aren't you?"

"Yes, we're just leaving," Skip said.

"There's a drugstore about six blocks south from here, just off Packard on the corner, past Shadford Road. You can't miss it."

"Okay. Let's go, Skip. Good day, Sister," Henry said.

"Good day," Sister Barnabas said. She watched them go down until they were out of sight, and then retreated into her room again, closing the door.

CHAPTER NINE

Later Saturday morning, October 7, 1950
The Neighborhood

When they reached the bottom of the stairs, they crossed to the entry doors. Henry gathered up his hat, and they went outside to the porch. When Henry had closed the front door behind him, Skip looked up at his face. "You were swell back there. Thanks to you, I got out of her room in time."

"Good. I'm new to this detective stuff, but I'm learning."

"You did great. Let's walk a bit."

"Okay, but we could go get the cigarettes right away and then come back. If we change our clothes, we could take a picnic lunch to a park or something by the river. I'm sure Miss Grant could arrange a basket for us, maybe a bottle of wine. It's warmed up, and according to the newspaper it's supposed to be in the mid to high sixties by this afternoon."

"I like the sound of that, Henry. It's been ages since I've had a picnic, but let's save that for tomorrow before we leave, okay?" he said, placing his straw hat at a rakish angle on his head. "There are a few other things I want to do today."

"Whatever you say, Valentine." He put on his own hat and strolled down the steps to the sidewalk with Skip by his side. "Just being with you is a picnic to me."

"I feel the same way. You're the bread to my butter, Henry. Let's go around the block, shall we? I love to look at all these big old houses."

"It seems to me we could have done that in Chicago. They have plenty of old houses back home," Henry said.

"But not these same houses," Skip said. "Come on."

They turned left at the end of the front walk and strolled casually and slowly down the tree-lined street, pausing now and then to comment on a house or its yard and garden, or to exchange pleasantries with a neighbor on their porch. When they reached South Forest Avenue they went left again, meandering slowly past the grounds of the Eberbach estate toward Wells Street, where they made yet another left.

"So," Henry said, as they passed under an old chestnut tree, "what exactly were you looking for in Sister Barnabas's room that you needed me to stand guard in the hall for, anyway? And did you find anything?"

"I wasn't sure what I was searching for, as I told you before, but I certainly did find something. In the sister's closet, which was locked, by the way, there were dresses, skirts, blouses, and fancy shoes, and in the medicine cabinet in the bathroom, which was also locked, I found, along with the expected toothbrush and toothpowder, a lipstick, a compact and some rouge, and a bottle of hair dye. There was a small glass bottle with something silvery and shimmery in it, too."

They stopped under the shade of another chestnut tree, this one not as large as the last. "Okay, I get it. Why would a nun have dresses, skirts, blouses, lipstick, rouge, and hair dye?"

"Exactly. It doesn't make any sense. And who locks their closet and medicine cabinet?"

"I agree with you, it does seem strange. Say, if the closet and the cabinet were locked, how did you get them open, anyway?"

"I have my methods," Skip said coyly.

"The paper clip and nail file, I bet."

"See? You're getting better at this detective business."

"Thanks, I have a good teacher. But if you're that talented at picking locks, why is the connecting door between our rooms still locked?"

"That one is trickier. It's been locked so long it may be rusted," Skip said with a sly smile.

"And that's how you broke your nail file."

"Guilty. I wanted to surprise you. I'll work on it more tonight. If I can get it open, it would certainly make sneaking back and forth a lot easier. But regardless, *if* we're going to do anything more, it will have to be in your room again, and we'll have to be quiet. Your uncle is already suspicious."

"Is he?"

"Yes. Last night he asked if I was funny, and told me he thinks you're impressionable and you shouldn't hang out with the wrong kinds of people, meaning me."

Henry scowled. "That's ridiculous. I'm far from impressionable, and you're definitely not the wrong kind of people."

"Thanks. It's not the first time someone has said I was funny, and probably won't be the last. I guess I'm just not the manly man type."

"You're man enough for me. Smart, funny, handsome, and sweet."

"I'm glad you think so, Henry. Anyway, now we have to figure out Sister Barnabas's secret."

Henry frowned. "Do you think that's a good idea, Skip? I'm sure there's a logical explanation."

"I'm sure there is, and I'd wager it's not a good one. I don't trust that woman. Let's keep walking, we still have lots to do."

"You keep saying that. Like what besides going for cigarettes?"

"Some of it remains to be seen. By the way, any thoughts on what the silvery, shimmery liquid in the bottle might be?"

"Mercury would be my guess," Henry said.

"Mercury? Why would she have a bottle of that?"

"Well, uh, it's used in thermometers and stuff, you know."

"Henry, I don't think Sister Barnabas has a hobby of making thermometers."

"Well, there are a few uses I can think of, but the one that comes to mind I hear penicillin is used more for now."

"Used more now for what?"

"Gee, Skip, it's not polite to talk about," Henry said, his cheeks flushing. "I only know about it from being a medic in the Army."

Skip stopped in his tracks and faced him. "Oh, fiddle faddle, Mr. Finch, tell me at once."

Henry's cheeks blushed a rosier red. "It was used to treat syphilis," he said quietly.

"Syphilis!" Skip said loudly, and Henry felt his cheeks begin to burn.

"Quiet, Valentine. You want all of Ann Arbor to hear you?"

"Oh, what do I care? This whole thing gets stranger and stranger."

"You can say that again," Henry said. "And I think that fella across the street heard you."

They both nodded politely and Henry tipped his hat to the older man working in his yard who had stopped raking and was staring at them, and then they continued their stroll up Wells Street, where the houses weren't quite so grand as they were on Woodlawn, but still large and mostly well kept.

"Why would a nun need a syphilis treatment, Henry?"

"She wouldn't, but like I said, there were other uses, too, mostly out of date now. It was also used as an antiseptic and diuretic. Most likely it's been in that cabinet for years, forgotten about, if that's what it is."

"Hmm, I suppose that's possible. And she is a nurse, so maybe if it is hers, it's something she used on patients."

"Could be," Henry said.

"But still, it's curious."

Eventually, they'd circled almost the entire block when Skip came to an abrupt stop, staring up at a tidy corner house with a white picket fence around it.

"This house must be directly behind your uncle's," he said.

Henry looked up at it. "Yeah, sure, that makes sense. This is the corner of Packard and Wells. My uncle's is on the corner of Packard and Woodlawn. We've almost made a complete circle, or rectangle, to be more precise."

"Yes. It's a smaller, simpler house but nice and well kept."

"I like how the front porch runs the full width of the house, perfect for sitting on a hot afternoon with a pitcher of lemonade."

Skip laughed. "Saying 'howdy, neighbor' to everyone who passes by."

"Well, sure, why not?" Henry said, grinning. "It pays to be neighborly."

"I agree. And on that note, let's go and say hello."

Henry raised his eyebrows in surprise. "To who?"

"Mrs. Savage, of course."

"Who?"

"Augusta Savage, the lady that must live here. The one that used to talk to Bitters over the back fence and called on Mrs. Rutherford every week."

"Ah, now I see what you're up to. More prying. You're going to get us into trouble with all this snooping about."

"I'm merely being friendly."

"Uh-huh. What do you hope to find out this time?"

"I'm not sure yet, once again, but we look silly standing here on the sidewalk debating. Let's go." He didn't wait for a reply, but unhitched the gate of the white picket fence and walked up the narrow, flower-lined path to the porch, where he rang the bell. Henry, he noticed, had followed behind.

"What are you going to say to her?"

"Hello, for starters."

"That's a pretty good start, I guess," Henry said.

Presently the door opened, and a woman wearing a simple house dress, her gray hair piled atop her head in a bun, stared out at them. She had deep lines on her suntanned face and bags under her brilliant hazel eyes. She was petite, her veins exposed under a thin layer of wrinkled skin.

"Mrs. Savage?" Skip said, smiling down at her.

"I'm not interested in anything you're selling, young man," the woman said, starting to close the door.

"Wait. Oh no, we're not selling anything. We're from the Rutherford house, right behind yours," Skip said, pushing back on the door, which was met with a fair amount of resistance. The little woman was surprisingly strong and tough, like a piece of barbed wire. Mrs. Savage stepped back and the door gave way, Skip almost tumbling into her arms.

"Careful, watch your step."

Skip straightened himself up and brushed off his trousers, stepping back next to Henry on the porch, somewhat embarrassed. "I do apologize, ma'am."

"It's all right. You say you're from the Rutherford house?"

"Yes, that's right. I'm Skip Valentine, and this is Henry Finch, Mr. Rutherford's nephew. We're up from Chicago for the weekend."

"I didn't know he had a nephew," she said, looking Henry up and down.

"Well, a distant relation. He's my mother's second cousin, but I've always called him uncle," Henry said. "I think he might be my second cousin once removed."

"Darn confusing, all those second cousins, first cousins once removed, and so forth," Mrs. Savage said.

"I feel the same way," Skip said.

Mrs. Savage smiled, revealing yellow teeth, one on the bottom right missing. "Well, come in, then, and have a cup of coffee with me and set a spell. Tell me why you've come to call."

"Thank you, Mrs. Savage, you're too kind," Skip said as they stepped into her front hall. The house was smaller than the Rutherford place, but it was clean and tidy if a bit dated. Nothing appeared to have changed much in the last thirty years or more.

"Just this way, my front parlor," she said, motioning them into a room on the left side of the hall. "My only parlor. You may put your hats on the table there."

"Yes, ma'am," Henry said.

"Sit, sit. I'll get the coffee. Back in two shakes of a lamb's tail."

Skip and Henry both sat dutifully next to each other on the green velvet davenport under the front windows overlooking the porch. Two matching chairs faced the sofa, their backs and arms draped with age-yellowed homemade doilies. Just past the chairs was a broad doorway into the dining room, framed with burgundy curtains. Vases full of colorful flowers made the place seem cheery. On the wall opposite the entrance to the hall stood a well-used fireplace and an old, battered upright piano, a string hanging from a front panel where a knob must have been at one time.

"I still don't understand why we're here, Skip," Henry said softly.

"As I said, just being neighborly, Henry."

"Uh-huh."

Presently the old woman returned, carrying a silver tray in need of polishing, upon which sat three porcelain cups of coffee with matching saucers, a sugar bowl, a creamer, three silver spoons, and a pair of silver tongs. Henry got to his feet to help her with it, but she shooed him back. "Sit, sit, Mr. Finch, is it? I'm quite capable."

Henry sat back down as she placed the tray on top of the coffee table and handed Skip and Henry each a cup of coffee and a saucer. "Help yourself to cream and sugar, as you like," she said, putting three sugar cubes and a dash of cream into her cup before settling into one of the green velvet chairs.

"Now," Mrs. Savage said, sipping her coffee, "why would two young men like you come to see an old lady like me?"

"Mrs. Rutherford mentioned you," Skip said, picking up one of the cups. "She said you used to call on her."

"That's right, I did. How is she?"

"Not well," Skip said.

"I didn't figure she'd gotten better since I last saw her. Sad. And all alone in that house, with no family except for her son. I'm a widow, too, and also by myself. My children have moved away. I have a grandchild, almost sixteen by now, a sweet girl. Clara's her name, my daughter Ethel's child. They don't visit much."

"I'm sorry," Henry said, taking a cup and adding a little cream to it.

"Oh, I keep myself busy. I don't have a television, too expensive, but I knit, crochet, volunteer at the church and the hospital, and I bake. Goodness, I've forgotten the biscuits and cookies. Would you like some? I just made them yesterday."

Henry shook his head and Skip said, "No, thank you, Mrs. Savage."

"Suit yourselves. So, are you two brothers?"

"No, ma'am, just good friends. Probably closer than brothers," Henry said.

"Oh, how nice, and you chose to sit closely on the davenport next to each other instead of in the chairs."

"Er, yes, I guess we did," Skip said.

"Good friends are the family we choose, you know. When were you born, dear?" she said, looking at Skip.

"January eighteenth. Why?"

"Ah, a Capricorn. And you?" she said, pointing at Henry.

"May fifteenth, ma'am."

"I knew it, a Taurus. Oh, you two are well suited to be good friends, I can see that. It's in the stars. Capricorns and Tauruses hold a significant amount of respect and love for one another. I'm an Aquarian, and my husband Jack was a Gemini. We were both strong-willed people, but we didn't let it hurt our relationship, no sir. We always knew we'd rather be together than apart. It's only a hunch, but I bet you two feel the same way."

"Uh, has your husband been gone some time?" Skip said.

"Nearly twenty years. Captain Savage, he was. He and his crew all lost in a terrible accident."

"How awful," Skip said.

"Yes. I still miss him. He was a good man. I contacted him once, through a séance my friend Velma held. He told me he missed me, but he was waiting for me in the afterlife."

"That must have given you some peace of mind," Skip said.

"Oh, indeed it did. After that, I didn't see the need to bother him anymore. But we'll have lots to catch up on when my time comes." She smiled wistfully. "He and I built this house right after we were married. We wanted a big family. We ended up with just two, a boy and a girl. There's a picture of them on the mantel there. They were just two and four when their father died."

"A lovely family," Skip said, looking over at it. "That must have been difficult for you, and for them."

"Thank you. Yes, it was. The last time they telephoned, I told them I spoke with their father via a séance, but they didn't believe me, unfortunately."

"I'm sorry. By the way, I understand your friend conducted a séance for Mrs. Rutherford, also," Skip said.

"Yes, she wanted to talk to the spirit of her dead son, Arthur, so I arranged it. Velma channeled the boy, and he told Mrs. Rutherford he was happy and content to play with his ball and roam the halls of the house, never far away from her."

"Was that the last time you saw Mrs. Rutherford? The night of the séance?"

"No, I called on her about two weeks ago, Friday, the twenty-second of September. After what happened that day, I'm done with her, I think. Every Friday for years I'd stop and visit, on my way home from my volunteer work, you see, even during the war."

"What happened that day that made you not want to return?" Henry said.

Mrs. Savage pursed her lips. "Oh, she's gotten so bad, you know, in the last few months. It all started in June, I think, or maybe it was July. She doesn't know me half the time lately or doesn't remember I was there. What's the point of my visiting? She gets angry, too, just like that." The old lady snapped her surprisingly nimble fingers. "The last time I was there, she threw a flower vase at me and nearly hit me in the head. And that is why it was the *last* time I was there."

"Oh my, that's certainly understandable," Henry said.

"Definitely," Skip said. "By the way, Mrs. Rutherford said you were friendly with Mr. Bitters before he died."

Mrs. Savage took a sip of her coffee. "Yes, that's right. We used to chat over the fence out back while I was working in my garden and he was mowing the Rutherfords' lawn or fixing something around their place. I'd bring him a glass of lemonade or a few cookies I'd just made, and he'd tell me all about the goings-on in the Rutherford household. In fact, we spoke just a couple of days before he passed away."

"Mrs. Rutherford told us you believe his death may not have been an accident," Skip said.

"My, it sounds like you two had quite a conversation with Gabria."

"It was fairly brief, but she was lucid at the time, at least for a bit, and it seemed she wanted to talk."

"I see. Well, the official verdict, of course, is that it *was* an accident, that Joe was most likely intoxicated and had passed out when the fire started. He certainly was a heavy drinker, but I do wonder. When Gabria told me about the pounding and barking she heard in the house late at night just after the fire, I put two and two together and figured it must be the ghosts of Joe and his dog Bullseye. And the only reason they'd haunt would be because they're not at rest. After all, they want someone to discover what actually happened to them. I told Velma about it, too, and she agreed."

"Not surprising," Henry said.

"No, Velma's very in tune spiritually. She told me they've taken to haunting the main house because their home was destroyed. Mrs. Rutherford told me she's the only one who's heard them, though."

"Um, how fascinating," Skip said. "Is that the only reason you think it may not have been an accident?"

"No, not entirely. You see, the fire was on August twenty-eighth. Two days before that, Joe told me he'd found something and was going to be coming into some money."

"He didn't tell you what he found?" Henry said.

"No, he didn't. But he did say he had found something important, and that if something happened to him, I should find his notes. He was rather cryptic and gave me a rhyme I simply can't figure out. And I've looked everywhere I could think of, but nothing has turned up."

"So, Mr. Bitters didn't explain what it was he had found or where to find these notes, or what they contained?" Skip said.

"No, as I said, he only gave me a puzzling rhyme that I've memorized. 'A sharp mind will find a major clue in these. Pull the cord, and you've scored the location of my keys. Unlock the quotes to find my notes, and the evidence you'll see.'"

"Huh?" Henry said.

Skip raised a brow. "You're right, that's quite a puzzle. You've no idea what he meant by all that?"

"None at all," Mrs. Savage said. "I've thought and thought about it. Regardless, the notes and evidence were most likely destroyed in the fire, so we may never know what he'd found."

"That's what Mrs. Rutherford thought, too. She couldn't fully remember the rhyme, though," Skip said.

"Still, my goodness, she *was* having a lucid moment. She didn't seem to comprehend anything I was saying at the time, so I'm surprised she recalled any of that."

"Did Mr. Bitters get along with Mr. and Mrs. Rutherford?" Skip said.

"Well enough, I suppose, but Joe didn't care for the lot of them, to be honest, and he'd say some rude things about them to me in confidence. He didn't like the sister much, either."

"Why is that?" Henry said.

"He told me he saw her the day she first arrived when Mr. Rutherford pulled up to the garage. Joe happened to be in the yard, and he went over and helped with her satchel. He said she was cordial, but then he ran into her again a few weeks later, and she barely spoke to him and was rude, keeping her distance."

"Maybe she was having a bad day," Henry said. "I imagine caring for Mrs. Rutherford got tiring quickly."

"Oh, no doubt. And Joe was not necessarily what one would call a nice man, but he was friendly enough to me. He'd visit me every so often, you know, and we'd sit right here in this room and have coffee and cake and chat. Sometimes he'd play for me."

"Play?"

"The piano," Mrs. Savage said. "He was good, and he also wrote music and poems. I never learned how to play myself, but my daughter, Ethel, took lessons. It's a player piano. You pump the foot pedals and it plays, but I could never figure out how to change the rolls, so I just leave it alone."

"I could take a look at it for you if you like," Skip said. "I took lessons for several years, and my uncle had an old player I used to fiddle with."

"Thank you, but it's fine. The knob on the compartment for the rolls broke off, too. I replaced it with a piece of twine but it's not so strong, so best to leave it be. I'm too old to fuss with it, but I can't bear to part with the piano, either."

"Sure, I understand. Lots of memories."

"Yes, some good, some not so good. Poor Joe. He was a bright man, but not the smartest. He liked his liquor, sometimes too much, as I said before, and they found quite a few empty bottles in the wreckage. That's why the police thought he may have been drunk and incapacitated, and I suppose he may have been. You know, a whole bottle of vodka went missing from my sideboard once after one of his visits."

"You think he took it?" Henry said.

Mrs. Savage laughed lightly. "Oh, my dear, of course. But I didn't mind. Joe didn't have much, you see, and I could spare a bottle of vodka. I only kept it on hand for visitors, anyway. He took other little things, too, nothing I minded. Rumor has it he was fired from his last job for dipping into the till, but that's just a rumor. I looked the other way."

"That's generous of you," Skip said.

"Oh, he repaid me many times over with his company, and his music and photographs."

"Photographs?"

"Yes, he was an amateur photographer," she said. "I'm a little embarrassed, but he took a picture of me this past summer out in my garden. I have it just here, inside my Bible." She reached over and picked up a well-worn leather Bible from off the side table, extracting a small black-and-white photograph, which she handed carefully to Skip.

"It's a good likeness, Mrs. Savage," Skip said.

"Yes, you look pretty," Henry said.

"Thank you. Still hard to believe he's gone," Mrs. Savage said wistfully. "And his old dog, too. Did you know Mrs. Rutherford also had a dog?"

"Yes, she mentioned him to us," Henry said.

"She got him a couple of years ago when she was still all right. She must have been lonely. Oh, she'd go out now and then, to church and whatnot, and folks would call on her, but she didn't seem to have any real friends. She was a stern woman, still is, and regretful."

"Regretful?" Henry said.

"That's right. She'd talk to me about her youth sometimes, before she got so sick. She was young and gay, vibrant and pretty, with lots of suitors where she grew up in Traverse City. She met Giles Rutherford when he was visiting his brother one summer, and soon they were married. She was only nineteen."

"So young," Skip said.

"Giles was older, in his late thirties, not much younger than Ambrose is now, come to think of it. But he was wealthy and charming enough, she told me. He brought her down here to Ann Arbor, where she knew no one. Unfortunately, his business kept him busy, and Gabria was left alone much of the time in that big old house with little to do."

"But she had children," Henry said.

"Yes, eventually. Her first child, a girl, was stillborn when she was twenty-eight. Her son Arthur was born several years later, and Ambrose came along a few years after that when Gabria was in her early forties, I think. I never met or saw Arthur, so protective of him, she was. Of course, she's told you Arthur died at the age of five."

"Yes, pneumonia. It claimed so many young lives back then."

"Indeed. And then, of course, her husband Giles died shortly after Ambrose was born. I suppose it's no wonder Mrs. Rutherford became a stern, strict woman, left alone with a toddler at her age, in a town that was all but foreign to her, even after all those years," Mrs. Savage said. "She told me she never liked Ann Arbor."

"I'm surprised she stayed here after her husband died," Henry said.

"I asked her that once. She used to wallow in self-pity, I'm afraid. She said nothing was left for her in Traverse City anymore. Childbirth had ruined her figure, she was over forty, worn out, and tired. Giles had arranged for her to be taken care of financially, and he had put the house in her name, so she stayed and raised Ambrose as best she could."

"But she was lonely, you said," Henry said.

"She was. Understandable, I should think. She kept to herself, never made any real friends here, and never remarried. She could be cold and distant with me. As I said, I called upon her every Friday like clockwork but she never once called upon me, wouldn't lower herself to walk to this side of the block."

"Her loss, of course," Skip said.

"Thank you. Anyway, I was pleased when, two years ago, Miss Grant found a puppy for her. Gabria took to the little runt right away, and the two of them became inseparable. I can't remember what she named him off the top of my head."

"Gipper," Henry said.

The old lady nodded, the bun on top of her head bobbing up and down. "Yes, that's right. So devoted to him she was. But the dog apparently ran away."

"She told us that, too," Skip said.

"Yes, but I'm not sure I believe it any more than I entirely believe Joe Bitters's death was an accident."

"Are you saying you think Mrs. Rutherford made it up about her dog?" Henry said.

"Oh no, I believe *she* believes he ran away, but I don't. I think that dog is dead."

"Why?" Skip said.

"I'm not one to gossip, but one night shortly after the fire, I couldn't get to sleep, I was restless. I was still upset about Joe dying, and I guess I had too much on my mind. I tossed and turned, and finally got up and looked out the bedroom window. I can see the Rutherfords' yard and old carriage house from there, you know."

"That makes sense. Your house is directly behind theirs," Henry said.

"Yes, and my bedroom is upstairs in the back. Anyway, I was standing at the window, staring down at the Rutherford place, lost in thought. There was a bright moon out, and it lit up everything almost like it was day. Everything was quiet and still, peaceful, even the crickets seemed to have gone to sleep. Then, all of a sudden, I saw a man come from the back of the Rutherford house, and it looked like he was carrying something, a box, maybe. He went into the garage and came back with a shovel, and then dug a hole beneath the old stairs near the fence. I couldn't see for certain, but it might have been Jake, Miss Grant's nephew. I'd bet money what he was carrying was a box with Gipper inside it, and I'm willing to bet dollars to doughnuts that someone killed that dog on purpose and told him to bury it."

"Why would someone do that?" Skip said, surprised and rather horrified.

"I don't know unless it was to punish Mrs. Rutherford, to get revenge on her. As you must be aware, she can be harsh and cruel. And as much as I hate to think it, it's also possible *she* may have killed the dog in one of her fits of anger."

"Oh my, that's an awful thought," Skip said.

"It is, but if she did it, I'm sure she doesn't remember. Afterward, they may have told her the dog ran away to spare her feelings and had Jake bury it." Mrs. Savage took a final drink of her coffee and set the cup and saucer back down onto the tray. "But as I say, I'm not one to gossip."

"No, of course not," Skip said. "So, you believe someone killed Gipper and buried him behind the carriage house, and Joe and his dog were locked in the night of the fire and now haunt the main house because of it?"

"That's correct, and Velma agrees. I can see Joe being the haunting type, but Bullseye was such a sweet old thing. Of course, maybe for the dog, the fire was a blessing."

"How so?" Henry said.

"Joe told me Bullseye had cancer real bad. He was an old boy, almost fifteen, and the veterinarian thought he only had a month or two at best to live. Maybe the smoke inhalation was a kinder way for him to go."

"Still, how sad," Skip said.

"Oh yes, indeed. And tragic for Joe Bitters. I miss him. I get lonely, too, sometimes."

"That's understandable, and please accept our condolences," Henry said.

"Thank you, my dear. Poor Joe. I think Mr. Bitters put his nose in where it didn't belong, and someone bit it off, so to speak."

"Yes, well, if that's the case, I hope justice is soon served," Skip said.

"So do I, though the police seem to consider the matter closed.

An accident, as I said, and they may be right. I could be letting my imagination run away with me."

"Maybe, but there have been a few 'accidents' around the Rutherford place lately," Skip said.

"Skip," Henry said.

Skip glanced over at him and then back to Mrs. Savage. "I guess we can talk about all that another day, ma'am. I think we've taken up enough of your time. You've been so awfully kind." He set his cup back on the table as Henry did the same.

"Oh, must you be going so soon?" the old woman said.

"I'm afraid so. The morning is slipping away, and we still have to get somewhere. But thank you so much for your hospitality," Skip said.

Skip and Henry stood up. "May we help you clear the coffee service?" Henry said.

"Oh no, I wouldn't think of it. It gives me something to do. But you must have a cookie each to take with you. I'll be right back." She sprang to her feet with surprising agility and disappeared down the hall, only to return presently with two cookies on a small plate. "Here you go, I hope you like chocolate chip."

"My favorite," Skip said, taking one off the plate.

"And mine, thank you," Henry said, doing the same.

"You're more than welcome. Don't forget your hats, and do come again, please. I'm eager to hear more about these accidents and such. And I do want Velma to hold another séance. Maybe she can contact Joe and ask him what happened. Have you ever attended one?"

"Ah, no, I haven't," Skip said.

"Me neither," Henry said.

"They must be done right, you see. It must be dark except for at least three candles, or any number divisible by three, and food. The candles and food attract spirits seeking warmth and sustenance."

"Intriguing. That makes sense, I suppose," Skip said, as they made their way to the front door, cookies in hand. "Thanks again, good day."

"Good day. Give my regards to the Rutherfords."

"Yes, ma'am," Henry said, putting on his hat.

"Well, that was something, and so was she," Henry said, latching the gate behind them as they stepped onto the sidewalk.

"She certainly was," Skip said, taking a bite of his cookie. "Mm, these are delicious."

Henry took a bite of his. "They certainly are."

"And that was an interesting visit. We certainly did find out things," Skip said, finishing the cookie as Henry did the same.

"We did? It doesn't seem to me we found out much except for the fact she saw a man digging in the yard late at night. Otherwise, all we heard were her opinions on things, not facts, and she admitted that most of it may just be her imagination. She believes in ghosts, too, so maybe she's a bit loopy. We don't even know for sure if this Bitters fellow really found anything or left any notes. Maybe he was making it all up to entertain her."

"Or maybe not. That's why we have to do some more investigating."

"I don't think that's a good idea."

"You don't have to be involved if you don't wish," Skip said matter-of-factly.

"You are a stubborn one, Skip Valentine."

"It's one of my best traits, as someone once said about himself, so that makes two of us. Do you suppose your uncle keeps a shovel in the garage? And I seem to recall a flashlight in the glove box of your friend's car. Does it work?"

"A shovel and a flashlight? What the—" Henry stopped abruptly. "Oh no, absolutely not! We are not going to go digging up that dead dog."

"Aha. Then you admit you think Mrs. Savage is right and Gipper is in that box Jake buried."

"First of all, we don't know it was Jake for sure. And second, if it was, and if Gipper is in that box, what would it prove?"

"That he didn't run away, and that somebody killed him."

"But why?"

"That remains to be seen. Maybe to punish Mrs. Rutherford, as Mrs. Savage said."

Henry sighed, exasperated. "Skip, *if* the dog is in the buried box, there could be a thousand explanations. He may have died unexpectedly, gotten into some kind of poison, or been hit by a car, and they didn't want to upset Mrs. Rutherford by telling her he was dead. Telling her he ran away at least gives her hope that he could come back."

"False hope. She's heartbroken."

"False hope is better than no hope. And if Mrs. Rutherford is the one who killed Gipper, it's way better than the truth. We're not digging up that box, understand? What if someone caught us? How would we explain that?"

"That's why we'll do it in the middle of the night, with your friend Bernie's flashlight from the car."

"Oh sure, that makes total sense. Never mind the fact that we could be seen by Mrs. Savage, Mrs. Rutherford, *or* Mr. Rutherford. All their rooms overlook the yard and old carriage house."

"But they'd be sleeping."

"No, Skip. I don't care. I'm not doing it."

"Fine. I'll do it myself."

Henry took off his hat and rubbed his forehead. "You are giving me a first-rate headache. Let me think about it, okay?"

"Okay."

"All right, then. Let's go get Mr. Rutherford's cigarettes."

"Yes, and I want to do some shopping."

"Shopping? Why do I have the feeling you have an ulterior motive or two?"

Skip smiled. "Why, Mr. Finch, you are beginning to know me well."

CHAPTER TEN

Saturday afternoon, October 7, 1950
Shopping

They walked south on Packard Street several blocks before entering Lund's Pharmacy just past Shadford Road. The swivel counter stools at the soda fountain were occupied by teenagers, the boys discussing the latest football game while the girls batted googly eyes at the handsome soda jerk or giggled loudly at a comment one of the boys made. They sipped on their sodas, malts, and shakes, seemingly oblivious to the problems of the world. The prescription counter was at the back of the shop, and Henry and Skip could see a handsome, older man in a white lab coat working there, busily filling prescriptions and mixing potions. A tall, younger, pretty blond woman, possibly his wife, was working next to him.

"I'll get the cigarettes. Anything you need?"

"Can't think of anything. I don't think they sell shovels here," Skip said.

"Skip…"

"Just a comment."

"Honestly," Henry said, rolling his eyes. "Hey, look, more penguins. I wonder if they know Sister Barnabas."

Skip followed his gaze to three nuns one aisle over and then looked back at Henry. "I believe I told you that you shouldn't call them that, Mr. Finch, it's rude."

"Sorry," he said. "But that's what Mrs. Rutherford calls them."

"Mrs. Rutherford is mentally ill. But I do wonder," Skip said. "Maybe they can shed some light on the mysterious Sister Barnabas."

"Skip, don't."

"There's no harm in talking to them, Henry. I want to find out her secret. I bet they've never heard of her."

"Skip, she's a nun."

"So she says, but I could say I'm Cary Grant."

"I think you're more of a young Van Johnson, myself."

"Thanks. Stay here if you like, I'll be right back." He turned and walked down and around to the three of them, but Henry stayed put, examining a display of Brylcreem and hair tonic.

The nuns looked curiously at Skip as he approached, clearing his throat. "Excuse me, Sisters, are you from the Convent of the Immaculate Heart of Mary by any chance?" he said, addressing all three.

The oldest of them spoke. "Yes, my child. I'm the Reverend Mother. May we help you?" She had steel blue-gray eyes that looked like they could see right through you into your soul.

"I don't wish to bother you, but I did wish to ask you something."

"No bother to us, we're just picking up some necessary items."

"Gee, it seems funny seeing you out of the church, in the real world and all, I mean, shopping just like regular people."

"We are not a cloistered order. We are Sisters of Charity. We teach and nurse."

"Oh, how commendable. Much needed, of course."

"Yes, much needs to be done in the world. How may we help you today?"

"Well, I was wondering about a Sister Barnabas. She's a bit heavy, wears thick glasses, and has bushy eyebrows. I believe she's from your convent."

The Reverend Mother showed no sign of emotion except for a slight raising of her thick eyebrows. "Sister Barnabas is one of our nursing sisters. She's on assignment caring for an ill woman."

"Where?"

"I'm afraid I'm not at liberty to disclose or discuss that. Why do you ask?"

"She's at the Rutherford house," Skip said.

Once more the eyebrows of the Reverend Mother went up a fraction of an inch. "If you knew that, why did you ask me?"

"I'm staying at the Rutherford house also. My name is Skip Valentine."

"I see. Or rather, I don't see. Is something wrong?"

"Oh, no, Reverend Mother, I don't think so. I mean, she does act a bit peculiar sometimes, I think."

"Is Sister Barnabas not performing her duties? Is there a problem of some kind?"

"Gosh, it's nothing like that. She seems to be caring for Mrs. Rutherford well, all things considered. It must be trying, maybe she just gets tired."

"Sister Barnabas is a child of God, a member of this order. But she is still a woman, a mortal being, not a saint. If she has behaved inappropriately, I suggest you bring it to her attention. Only with guidance will we grow, and I'm certain any perceived misconduct was not intentional."

"Oh dear, no, I didn't mean to imply any misconduct. It's only that she's been complaining about headaches, and she's always peering at us over the top of her glasses."

"Headaches? Sister Barnabas does have poor vision. Perhaps she needs a new prescription. She has been at the Rutherford home for some time now, and it may be time for me to drop in and see how things are going."

"Er, yes, well, if you do, please don't mention I said anything. I wouldn't want Mr. Rutherford to think I was interfering."

"Go with God, my child. We will pray for you, as we have been doing for Mrs. Rutherford."

Skip bowed his head. "Thank you, Reverend Mother, Sisters." He backed away slowly, and then turned at the end of the aisle and walked hurriedly back to Henry, who looked annoyed.

"Well, Valentine, did you uncover Sister Barnabas's deep, dark secret?"

Skip frowned. "No, I didn't. She *is* a nun, and she *is* from the convent and they *did* send her to take care of Mrs. Rutherford, *and* she has bad eyesight."

"I told you so."

"Ugh, I hate that phrase. But yes, you did. It still doesn't explain the makeup in the medicine cabinet and clothes in her locked closet."

"No, but I'm sure there is an explanation."

Skip shrugged. "Maybe I do have too active an imagination, like Mrs. Savage. Ugh, that Reverend Mother thinks I'm a dolt. Come on, let's find those cigarettes."

They strolled down the narrow aisle, past soaps and hot water bottles, tonics and bandages, hair pins, hat pins, curlers, and candy. At last, they found the cigarettes, and Henry plucked out a package of Lucky Strikes from the display, going to the register opposite the soda fountain. He gave the girl a quarter and put the cigarettes into his pocket.

"Need any matches?" she said, smiling as she handed him back his change. "They're complimentary."

"No, thank you," Henry said.

"Know of any good places for a bite to eat?" Skip said.

"Oh, sure, my favorite place is Drake's up by the university," the girl said. "They make a great orange marmalade sandwich and heavenly pecan rolls, but there's a game today against Dartmouth and over thirty-seven high school bands performing at halftime, so it will be crowded everywhere."

"Thanks, miss," Henry said. "I hope Michigan wins."

"Me too, go Wolverines! Enjoy your day."

"You do the same," Skip said as he followed Henry back out onto the sidewalk and the early afternoon sun.

"Why'd you ask about a place to eat?" Henry said.

"I was just curious, and I guess I'm hungry."

"Miss Grant is expecting us for lunch."

"I know, but she's serving meatloaf, ugh."

"It will be fine."

They walked back north on Packard Street, Skip occasionally stopping to admire a house or point out a particular bird in a tree.

"Oh, look," Skip said. "Clif's diner has a lunch special, ground U.S. sirloin steak with mushroom sauce, fried potatoes, vegetables, and coffee, tea, or milk, for $1.25."

Henry glanced at his watch. "Yes, but as I said, we're expected back at the house. It's almost twelve thirty."

Skip made a face. "But as *I* said, Miss Grant is serving meatloaf, and the sister said it wasn't her best dish. Wouldn't you rather have steak with mushroom sauce?"

"Well, sure, but what would we tell my uncle?"

"We could call from the diner and give an excuse of some kind. And since you drove us to Ann Arbor, lunch will be my treat. What do you say?"

"I say I'm not the only one who's persuasive. All right, let's go in. You order for us while I telephone Uncle Ambrose."

It was one fifteen when they had finished eating and were walking back to the house once again.

"Gosh, Henry, that was delicious. Thanks for indulging me."

"Thanks for picking up the bill. For a little guy, you sure can eat."

"Hey, I may not be six feet tall like you, but I'm not little. I'm average, five foot eight."

"That's about the only thing average about you, Skip."

"Thanks, I think. Anyway, I was hungry. I noticed you didn't leave a morsel on your plate, either."

"Guilty," Henry said.

"What did they say when you telephoned, by the way?"

"I spoke with Miss Grant and told her we'd been delayed and we were going to eat out. She said she'd let my uncle know."

"Okay."

"So, now what?"

"Now we stop at that haberdasher we passed earlier and have a look at that bowler hat in the window," Skip said.

"Only if we also go into Smooch's Mercantile on the corner," Henry said.

"You mean the one with the display of fishing equipment on sale?"

"Yes, well, it is near the end of the season, so I could save money."

"Perfect, there are a few things I want there, too. While you peruse the fishing equipment, I'll look at clothes. Here's the hat shop. Coming in?"

"No thanks. I see a newsstand over there. Think I'll buy a newspaper and catch up on things."

"All right, I won't be long."

Half an hour later, Skip emerged carrying not one but two hatboxes.

Henry had finished his paper and was leaning on a lamppost, waiting for him.

"Two new hats, Skip? You are indeed a dandy."

Skip laughed. "I guess so. Do you mind?"

"Nope. It's one of the things that first attracted me to you on the bus, remember?"

"I do. I bought the bowler plus a new Hamburg. They were on sale."

"Marvelous, can't wait to see you wearing them. And speaking of sales, come on, let's go to the mercantile."

They spent over an hour in Smooch's. Skip bought a pair of dungarees, basic work shoes, a flannel shirt, and a few pair of underwear, and Henry treated himself to a new set of bobbers, marked down to half price.

"Well, my friend, any other stops?" Henry said as they stepped back out onto the street.

"I don't think so. Let's go back to the house so I can try on my things."

"Okay. Let me carry some of that," he said, taking a few of the packages. "Rather curious purchases, I must say. In the albeit brief time I've known you, you've never worn dungarees, flannel shirts, *or* work shoes."

"A first time for everything. And don't forget, I *did* buy new underwear."

"Now, that I definitely look forward to seeing you model. I like spending time with you."

"I'm glad. I like spending time with you, too, Mr. Finch," Skip said, wishing they could hold hands. They walked back at a leisurely pace, climbing the front steps to the house slowly.

Chapter Eleven

Later Saturday afternoon, October 7, 1950
The Rutherford house

Henry and Skip put their hats on the hooks in the entryway and entered the main hall.

"I wonder where everyone is," Skip said. "The house is utterly silent. I can't hear a sound but the ticking of the grandfather clock."

"Maybe they're all taking afternoon naps."

"Hmm, that could be helpful."

"Helpful?"

"Oh, well, sure, restful, I meant."

"Do you want to nap?" Henry said.

"I'm not tired, but you go ahead if you like."

"Nah, I'm okay. So, what do you want to do?"

"Put these things away at the moment."

"All right, then we can figure something out, or maybe you could work on that lock on our connecting door some more."

Skip smiled. "Maybe."

They went quietly upstairs to their respective rooms and Henry handed off the packages of Skip's that he'd been carrying.

"Meet me downstairs in a few minutes, okay?" Skip said.

"Downstairs?" Henry said. "You don't want to fiddle with the lock?"

"I promise I'll do that later. Put your bobbers away and meet me in a few minutes. Let me know if you see anyone, okay?"

"Hmm, okay. But why do I have the feeling you're up to something again?"

"Aren't I always?" Skip said, disappearing into his room. He stripped down and put on his new flannel shirt, dungarees, and work shoes, leaving the new underwear for later. Satisfied, he went quietly down the stairs to the hall, where he noticed Henry staring at the portrait of the woman above the settee.

"She's a beautiful young woman, and those dark curls about her soft, smiling face make her more so," Henry said as Skip approached.

"Yes. An old Rutherford relation, perhaps," Skip said, looking up at her. "Thanks for waiting for me. I had to try on my new things."

"Looks like they fit pretty well."

"Yes, not bad. Have you seen anyone about?"

"Just you and this mysterious lady," Henry said.

"Glad she kept you company."

"She doesn't talk much, but she sees all. How are the new shoes?"

Skip looked down at them. "A bit stiff, but they'll loosen up. Decent arch support for my flat feet, at least."

"Good. So why the new attire? As I said before, it's not what you typically wear."

"They fit with what I want to do."

Henry frowned. "I don't think I like the sound of that. What do you plan on doing?"

"A walk about the yard. It's a lovely afternoon."

Henry raised his eyebrows. "What for? We've just had a long stroll around the block, and all the way to the drugstore and back."

"I know, but I want to have a closer look at the old carriage house and the area behind it."

Henry put his hands on his hips. "Skip, no. Enough already. I thought we'd discussed this. You're going to get us into trouble."

"You keep saying that. I'm just going to have a look. I won't do any digging out back until after dark. Stay here if you want."

"I intend to."

"Fine. I'll be back in a bit. Go see if you can find your uncle and give him his Lucky Strikes. Don't forget he owes you for them."

"Plus the eight cents from his half of the cribbage games last night," Henry said.

"Right. He might still be up in his room or in the library, I see the door is closed. If you do find him, keep him occupied. I'll be back in a few minutes." Skip went through the door under the stair landing, into the small hall, and out the side door of the house.

The pea gravel crunched beneath his work shoes as he walked slowly to the back of the partially burned building. It was in shadow, and it felt cool and damp. He bent down and examined the ground beneath the remains of a wooden staircase that leaned precariously out from the structure. A small mound was next to the fence, and it appeared someone had definitely been digging there. Skip stood up and dusted himself off before walking to the far, unburned side of the building where a service door was located. He assumed it would be locked but tried it anyway, smiling to himself as it swung open with a low creak.

Stepping inside, he noticed a burnt, charred smell that hung thick in the stagnant air. He could see the Rutherfords' black Studebaker, and on the back wall various tools, shovels, rakes, and garden equipment had been arranged neatly. Skip walked cautiously around the car to the center of the room, peering ahead into the darkness on the other side where the fire had been. He proceeded slowly, tentatively, as the floor was dirt and had deep ruts here and there. A cobweb brushed his face, but he shook it off. Dust particles he kicked up danced in the sunbeams that shined through the cracks in the ruined wall to his left and made him sneeze.

"Bless you," a deep male voice called out from the shadows.

"Who's there?" Skip said, taking a step backward as his heart leaped into his throat, his fists clenched, ready for a fight if necessary. "Who said that?"

No reply, but rather slow, heavy, deliberate footsteps coming toward him, billowing up bigger clouds of dust from the floor.

Skip took two more steps back as he stared straight ahead into the murky darkness. A menacing figure slowly emerged from the deep recesses.

"Who are you?" the voice said, stopping just a few feet in front of him, still mostly in shadow. Skip could feel the man's stale breath on his face.

"I'm Skip Valentine from Chicago. My friend and I, Henry Finch, are visiting the Rutherfords. Who are you?"

"Oh, yeah. I saw you before," the voice said.

"Who are you?" Skip said again.

"I'm Jake Bartlett," the man said, taking another step toward him. Skip could see now that Jake was dressed in a blue work shirt, overalls, and dirty leather boots, a red bandana around his neck and another protruding from his front pocket.

"Jake? Oh, Miss Grant's nephew," Skip said, relieved and yet still terrified, all at the same time.

"You know me?" Jake took another step forward.

"Well, I've heard about you. And I saw you briefly in the dining room last night when you brought in the soup."

"I didn't do that so well. Mr. R was upset."

"Oh, I don't know. I think you managed okay. That tureen had to be heavy."

"It *was* heavy. It wasn't my fault. He shouldn't have yelled at me."

"I agree."

"It made me mad."

"I don't like it when people raise their voice to me, either. I recall you were also in the hall last night after the chandelier fell."

"Yeah. Almost killed him," Jake said, his voice surprisingly calm.

"Yes," Skip said. "He was lucky. What are you doing in here?"

"There's some squirrels that built a nest upstairs. I bring them out old apples and stuff sometimes."

"I see. That's kind of you, Jake."

"I like animals. Do you?"

"Yes, very much."

"Me too. How come you're in here?" Jake said.

"I was just being curious. I see this is where the shovels and tools are kept."

"Joe Bitters used them. He was the handyman. He took care of the yard, too."

"I see. The fire must have been terrible."

"Yeah. Old Joe and his dog didn't make it. They couldn't get out in time. He lived above here."

"I heard that."

"There's stairs out back that go up there, but they ain't safe anymore. I use a ladder and go through a hole in the floor back in the corner," he said, jerking his left thumb over his shoulder.

"You should be careful," Skip said.

"I always am, not that anyone would care much if something happened to me."

"Oh, I'm sure that's not true, Jake. Your aunt would be most upset, as well as Mr. Rutherford and his mother."

The boy laughed bitterly. "My aunt, maybe. She's all right. But Mr. R and his mother, they don't like me much, and I don't much care for them. The old lady calls me Jake the mistake, on accounta my mom not having been married when I was born."

"You're not a mistake, Jake, you're the product of two people who loved each other, if only for a moment, and that can never be a mistake."

"That's a real nice thing to say, Mr. Valentine. Maybe I like you."

"And maybe I like you, too, Jake. *I'd* be upset if something happened to you."

"Would you?"

"Of course I would. I don't like to see anyone get hurt."

"Not even Mr. R. and the old lady?"

"No, of course not. Why would you say such a thing?"

Jake heaved his large shoulders up and down. "I wouldn't mind if they was to get hurt. They're not nice to me or to Aunt Jane. Old Joe wasn't too nice, either."

"Well, be that as it may, I still wouldn't want anything to happen to them."

"Not me. The old lady was rude to my mama, too. Ma died when I was twelve, but I remember."

"I'm sorry. That is a difficult thing to have happen to you, especially at such a young age."

"Thanks. She was real pretty. Prettier than Aunt Jane. Aunt Jane got her a job here, so we came and lived in the big house when I was a little kid. Jane and Ma had rooms above the kitchen, though they usually just stayed in one, sharing a bed to keep warm. I stayed in Ma's room at first but eventually got a place in the attic. It's okay up there, but it's hot in the summer and cold in the winter."

"I bet you miss your mom. My mom and dad are both gone. My only relations are a few cousins in Milwaukee, as far as I know."

Jake looked thoughtful, his face now out of the shadows. "I think about my ma sometimes, you know? All the time, sometimes, if that makes sense. Aunt Jane misses her, too."

Skip nodded.

"Aunt Jane says Ma was going to have another baby, and they was trying to get rid of it when she died."

"Oh, that's horrible. Who was trying to get rid of the baby?"

"She told me it was Ma and Mr. Rutherford."

"Mr. Rutherford?"

"Yeah. He used to visit Ma sometimes late at night or real early in the morning. That's what Aunt Jane told me, anyway."

"Ah, I think I see. Oh, Jake, I'm so sorry."

Jake shrugged. "Aunt Jane says it's Mr. R's fault Mama died, and I think she's right. I ain't so smart, but I ain't stupid, neither."

"Why do you and your aunt stay here?"

Jake scuffed his feet, causing more dust to billow up.

"I've been here since I was a little kid. I don't know nothin' else. And Aunt Jane says Mr. Rutherford pays real well, and he doesn't ask for much. She don't like him much either, though, I don't think."

"Understandable," Skip said, fighting back another sneeze. "By the way, Jake, did you bury something a while back behind this building?"

The boy stared at Skip for a few moments, then looked down at his feet. "Why you ask that?"

"Because someone told me they saw you burying something late at night not too long ago. A box."

"I didn't bury no box." He took another step toward him, a scowl on his face.

"I think you did."

"You calling me a liar?" His tone was angry.

Skip took two steps back this time, edging around the Studebaker. He was almost at the door, he figured. "No, I just think maybe someone told you not to say anything, and you're good at keeping secrets, I bet. What was in that box, Jake? You can tell me. You can trust me."

"I don't trust nobody. I take it back, I don't think I like you after all. Go away." Jake scuffed his feet against the floor once more, and then pushed past Skip and out the door, raising another cloud of dust. Skip sneezed again, but this time there was no one to bless him.

"Wowzer," Skip said to himself, breathing hard. He sneezed once more and wished he had a handkerchief. He waited until his breathing had slowed and his heart had stopped racing. Then, slowly, he went to the left side of the building where he could just make out an old wooden ladder toward the back rising to a makeshift hole in the ceiling. "I hope those squirrels are friendly," he said and began to climb, thankful he had on his work shoes, flannel shirt, and dungarees. When his head emerged through the hole, he saw the remains of what had been simple living quarters, now in ruins. The smell of ash and burned wood was more potent and most everything was charred. A single metal bedstead stood against the far wall, the springs of what had been a mattress resting atop it. "If there *were* any notes hidden up here, they'd have been burned to a crisp all right, but maybe the keys?" Skip said again. He hoisted himself the rest of the way through the hole and explored the space carefully before giving up and climbing back down. The lower level, while in better condition, yielded similar results.

❖

Henry, meanwhile, was in the library, pacing back and forth, while his uncle sat in his chair smoking one of his cigarettes, his leg still propped up, a fresh bag of ice upon his ankle.

"Why do you keep pacing, my boy?"

"What? Oh, no reason. I was surprised to see you still sitting in here. I thought perhaps you'd be napping up in your room."

"No, I wasn't in the mood to climb the stairs with my ankle the way it is. I've been sitting here relaxing. I never heard you and Mr. Valentine come in, so I must have dozed off for a bit after lunch, but I'm wide awake now."

"Oh, that's good, I suppose," Henry said. He walked once more to the window overlooking the yard and garage but couldn't see Skip. He walked to the rear of the room, where French doors opened onto a small patio, but there was no sign of him back there, either.

"You said Skip was out getting some air? He'll be back soon, I imagine."

"Hmm? Oh, right."

"You know, I'm surprised neither of you has a girlfriend."

Henry stopped pacing and turned to his uncle. "I guess we're both happy being single at the moment. You never married."

"My circumstances were different. There was a woman once, but that was long ago. And just because I haven't yet doesn't mean I won't. I'm seeing someone now, to tell you the truth."

Henry raised his eyebrows. "Uncle, you surprise me."

"I may be older, but I'm not dead yet, as they say. A pretty girl can still turn my eye. And she's awfully pretty, an actress."

"I heard about her," Henry said.

"Marjorie?" Mr. Rutherford said, his eyebrows raised in surprise.

"Yes, your mother wrote my mother. She wasn't too keen on her, it seems."

Ambrose blew out a cloud of smoke from his nostrils. "She's never been keen on any of my friends or anyone I've dated. She finds fault with any woman I bring home, including Marjorie Banning. Mother thinks she ran her off."

"I'd heard that. You mean she didn't?"

"Oh, at first, yes. But we've recently become reacquainted, and we've started courting again."

"Does your mother know?"

"Not yet, and I don't think there's any reason to tell her now. She'll be in a nursing home by this time Monday, and I doubt she'll ever come back. I love my mother, of course, but Marjorie is important to me, and I don't want her being scared off again."

Henry paced to one of the windows and looked out. "Relationships are important. All kinds."

"Of course," Mr. Rutherford said. "Skip's a good friend, isn't he? You've grown close over a short period of time."

"Well, yes. He's quite a character, but he's also witty and smart as a whip."

"You have to watch those smart ones, you know."

"What do you mean?"

"Sometimes they try to use their intelligence to get something."

"You sound like your mother. She said something similar earlier."

"Well, I am my mother's son. Skip knows you stand to inherit this house and the Rutherford money someday."

Henry frowned, the hair on the back of his neck standing up. "He only found that out last week. And what's that got to do with the price of eggs?"

Mr. Rutherford ground out his cigarette and lit a fresh one. "Oh, don't get defensive, my boy. You're young and you have a good friend, a fairly new friend, I think. I'm just suggesting you be careful."

"I'll have you know Skip has more money than I do. His parents are gone, and they left him fairly well off. He also has a good job with the Chicago Public Library."

"Bully for him. But a young man like Mr. Valentine is used to nice things, it seems. He wears nice clothes and probably has a nice apartment, perhaps a nice car…"

"All of which he provides for himself."

Mr. Rutherford blew a cloud of smoke toward the coffered ceiling. "Inheritances only last so long, and he can't make all that much at a library."

Henry scowled, crossing his arms in front of him. "What's that supposed to mean?"

"Just that sometimes people want to be your friend not because they like you particularly, but because you're wealthy or famous or well connected. I learned that lesson early on. Everybody wants something from you when you have money or are related to someone wealthy."

"Skip and I are friends because we have similar interests, and we genuinely like each other. We want nothing from each other but companionship. Besides, our friendship is none of your business."

"I'm only looking out for your concern."

"Well, don't."

Ambrose stared at Henry. "I don't know if you've noticed, but he also strikes me as a bit funny. You should proceed with caution. Those types can be dangerous. He may try to influence you, recruit you."

"That's absurd and utterly ridiculous. And Skip's not dangerous. Besides, if he was interested in your money, don't you think I'd know?"

Mr. Rutherford blew three perfect smoke rings into the air. "Perhaps. You said he's a smart cookie."

"So, you think he somehow knew about my potential inheritance before I did and befriended me because of it?"

"I know it sounds improbable, but it's been known to happen."

"Not where Skip is concerned. I said he was smart, not diabolical." Henry turned back to the window, but there was still no sign of him and he was getting worried.

❖

Back in the partially burned-out building, Skip was getting worried, too. Something, he felt, just wasn't right. Two attempts on

Ambrose Rutherford's life, a strange nun who wasn't all she appeared to be, a runaway dog that might actually be dead, a ghost and his ghost dog pounding and barking in the night, and the mysterious fire that killed them. And then there were the notes that Bitters supposedly left behind, but where? Were they burned and gone, or were they still hidden somewhere, waiting to be found? And if they were found, what would they show? What was it Bitters discovered, if anything? And finally, what role did Henry play in all this? That was the most troubling of all.

Skip left the old carriage house, glad to be out in the fresh, brisk air, and walked slowly back toward the house, deep in thought. He came in through the front door, wondering where Henry had gone. No one was in either drawing room, but the door to the library was now open, he noticed, and he could hear voices from within. Mr. Rutherford looked up, a rather startled expression on his face as Skip entered.

"Good heavens, boy, what have you been into?"

Skip stared back at him, perplexed as to what he meant.

"You're covered in soot and ash, Skip. It's on your face, your clothes, your arms…" Henry said.

Skip looked down at himself, and then at his reflection in the mirror above the fireplace. "Oh. Jeepers, I wasn't aware."

"Have you been nosing about in the garage, Mr. Valentine?"

"Well, yes, as a matter of fact," he said. He couldn't think of any other plausible answer for being covered in soot.

"Whatever for?" Mr. Rutherford said, grinding out the second cigarette next to the first in the ashtray.

"Well, er, to be honest, things just don't seem right. Two attempts on your life, so close together…"

Mr. Rutherford threw his head back in frustration. "Good grief. Parts of that building aren't safe. I don't like you poking about where you shouldn't."

"With all due respect, sir, I think someone in this house wants to hurt you, maybe kill you, and I'm only trying to help. I ran into Jake out there. You mentioned he doesn't like you, that he blames you for his mother's death, and he pretty much told me the same thing," Skip said.

"He shouldn't have been out there, either. I shall have to talk to Jane about it again. Jake's a troubled, angry young man, and he's not right in the head, you know. He has a volatile temper. You'd do well to stay away from him."

"Shouldn't you telephone the police and have them investigate?" Henry said.

"I don't think there's enough proof just yet to involve the police. It would only make Jake angry, perhaps push him to do something more serious, and frankly, I'm becoming a bit afraid of him. He intensely dislikes me and my mother. He didn't care for Bitters, either, not that I blame him there. Bitters was a bit of a bully when it came to Jake, always picking on him, mocking him, and making fun of him. Frankly, it wouldn't surprise me if Jake had something to do with that fire, too."

"Maybe it's time you discharged Jake," Skip said. "Before that something more serious does occur."

"It's crossed my mind. I want to get Mother settled and out of the house first, though. I want to make sure she's safe."

"But if he was involved in the fire, the police…" Skip said.

"The police investigated. They found no evidence of wrongdoing, and yes, they did question Jake, and it just made him more sullen and angry."

"Well, Jake may be a suspect, but there's someone else, too, I think," Skip said.

"And who might that be?" Mr. Rutherford said, surprise in his tone of voice.

"Sister Barnabas. I know she's from the convent, but I don't think she's everything she appears to be."

"Skip…" Henry said.

"What do you mean by that?" Mr. Rutherford said. "What possible motive could she have for wanting to harm me? She has absolutely nothing to gain."

"Not that we know of," Skip said, "but I don't trust her. I found some rather interesting items in the medicine cabinet in the hall bathroom. Things like hair dye, lipstick, a compact, and some rouge. Why would a nun have those things in her possession?"

Mr. Rutherford looked at him sideways. "She wouldn't. And she doesn't. Those all belong to my mother."

"Your mother? Then why are they in the hall bathroom and not Mrs. Rutherford's?" Skip said.

"Not that it's any of your concern, but we had to take her cosmetics away from her. The last time she attempted to fix herself up, she had lipstick all over her face and powder throughout the room. We've taken most of her clothes away and locked them in the sister's closet, too. As you may recall, when Mother dresses herself lately, she doesn't do a very good job. Not to mention she rips the zippers and fasteners and has ruined much of her clothing as well as the items she stole from Jane. When and if Mother needs to go out or someone comes to call, Sister Barnabas helps her dress now and do her makeup."

Skip looked embarrassed. "Oh, I see."

"I am very disappointed you were snooping in the bathroom, and now that I think of it, Sister told me she keeps that medicine cabinet locked to keep my mother out of it. How did you know the contents?"

"Oh, well, I, uh, just happened to find it unlocked earlier when I was looking for a drinking glass. She must have accidentally left it open."

"That, Mr. Valentine, seems unlikely. But I'll take your word for it for now."

"Thank you, sir," Skip said. He felt sick to his stomach.

"I do hope you won't go snooping about anymore. Parts of the garage aren't safe, as I said, and Jake is an unlit fuse waiting to be ignited."

"I understand," Skip said.

"And one more thing. Leave Sister Barnabas alone, please. She's under an unbelievable amount of stress, as am I, taking care of my mother. She came highly recommended by the convent. I selected her myself out of several candidates."

"Yes sir, I'm sorry," Skip said. "I was only trying to help."

"Help by going upstairs and washing off that soot and dirt, changing your clothes, and minding your own business, understand? No more shenanigans."

"Yes, sir. Henry had nothing to do with any of this, by the way. He told me not to snoop."

"I should hope so," Mr. Rutherford said.

"On the contrary, Uncle, I had everything to do with it. I was in here with you now to keep you occupied while he had a look around."

Mr. Rutherford stared up at him, a cold look in his eyes. "Henry Finch, I thought better of you, I did. I shall have to write your mother."

"Go ahead. I'm not a little boy, I'm twenty-five years old and responsible for my own actions."

"He's just trying to protect me, Mr. Rutherford. Honestly, he had nothing to do with any of this," Skip said.

Mr. Rutherford ground out his cigarette and took out another from the pack Henry had bought for him. "And you're trying to protect him. How noble of you both. Go, both of you. I want to be alone with my thoughts. We can discuss this more at dinner."

"Yes sir," Skip said.

"Fine," Henry said. He turned and left, Skip following behind and up the stairs with him.

"Henry, why did you say that? You tried to talk me out of snooping," Skip said as they reached the second landing. "Several times. I know I told you to keep your uncle occupied if you found him, but you didn't have to implicate yourself. It's all my doing."

"Maybe, but we're in this together, and we stick together, regardless. That's the way I see it. That okay with you?"

Skip stopped and looked at him, gazing up into his green eyes. "That's more than okay. Thanks. It means a lot to me." He glanced about but they were alone, so he quickly reached up and kissed Henry, smudging his cheek with ash. "Oops, looks like we both need to clean up now."

"I don't mind," Henry said. "By the way, while you were outside, Uncle told me he thought you were dangerous, and I should proceed with caution."

"Yeah, like I said before, he thinks I'm a bad influence on you. I don't think he likes me too much."

"Maybe not, but I do, and I don't give a fig what he thinks."

"Thanks, Finch, truly."

"You bet, but maybe just try not to ruffle his feathers anymore while we're here, okay? Leave things be and stay out of his way."

"Okay, I'll try, I promise," Skip said, taking out his pocket watch. "It's almost five thirty. Meet you here in the hall at seven?"

"Deal."

Chapter Twelve

Saturday evening, October 7, 1950
The Rutherford house

Skip retrieved the robe from the closet in his room before going to the hall bathroom, which was fortunately unoccupied. He undressed, set his pocket watch and fob on the edge of the sink, and hung the robe next to the door while he drew a hot bubble bath. He climbed into the warm water, closed his eyes, and relaxed, lost in thought about everything that had happened. He soaked and scrubbed for a good twenty minutes and was just about to climb out and towel off when the hall door opened abruptly.

"Oh, you're bathing now, are you?" the nun said, stating the obvious as she stared at Skip over the top of her glasses.

"*Excuse me*, and yes, I got a bit dirty," Skip said, sinking lower into the tub, immersed in the few bubbles that remained.

"Poking about in the old carriage house. Mr. Rutherford told me," she said.

"I wasn't poking about, exactly. Just seeing what was what. Did you need something?"

"I was going to wash my face and hands before dinner, but I can wait until you're finished."

"I'll try to hurry," Skip said. "Don't you ever knock?"

"If you wanted privacy, you should have locked the door."

"I forgot. But I *am* naked under these bubbles, you know."

"I should hope so, that is how one usually bathes. Don't forget I'm a nurse. I'm used to the human body, male and female, and I'm also a nun, so no need to be embarrassed."

"Maybe so, but I'd still prefer it if you'd leave me alone to finish."

"If you wouldn't go snooping around, you wouldn't have to bathe in the late afternoon, Mr. Valentine, *and* monopolize the bathroom," Sister Barnabas said.

Skip resisted the urge to throw a wet sponge at her. "I told you I was just seeing what was what."

"And what what was what?" Sister said.

"What? Oh, well, I talked with Jake a bit."

"Miss Grant's nephew."

"That's right."

"You should be careful around him. He's an angry, troubled young man. I think Jake had something to do with those accidents, *if* that's what they were."

"What do you know about Jake, Sister?"

"Miss Grant told me he was just twelve when his mother passed away."

"I had heard that."

"Then you probably also heard she was with child again, and was at the doctor's office trying to get rid of it when she died. The unborn child died, too."

"Yes, how awful."

"It's against the teachings of God to abort a child, of course, and it's certainly a sin to have relations outside of marriage, but she seemed to be a sinful person from what I've heard."

"Sin is in the eye of the beholder, I think."

"I'm not surprised you'd think that. Regardless, Jake believes Mr. Rutherford was the father of the unborn child. It's absurd, of course. Certainly, Mr. Rutherford was kind to her, but nothing more. The father was probably a door-to-door salesman."

"But Jake told me Miss Grant said Mr. Rutherford used to visit his mother late at night." The bath water was cooling off.

"As I said, he's a troubled young man. You can't believe everything he says, and I wouldn't believe everything Miss Grant says, either."

"Why would she lie about it?"

"Oh, I don't think she lied. But you have to understand, she was just repeating what her sister had told her."

"I see, and her sister was unmarried and with child again. You think perhaps she told Miss Grant Mr. Rutherford was the father because she wanted money from him, is that it?" Skip said.

"It's certainly possible. And I believe Jane was trying to comfort Jake about his mother's death when she told him, hoping he wouldn't blame himself, but instead Jake became angry, most of it misdirected at Mr. Rutherford, who was only trying to help."

"I could tell Jake was emotionally unbalanced, perhaps, but he doesn't seem capable of murder."

The sister leaned against the sink and stared at Skip as she picked up his pocket watch and fob and studied them. "You'd be surprised what people can do. This is a lovely watch and fob. Expensive looking."

"Thank you, a gift from my parents."

"Generous of them." She set them back on the edge of the sink and gazed at Skip once more. "There are also others, of course, that would wish Mr. Rutherford harm, though he doesn't realize it."

"Such as?"

"You'd better make a list. There's the neighbor, Mrs. Savage, who we were talking about last night."

"Yes, we met her earlier this afternoon. She seems nice enough."

"Mr. Rutherford told me he wants to buy her house and tear it down to make room for a tennis court. She doesn't want to sell, but he thinks he can use his influence with the city to force her."

Skip raised his eyebrows in surprise. "She never said anything about that."

"I'm told she's upset and angry about it."

"That's understandable. Do you think he'll succeed?"

"He says it's up to God, but I suspect he will, and I imagine she does, too."

"He says it's up to God?"

"Yes. Mr. Rutherford and I are both religious, but we have, shall we say, different views."

"Different how?" Skip said.

"He believes just about anything that happens is God's will. If a child is hit and killed by a car, he feels it was meant to happen. If someone contracts an illness and dies, the same thing. He doesn't believe much in doctors or modern medicine."

"That's ridiculous."

"It's not for me to judge, Mr. Valentine. But I will say I believe God gave us the brains and the abilities to overcome such things. He wants us to. Perhaps he is challenging us to see how we can help each other, and if we will."

"Perhaps he is," Skip said. "So, is there anyone else who doesn't like Mr. Rutherford?" he said, his mental pencil poised in midair.

"Naturally. Jane Grant, for one. She resents him, I think, for the way he treats Jake, and there's bad blood between Mr. Rutherford and Jane that goes back many years. As I said before, she believes he's the father of her sister's unborn child and the cause of her death, and she willingly tells people about it. He, of course, denies it."

"But if it isn't true, why hasn't she been discharged? Why would he keep her on after an accusation like that?"

"Mr. Rutherford said if he discharged her, it would be like admitting guilt. Besides, she does her job well enough, and that was all many years ago. Good housekeepers are hard to find nowadays."

"That may be true, but then why hasn't she quit? If there's a domestic shortage, she shouldn't have a problem finding another job. Jake said Mr. Rutherford pays his aunt well, but that can't be the only reason she stays."

"I think it's because Jake's a bit slow, you see, a detriment. Not many other employers would take both of them on, I imagine."

"Then back to my original question. Why would she wish to harm Mr. Rutherford? What would she have to gain?"

"Revenge, perhaps, after all these years. Doesn't the saying go 'revenge is a dish best served cold'?"

"Goodness. Anyone else?"

"Mr. Rutherford's mother. I'm here to nurse her, but also to protect her from herself, and possibly, to protect others from her."

"Why on earth would she want to harm or kill her son?" Skip said, shivering in the ever-cooling water.

"No one knows what goes on in the minds of the mentally ill, Mr. Valentine. Paranoia, anger, depression, fear, so many things. Her other son, Arthur, died tragically at just five years of age. She's told me that the wrong son died, and she blames Ambrose for Arthur's death."

"But Arthur died of pneumonia," Skip said.

"Yes, but Mrs. Rutherford claims he caught a cold from Ambrose, and that led to pneumonia. I believe she's angry with her son and highly capable of committing murder."

"If that's true, she definitely needs to be in an institution." The bubbles were nearly gone.

"I agree. It's taken his aunt Lillian this long to convince Mr. Rutherford of it, however. She's supposed to be arriving today. Mr. Rutherford got a cable a short while ago saying her train has been delayed."

"Has Mrs. Rutherford been this way long?"

"A few months, perhaps longer. Apparently, things started to get worse in July and August. Finally, I was asked to come here to take care of her. But as you can see, she is beyond my capabilities at this point. There's nothing more I can do."

"How terribly sad."

"Yes. She's an intriguing woman. And strong, at least physically. She may appear small and frail, but she's not. She could have easily pulled that trip wire, then slipped up the back stairs to her bedroom. And she's fully aware of the workings of the hall chandelier. There's something else, too. I suppose there's no harm in telling you at this point."

"What is it?"

"No one besides me and Mr. Rutherford knows this, but his mother also set fire to Mr. Rutherford's bed while he was napping not long ago."

"You're joking."

"I wish I were. Fortunately, he woke up before it had spread. We've taken all the matches away from her now, but it does make one wonder if she may have been responsible for the fire in the carriage house."

"It's hard to believe, but I suppose it's possible."

"Yes, and I'm afraid there's one other threat to Mr. Rutherford."

"Oh? Who?"

"There's also your friend, Mr. Finch, if I may say so."

Skip looked at her crossly, gripping the sponge beneath the water. "You may not." One good fling and he was sure he could hit her right in the face with it.

"I see. You're the blindly loyal type."

Skip stared into her eyes. "Fine, I'll play along. Why would Henry want to harm his uncle?"

"Because Mr. Finch is the main heir to the fortune, of course. And besides the bank account, there's this house, the land, and more. With Mr. Rutherford out of the picture, it would just be a matter of time before his mother is deemed mentally unstable and he could take over."

"Don't be ridiculous. I know Henry Finch, and he'd never hurt anyone unless it was to defend himself or a loved one."

"How well do you know him, Mr. Valentine? Didn't you say you'd only met a few months ago?"

"Well, yes, earlier this year, but we've spent quite a bit of time together."

"The devil wears many disguises. Don't take anything, or anyone, at face value."

Skip shivered again. The bath water had become cold. "I'll take that under advisement, Sister. Now if you'll excuse me, I'd like to rinse off and get dressed."

"Of course, I'll leave you be. The bubbles are pretty much gone, and I can see your shortcomings." She turned surprisingly quickly and left, closing the hall door behind her.

After she'd gone Skip drained the water out of the tub and dried off, still shivering. He slipped on the robe, gathered up his watch, fob, and dirty clothes, and returned to his bedroom where he dressed as quickly as he could, putting on an ivory-colored shirt, red tie, gray pleated trousers, and black penny loafers. After combing his hair, he hurried down the back stairs to the kitchen, eager to talk with Miss Grant.

CHAPTER THIRTEEN

Later Saturday evening, October 7, 1950
The Rutherford house

The housekeeper cocked her head at the sound of footsteps on the stairs.

"Oh, Mr. Valentine, I thought you were Jake. Why are you coming down the back way?"

"I was hoping to speak with you briefly before dinner."

"Something wrong?" she said as she opened the oven door to baste the roast.

"No. Yes. I'm not sure, exactly," Skip said.

"Well, that clears it up. I'm afraid I'm rather busy right now."

"Gee, maybe I could help and we could talk while we work. I'm handy in the kitchen."

She considered that briefly, then nodded. "All right, I suppose that would be okay if you're sure you don't mind. Grab that knife there and slice those carrots for the top of the salads, please."

"Sure," Skip said, picking up the knife and cutting the freshly washed carrots as instructed.

Miss Grant closed the oven door and glanced over at him. "Thinner, Mr. Valentine, they're a garnish, not a snack."

Skip obliged, and Miss Grant inspected his work. "A little better. Now, what did you want to talk to me about?"

"Um, er, I was just wondering. About Jake's mother, your sister."

Miss Grant looked at him sharply. "Annabelle? What about her?" She began shredding the lettuce with her hands and putting it into a large blue ceramic bowl along with tomatoes and cucumbers she had already cut.

"I heard how she died, more or less. I mean, I heard stories about her and Mr. Rutherford."

"What about them?" Jane added some of her homemade dressing and started tossing the salad in the bowl vehemently.

"I mean, I was told he may have been the father of her baby."

"I don't see as how that's any of your business, sir, but yes, I believe he was, or at least he certainly could have been. Annabelle told me he was, anyway."

"If that's true, how could you stay here? How could you continue to work for him?"

Miss Grant finished the rest of the salad and placed it into individual bowls. "Mrs. Waters hasn't shown up yet, but I made a salad for her and set a place just in case. Those carrots still aren't fine enough, but they'll have to do. Put some shavings on top of each."

"All right. I'm sorry, I did the best I could."

She put her hands on her hips and stared at him. "That's all any of us does, isn't it? The best we can? You asked me how I could stay here after what happened to Annabelle. It's not a simple question. Annabelle was a free spirit in every sense of the word—a kind, beautiful woman, but not smart. We butted heads many times over the years, though we loved each other. Her folks died when she was sixteen. She had Jake by some neighbor boy when she was seventeen. A year or so later she took a job as a cook in a roadhouse where I worked. They gave her and the baby room and board, and I tried to help out as much as I could. I was twenty-three. Then I got this job, so I left, but we kept in touch and visited back and forth. When Mr. Rutherford's old cook quit, I convinced him to hire Annabelle, which wasn't hard. She always was a pretty girl, and Mr. Rutherford likes pretty girls. He took Annabelle on, little two-year-old Jake in tow, and at first, it wasn't so bad."

"You said her folks died when she was sixteen," Skip said, as he finished garnishing the salads with the carrots.

"That's right, she was so young."

"But she was your sister. Wouldn't they be your parents, too?"

Miss Grant's face flushed. "Oh, well, yes, of course. I meant, *our* parents."

"Hmm, okay. Then what?"

"Well, as you know, Annabelle got in the family way again, and as I said, she told me Mr. Rutherford was the father. She died at the hands of some butcher doctor he arranged for her to see, claiming he just wanted to help. After that, I did think about quitting, but I had Jake. I applied as a housekeeper at other places and was offered a few positions, but always without Jake. No one wanted a twelve-year-old boy to feed and house. Mr. Rutherford was willing to keep him on here, so I stayed. It wasn't all Mr. Rutherford's fault; Annabelle was a legal adult and she knew what she was doing. And she agreed to go to that butcher doctor against my wishes."

"Mr. Rutherford said Jake blames him for his mother's death."

"That's my fault. I foolishly told him what Annabelle had told me because Jake was so distraught when she died. He was angry with me for not protecting her. He didn't understand there was nothing I could have done."

"So, you told him Mr. Rutherford used to visit her late at night and may have been the father of her unborn child."

"Yes. I realize now that was stupid, but I didn't want him to be angry with me. Besides, I thought it was the truth at the time. I still think it's probably the truth."

"But Jake said you and your sister shared a room. How could Mr. Rutherford visit?"

"You spoke with Jake?"

"Yes, out in the garage, the old carriage house, earlier."

"I see. Mr. Rutherford told me again to talk to him about that, and I've told him to stay out of there many times. It's not safe, but he's stubborn. There are squirrels out there he takes care of."

"He told me. So, you and your sister slept together?"

"Er, yes, well, she didn't like sleeping alone, you see. Most of the time Annabelle and I shared a bed, but occasionally she went to her room for the night if one of us was restless. That's probably when she got in the family way again."

"Hmm. Do you think Jake hates Mr. Rutherford enough to try to kill him?"

"Jake is like a son to me, Mr. Valentine. I would never think such a thing of him, and I would defend him to my death."

"What about Mrs. Rutherford? Jake told me he doesn't like her much."

Miss Grant scowled. "With good reason. I'll be glad when that crazy woman is gone, frankly. I despise her. She wasn't kind to Annabelle, and she's always been rude and abrupt with Jake. You heard what she said about him at dinner last night. I keep him out of her sight as much as possible."

"Sounds like a smart idea. How well did you know Joe Bitters?"

"Joe? He started after Annabelle died. He was the handyman here. Kept to himself mostly. Our paths didn't cross much. The last time I saw him was a week or so before the fire. He came here to the kitchen to fix a clogged sink."

"So, you got along with him?"

"We got along, I guess, though I didn't care for the way he treated Jake, not one bit. And I never trusted him."

"Why not?"

"Because he was a liar, a drunk, and a thief."

"A thief?"

"Oh, nothing major, you understand. But he liked to help himself to Mr. Rutherford's cigars when he got a chance, or some of the vegetables from the garden, or a book from the library."

"I see."

"But the worst was when he'd drink Mr. Rutherford's expensive vodka without permission."

"That doesn't sound good. Mr. Rutherford never caught him?"

"No. I think he blamed his mother for some of the missing things, even the cigars, which is rather funny in a way."

"Where is the vodka kept?"

"In the cellar in the walk-in freezer of the old ice room. Mr. Rutherford took it over for his vodka collection last year, but someone kept nipping into it, so he had to lock it."

"And the someone who was nipping it was Mr. Bitters."

"That's right, though I never ratted him out, as much as I would have liked to at times. In fact, that day he was here for the sink, he went down to the cellar to have a look at the pipes, but I knew what he was actually after."

"But you said the freezer was kept locked at that point."

"Yes, but I don't think there's a lock made that could keep Joe Bitters out. He went down, toolbox in tow, and when he came back up with a queer expression on his face, his cheeks rosy, I could tell he'd had a nip, though he denied it. The next day he came back with his camera, under the guise of wanting to get some candid photographs of me working. I noticed he'd purloined Mr. Rutherford's morning newspaper, too, had it tucked under his arm. Of course, he came up with another excuse to go down to the basement. Something about forgetting his wrench or something the day before. I knew he was going to the freezer again, but I kept my mouth shut."

"Did he take a lot of photographs?"

"Oh, he was always taking pictures. I rarely saw him without that thing slung around his neck. Joe said he never knew when the perfect picture was going to present itself. He had a darkroom in his quarters."

"Yes, I heard the developing fluid may have caused the flames to spread."

"It was an awful fire. He wasn't a remarkable man, but he deserved a better death," Miss Grant said, wiping her hands on her apron.

"It had to have been awful. By the way, there's one other thing I find puzzling."

"What's that, Mr. Valentine?"

"When I ran into Jake earlier, he told me his name was Jake Bartlett, yet you said Annabelle was never married, and that she was your sister. Shouldn't his name be Jake Grant?"

Jane stared at him. "She, uh, gave him a different last name so it would appear he wasn't born out of wedlock."

"Oh. Well, can I help you with anything else? I'm happy to assist, even if I can't slice carrots very well."

A bell rang above their heads then, and they both turned to stare at the indicator box on the wall. "There's the front door. Must be Mrs. Waters, and just in time for dinner. If you want to help, you could fetch two bottles of red wine from the cellar. It's the third door on your right."

"Sure, I'd be happy to," Skip said. He was eager for a chance to explore the basement.

"Mr. Rutherford keeps the wine room locked, like his vodka freezer, but unlike the freezer, I have a key for the wine room. Here." She handed Skip a small key on a lavender ribbon she'd gotten from her apron pocket. "Put the bottles on the table. Jake will open them. Excuse me." Miss Grant took off her apron, reset the call box, and exited the kitchen, leaving Skip standing over the salad bowls. He rinsed his hands and opened the cellar door, flicking on the dim light over the stairs and hallway below.

He descended slowly, each step creaking beneath his feet, the smells of must, mold, and dampness filling his nostrils. The floor was dirt, and the walls were made of quarry rock, thick and jagged. The ceiling was low and unfinished, full of stains and cobwebs. The first door he came to, made of planks nailed together, was vegetable storage, with bins of potatoes, carrots, and onions. Next was the fruits and stores room, lined with shelves of crockery. Beyond that was the wine cellar, but Skip decided to leave that be for now, choosing instead to explore the old ice room across the hall.

The door was unlocked, and he pulled the cord on the ceiling light. The small space was empty except for the upright freezer, its door padlocked. Everything seemed to be in order and all was eerily quiet, not a sound to be heard. He tugged on the light cord once more and closed the door, continuing to the laundry next door. Beyond that was the workshop, smelling of wood and sawdust with various tools on a pegboard above long, low tables. At the end of the hall was the wood and coal room, the coal chute leading up to an iron door at the top of the ceiling. Then there was the large furnace room, situated under the main hall. The furnace had many metal tentacles reaching this way and that into the ceiling, twisting and turning as they climbed. A large oil tank sat against the far wall. Skip walked across to the door opposite and found the final two rooms in the catacomb of chambers, the well and cistern quarters, now boarded over, and an empty storage room. A side door from the latter led him back into the furnace area, and he was crossing over to the hall when he heard a heavy footstep in the shadows. Skip froze, his heart racing. The dark outline of a large man appeared and lumbered toward him.

"What are you doing down here?" Jake said.

"Oh, Jake, you startled me," he said.

He took another step, moving close. "Aunt Jane sent me to look for you. You were supposed to get some wine."

"Oh yes, I'm afraid I got a bit turned around down here. There are so many rooms, and it's dark."

"You walked right past the wine cellar. Third door on the right from the bottom of the stairs. Didn't she tell you that?"

"She may have, I guess I wasn't paying attention. I'll get the wine now and go up."

Jake stared at him, his fists clenched. "Did you tell Mr. R that I was in the garage again?"

Skip sidled sideways toward the door to the hall. "Not intentionally. I didn't mean to get you in trouble."

"That wasn't very nice of you. He's mad at me, and so is Aunt Jane."

Skip went quickly now, flinging open the door as he spoke over his shoulder. "I spoke with her a short time ago. She's only concerned you might get hurt." He scurried quickly along the narrow passageway that ran alongside the stairs.

Jake was following him closely. "I guess she is, but he's mad. I don't like him. He told me to stay out of there, but I have to take care of the squirrels."

"I'm sure he's just worried about you, and the squirrels will be okay." He stopped abruptly at the door to the wine cellar and fumbled with the lock as Jake came up beside him.

"Give me that." He took the key effortlessly out of Skip's hand and opened the door as he turned on the light. "There. Go on in."

Skip looked up at him dubiously. "Thanks, Jake." He stepped a couple of feet in as Jake followed closely, blocking the doorway. Quickly Skip grabbed the first two bottles of red he could find and thrust them at Jake, who took them in his arms, a surprised look on his face. "You lock up, okay? I need to get back upstairs," Skip said, darting around him. He didn't wait for a reply but raced down the hall and up the stairs to the kitchen, out of breath. Miss Grant, he noticed, was carving the roast.

"There you are, Mr. Valentine. I sent Jake to look for you. Are you all right?"

"Yes, I'm fine. I got a little turned around is all. Jake will be right up with the wine. I need to get upstairs and put on a sport coat. Excuse me."

He hurried up the back stairs to the second floor and out to the upper hall, where Henry was waiting for him.

"Where were you?"

"Just in the kitchen, talking to Miss Grant." He paused to catch his breath.

"About?"

"Jake and his mother and Joe Bitters."

"Skip, it's time to let it all drop. Uncle is furious, and you promised."

"I know, I'm sorry, but I feel like I'm trying to put a jigsaw puzzle together, and none of the pieces fit, or pieces are missing."

"That's a good indicator that there's no puzzle to solve. It's just a bunch of odd people and queer accidents, that's all. Let's get through dinner, say our goodbyes early tomorrow morning, and head back."

"What about our picnic? And the fishing?"

"I think we've worn out our welcome here, Skip. We can picnic and fish another time. Come on, let's go down."

"I suppose, though I still say not everything is what it seems. I'll be right out, I just need to put on a jacket."

"What for? I'm not wearing one."

"Mrs. Waters has arrived. I want to make a good impression."

"Oh, in that case, I guess I should put one on, too. You should also run a comb through your hair. Looks like you've got part of a cobweb in your ginger tresses. Where did that come from?"

Skip blushed. "Miss Grant asked me to get some wine from the cellar for dinner."

Henry sighed and shook his head. "And while you were down there you couldn't resist the urge to poke about."

"You do know me, Mr. Finch."

"For better or worse. So, what did you find?"

"A lot of little rooms, dark and spooky. Nothing of consequence, I'm afraid."

"I'm not surprised."

"There is something I'm curious about with Miss Grant, though."

"What's that?"

"I wonder if Jake's mother Annabelle really was her sister. She made what I think is a slip of the tongue and referred to *Annabelle*'s parents rather than *their* parents. And Jake told me his last name is Bartlett, not Grant. And he doesn't look anything like Miss Grant."

"Why would she lie about being sisters?"

"Maybe because they were actually lovers."

"This Annabelle was in the family way twice, Skip. I don't think she was like us."

"She may have liked men *and* women, or the men may have forced themselves on her. Jake also said that they each had their own room, but most of the time they only used one, sharing a bed."

"Hmm, well, maybe they *were* lovers, I guess, but it's none of our business. Anyway, I'll grab a jacket while you clean up. Hurry or we'll be late."

"Right, back in a flash."

True to his word, he was only gone a few minutes.

Henry smiled upon his return. "Handsome as ever. It's hard to stay mad at you. All set?"

"All set."

Chapter Fourteen

Still later Saturday evening, October 7, 1950
The Rutherford house

Together they descended the stairs to the hall, where they found Mr. Rutherford speaking to a lady they both assumed was Mrs. Waters. Her skin and body were time ravaged, but her watery steel-gray eyes were still fierce. Her hair, piled upon her head in a tight bun, was the color of a frozen river in winter, all silvery blue and ice.

"Do we go into the dining room or introduce ourselves first?" Skip asked Henry quietly as they paused at the foot of the steps.

"I'm not sure," he said, but he needn't have worried, as Mrs. Waters saw them.

She walked toward them somewhat unsteadily, leaning heavily upon a beautifully carved wooden walking stick and leaving Mr. Rutherford near the settee. She smiled amiably as she held out her right hand, her fingers inflamed and contorted. The odor of mothballs and lavender about her was not altogether unpleasant, though.

"I'm Lillian Waters, Ambrose's aunt, his mother's older sister, down from Traverse City."

Henry took her hand in his gently. "A pleasure, ma'am. We heard you were coming. I'm Henry Finch, and this is my friend, Mr. Horace Valentine. He goes by Skip. We're visiting from Chicago."

"Ah, so you're Henry Finch, all grown up. I haven't seen you since you were a toddler, but you probably don't remember. I wrote your mother a letter not long ago discussing you. She's written me many times about you and your siblings, and during the last war, she wrote about your service in the Army. I'm so glad you came home safely."

"Thank you, me too. I served from 1943 to 1947, over a year of that in France. No physical scars or damage, anyway."

"War is a terrible thing," she said. "And now we're in one again, in Korea, of all places. Such a tragedy."

"I agree. World War Two was supposed to be the war to end all wars."

"They say that about every war, I think," she said, shaking her head slowly. "Anyway, Louise told me you've had difficulty finding a steady job since you've been home."

"It's been challenging. I'd actually like to go back to school, maybe even medical school since I was a medic in the war, but I'm short on funds at the moment," Henry said, shooting Ambrose Rutherford a look over Mrs. Waters's shoulder.

"I imagine medical school is expensive," Mrs. Waters said.

"It is, but I start another job on Wednesday, so hopefully I can save up."

"I'm sure you'll manage just fine. What brings you to Ann Arbor?"

"I came here because you had said in your last letter that there were papers for me to sign."

"Goodness, yes, that's right, I'd forgotten already. At the lawyer's office. Lawyers, nasty fellows, but a necessity, I'm afraid."

"I stopped by yesterday afternoon and took care of everything."

"Splendid," she said. "I didn't know you would be here this weekend. Ambrose never said."

"Mother invited them, Aunt Lillian," Mr. Rutherford said, walking up behind her with just the slightest limp. "We only found out they were coming this past Thursday, the day before they arrived."

"Oh, dear Gabria. She forgot to mention it, I suppose," Mrs. Waters said.

"She did until the last minute," Mr. Rutherford said.

"Poor thing," Lillian Waters said, shaking her head slowly. "Will she be down for dinner?"

Mr. Rutherford rolled his eyes. "One never knows. She made an appearance last night, but Jane generally takes a tray up to her."

"I should like to go up and see her. If she doesn't join us in the dining room, I shall do that afterward."

"I'm sure she'll be pleased, though she is unhappy about the prospect of going into a nursing home."

"I can imagine. She'll feel better about it once I talk to her. I just wish I didn't have to climb all those stairs."

"Well, as I said, she may come down, especially if she knows you're here. I'll have Jane inform her. Physically, she is still rather strong," Ambrose said.

"That's good to hear, but Dr. Grimes said she needs a complete physical, possibly a change of medications, a psychiatric evaluation, and all new treatments. You've done all you can for her here, Ambrose. It's time to let the professionals at Forest Grove handle her. You may be surprised at what modern medicine can do."

Ambrose looked at his aunt. "Yes, perhaps so. I shall be glad if they can do something to alleviate her suffering *and* mine." He glanced at the clock standing against the wall. "I can't imagine what's keeping the sister. As soon as she's down, we'll go in."

"How's your ankle, Mr. Rutherford?" Skip said.

"Oh, much better, thank you. The swelling's gone down. Should be back to normal by morning."

"What happened, Ambrose?"

"Oh, I took a little tumble is all," he said.

"Are you staying here in the house, Mrs. Waters?" Henry said.

"Call me Aunt Lillian, please, and no, I'm not."

"I'm afraid there's no room for her here," Mr. Rutherford said. "The two of you are taking up both of the guest rooms, and Sister Barnabas has the old nursery room."

"Oh, I'm sorry, I didn't know," Henry said. "If it would help, I could sleep in with Skip tonight and you can take my room, Mrs. Waters. Aunt Lillian, I mean."

Mr. Rutherford scowled. "That would not be prudent or wise, and in any case, it's not necessary."

"That's right," Mrs. Waters said. "I reserved a room at the Allenel Hotel on Main and Huron. I prefer staying there because they have an elevator. Besides, this house gives me the heebie-jeebies."

"I'll drive you to the hotel after dinner, Auntie. You should have telephoned so I could have picked you up from the station."

"Oh, it wasn't a problem to take a taxi, Ambrose, and I didn't want to have to wait for you, but yes, a ride to the hotel later would be pleasant."

"My pleasure, and thankfully my ankle is nearly back to normal, so it shouldn't interfere with driving. Ah, here's Sister Barnabas, at last," Mr. Rutherford said, as she came down the stairs, moving slowly from side to side, as always, gripping the banister.

"My apologies, Mr. Rutherford. Your mother was being somewhat difficult," Sister said.

"That's all right. Aunt Lillian, you remember Sister Barnabas, mother's nurse?"

"Yes, how do you do?" Lillian said. "We met a month ago or so."

"How do you do?" the sister said. "It's nice to see you again, Mrs. Waters."

"Thank you, it's nice to be seen."

"Well, why don't we all go in to dinner? Miss Grant won't be happy that we're late."

The five of them ate and talked, and Mrs. Rutherford stayed in her room with her tray. Lillian Waters entertained the table with stories of Ambrose as a small child, her memories of her sister, and the goings-on in Traverse City. When dessert, Henry's mother's peach cobbler with freshly made vanilla ice cream, was finished, Mr. Rutherford stood.

"That cobbler, Henry, was outstanding, just as I remember it. Please give my compliments and thanks to your mother."

Henry smiled. "I will. She'll be pleased."

"Good. Well, Sister Barnabas and I have some things to discuss in the library, so if you'll excuse us, perhaps the three of you could retire to the blue drawing room."

"I think I shall go up and say hello to Gabria," Mrs. Waters said.

"Fine," Mr. Rutherford said. "We'll join everyone shortly." He held the hall door open for Sister Barnabas and Mrs. Waters, and Skip and Henry went through the connecting door into the blue drawing room.

"Well, here we are again," Henry said.

"Yes. It's even more dreary in here at night."

"I agree. Well, Valentine, it's just coming nine. Looks like we have time to kill until the others join us. What shall we do?"

Skip paced about the room like a lion in a cage. "Good question."

"We could get the cards from the yellow drawing room and play gin rummy."

"Hmm. Or maybe we could sneak down to the cellar."

Henry raised his eyebrows in surprise. "Whatever for? You were already down there before dinner. You said it was just a lot of dark, spooky rooms."

"I know, but it's something Miss Grant said earlier about Joe Bitters going down to nip some of your uncle's vodka from the freezer."

"He stole vodka?"

"Among other things—cigars, newspapers, vegetables, books, and such. I guess your uncle never caught him, but Miss Grant knew all about it. And remember, Mrs. Savage said he took a bottle of vodka from her."

"Okay, so he was a petty thief. So what?"

"I don't know, exactly, but Miss Grant said Joe went down to the cellar a couple of times right before the fire. Maybe that's where he hid his notes, somewhere in the freezer. Maybe he wants us to find the key to the padlock on the freezer. Remember the puzzling rhyme? It said, 'Pull the cord, and you've scored the location of my keys.'"

"So?"

"So, the room has one of those pull chain lights. Maybe what he meant was to pull the cord on the light to find his keys to the freezer. Maybe the keys are hidden up in the rafters by the bulb."

"No, Skip. No. I don't think there are any notes to be found, not anymore, anyway, and it's none of our concern."

"Well, it wouldn't hurt any to have another peek down there, would it? I'm not afraid of spiders."

Before Henry could answer, the hall door opened, and Mrs. Waters wobbled in, her walking stick clunking on the floor ahead of her with each step.

"Oh, hello, Aunt Lillian," Henry said. "That was a quick trip upstairs."

She nodded as she shuffled to one of the upholstered chairs near the fireplace, breathing rather heavily. "Yes, Gabria was in a mood, to say the least, as the sister had mentioned. I'm not sure she realized who I am. It's heartbreaking."

"I'm so sorry," Skip said, taking a seat near her as Henry settled onto the sofa.

"So am I," she said. "But at least I'm here now."

"Did you have a pleasant trip?" Henry said.

"Ugh, the train was delayed, dreadful waiting, sitting about, most frustrating. I wanted to get here much earlier in the day." She shook her head slowly. "Poor Gabria. Ambrose wrote me about her illness in August. I visited in the middle of September and was flabbergasted at how bad a turn she'd taken, even with Sister Barnabas's care. When I telephoned a little over a week ago and learned she'd deteriorated further, I took the liberty of mentioning her condition to my doctor in Traverse City. He agreed she should be in a long-term hospital, a nursing home, as it were. So, I made arrangements to move her to Forest Grove on Monday. Fortunately, they were able to take her on such short notice."

"What did Uncle Ambrose say to that?"

"Oh, he disagreed initially, saying it was God's will or some such hogwash, but I insisted. And after seeing her just now, I'm certain it's the right thing to do. Ambrose has agreed."

"He and his mother seem to have a strained relationship," Skip said.

"Yes, I'm afraid, sadly, it was always that way."

"She seems to glorify the memory of her other son, Arthur," Henry said.

Lillian opened her mouth to speak, then closed it again. She put her head back against the chair and closed her eyes as if lost in thought. Finally, she opened them again. "Gabria still talks about Arthur to this day."

"Yes. I suppose losing him at such a young age was devastating. Losing a child at any age must be difficult," Henry said.

Mrs. Waters clucked her tongue. "Yes, but my sister was, unfortunately, not a good mother. I've no children of my own, so I suppose I shouldn't criticize, but she didn't do right by Ambrose, comparing him to Arthur."

"I agree," Skip said. "No child should ever be compared to another."

Mrs. Waters breathed in slowly, then out, then in again, her head still resting against the back of the chair. "Yes, especially to Arthur. Arthur was the perfect child, you see. Ambrose still doesn't know. No one knows, I don't think, except Gabria and myself. It's been a heavy secret to carry."

"Knows what?" Henry said.

She brought her head forward and leaned on the arm of the chair, gazing at them. "I suppose it would be all right to tell you, I feel I must tell someone, but you must promise not to tell anyone else, especially Ambrose."

"I promise," Skip said. "But tell him what? Or not tell him, I guess I should say."

"I promise, too," Henry said, leaning forward.

Mrs. Waters nodded, satisfied. "And I trust both of you to keep your promise. No good will come from Ambrose knowing the truth after all this time. You see, Arthur should never have been born in the first place, and he certainly shouldn't have lived as long as he did."

"I'm sorry?" Skip said. "That sounds harsh."

"Oh, pish posh, it's not like that. You don't know the real story behind Arthur Rutherford. Remember, not a word of this to Ambrose. It would drive a stake further between him and his mother."

"I'm afraid I don't understand," Henry said.

"It's like this, my dears. Gabria was never the maternal type, as I said before. She was a lovely girl, far prettier than I and several years younger, but I didn't mind. That painting over the settee is her, done just after she and Giles were married."

"I was admiring it earlier. She wasn't just lovely, she was beautiful. I had no idea it was Mrs. Rutherford," Henry said.

"Yes, but too pretty for her own good, I think. She didn't want to get married. She wanted to get out of Traverse City and be an actress, you see."

"I remember hearing that, and she referred to herself as an actress earlier," Henry said.

"Not surprising. She longed to be on the stage, but of course, that was before the turn of the century. Polite, well-mannered young women wouldn't dream of going into the theater. It was considered immoral. Our parents wouldn't entertain the idea of allowing it. When Giles came along, with his good looks and his money, they were only too happy to marry her off, and Gabria for her part was eager to accept. She saw it as a way to escape.

"She thought she could get Giles to agree to let her perform in local plays and theater here in Ann Arbor, but he refused. Then she became pregnant, which ended in a stillbirth. She vowed never to have any other children, but Giles had other ideas. Unfortunately, she suffered a series of miscarriages after the stillbirth, but it wasn't too many more years until Ambrose was born, a healthy baby boy. Giles was thrilled, but Gabria became more depressed, melancholy, and lethargic. She wanted nothing to do with the baby. She mourned her figure, her youth, her carefree days, her missed opportunities. She believes she could have been a tremendous actress, and she's probably right."

"How terribly sad," Henry said.

"Oh, absolutely. And it didn't help that Giles died the following year when Ambrose was not quite a year and a half."

"But what about Arthur? He was older than Ambrose," Skip said.

"That's right. But Arthur only existed in Gabria's mind and, to some extent, in Ambrose's mind because of that."

"I'm afraid I don't see. I still don't understand," Henry said.

Mrs. Waters leaned back into the chair once more, trying to get comfortable. "It's difficult to comprehend, I suppose. As Ambrose grew into his twos, I think he sensed his mother's distance, her coldness, and he became more unruly and troublesome than children that age normally are. Gabria, a widow by then, didn't know how to deal with a rambunctious toddler. So she invented an older brother, Arthur, who she said died at five years of age, supposedly when Ambrose was almost two years old, just after her husband died."

"Why would she do that?" Henry said, looking intrigued.

"Because she used the character of Arthur as a way to control Ambrose. She led Ambrose to believe Arthur was the perfect child and Ambrose had better live up to his memory. And she hinted that he caused Arthur's death by giving him germs."

"That's a horrible thing to do to a child," Skip said.

"I know. Gabria wasn't mentally well, I see that now. Perhaps it was the beginning, but I'm not sure. I was so far away up in Traverse City, I didn't know the extent of what she was doing. She told me it was just a game to get Ambrose to behave. She swore me to secrecy, and over the years, I think Gabria forgot it was make-believe. She speaks of him now as if he had been a real child, and I think she truly mourns him."

"But she showed us a lock of Arthur's hair she keeps in an old silver box in her room. The hair was red and curly," Skip said.

Mrs. Waters nodded slowly, her eyes half closed. "The lock of the dead. I don't know for certain where she got it, though I've seen it, too. My thought is she purloined it from the floor of the beauty parlor one day when she first came up with the idea."

"And Ambrose doesn't know any of this?" Henry said.

"No, he was never told. I thought as Ambrose grew, Gabria would drop the whole Arthur tale, but she never did. She kept at it. She *still* keeps at it because, as I said, in her mind I think she believes Arthur existed. If Ambrose knew the truth now, it would devastate him."

"Or set him free," Henry said. "Living in the shadow of a perfect, dead brother has to be incredibly difficult. If Uncle Ambrose knew the truth, it might lift a weight off his shoulders he's been forced to carry since birth."

Mrs. Waters seemed to contemplate Henry's words, pondering them as she rolled them around in her mind. Finally, she nodded almost imperceptibly and spoke, her voice quavering, her eyes almost completely closed. "Perhaps there's something to what you say, Henry. God knows I've wrestled with my conscience over the years. There was a time I encouraged Gabria to tell him the truth, but she always refused. Maybe I'll tell him when she's gone."

"I think you should," Skip said.

She breathed in and out deeply, wheezing a bit and coughing, finally opening her eyes. "Yes, when Gabria's gone, perhaps I will, though I know he'll be angry with her for the deception." Mrs. Waters looked about the room, and then at the clock on the mantel. "It's coming ten o'clock. I suppose I should be getting back to the hotel. It's been a long day, and I'm tired."

"I'd be happy to drive you," Henry said, "if you don't wish to wait on Uncle Ambrose."

"Thank you, but he shouldn't be long. I should be glad of a chance to chat with him for a bit without any distractions."

Almost as if on cue, Mr. Rutherford came in via the hall door. "Ah, there you three are. Anyone up for an after-dinner drink?"

Mrs. Waters looked up at him, a weary expression on her face. "Thank you, Ambrose, but I was just telling these young folks I should like to go back to the hotel if you'd be so kind as to drive me. I will see everyone in the morning, after breakfast, I think. I plan on sleeping late."

"All right, Auntie, I'll get the car out. Sister has gone up to tend to Mother but will be down shortly."

Henry stood up and helped Mrs. Waters to her feet.

Mr. Rutherford looked at Skip and Henry. "Don't wait up if you don't want to, boys. It may be a while before I get back, as I'll see Auntie safely to her room."

"All right, Uncle, I guess I'm getting tired also. We'll see you in the morning."

"Sleep well. I'll lock up when I return," Mr. Rutherford said, as he left to get his car out of the garage.

Mrs. Waters leaned heavily on her walking stick, wetting her lips. "Thank you for letting me tell my tale. It's weighed me down for many years."

"I can imagine," Skip said.

"I'll walk you out, Aunt Lillian," Henry said as she took his arm. They moved slowly out into the hall, Skip remaining behind, lost in thought. After a few moments, he got to his feet and watched out the window as Mr. Rutherford's car drove away from the curb, with Mrs. Waters in the passenger seat. Soon after, Henry returned.

Skip turned to him as he entered. "Well, here we are again, alone in this dreary room."

Henry smiled wryly. "Yes, it's a bit odd how it keeps happening. I'm sorry, Skip, about the way this weekend has ended up. It's all so strange."

Skip walked closer to him. "You can say that again, but it's all right, Henry. It's not your fault."

"Thanks. If you still want to poke about the basement, I guess now would be the time, while Uncle is out and everyone else is occupied. I can stand guard."

Skip sucked in a breath and let it out slowly. "It's tempting, but I've been thinking about it. If Bitters wanted only Mrs. Savage to find whatever it is he hid, why would he hide it in a place your uncle goes to, and in this house, which she probably can't access easily? Besides, you told me a short time ago it was none of our concern."

"I know, it isn't, and I agree with you about the basement. But after finding out Arthur never existed, well, it's definitely all a puzzle."

"I agree. A puzzle with a lot of odd pieces that don't seem to fit together."

"Or maybe we just don't have all the right pieces yet."

Skip laughed. "Now you sound like me."

"Is that a bad thing?"

"No, I'm just surprised."

"Aunt Lillian's story got me thinking about what you've said, and about all the crazy things that have happened in the short while we've been here."

"I can't *stop* thinking about it all. Do you think Mrs. Rutherford is really mentally ill, Henry?"

"What do you mean?"

"Well, Mrs. Waters told us Mrs. Rutherford wanted to be an actress as a young woman, and she referred to herself as one earlier. Maybe this is all an act."

"It would be a pretty convincing act, and for what purpose?"

"I'm not sure. Attention, maybe? She's the type of person who craves it and stops at nothing to get it."

"Seems rather extreme, though, especially since they're going to put her in a home."

"Hmm, yes, I suppose so. But if it is an act, maybe in the morning she'll have a miraculous recovery."

"After everything that's happened this weekend, nothing would surprise me, Skip."

"Me neither. Something to think about, anyway."

"Yes, but there's something else I've been pondering, too," Henry said.

"What's that?"

"The contents of that box that's buried behind the carriage house."

"Why, Henry Finch, you told me to leave that thought alone, too."

"I know I did, but maybe if we knew what was in it or *not* in it, other things would start to make more sense."

"What do you mean?"

"Maybe Jake didn't bury the box. Maybe it was Joe Bitters, and he put his notes and evidence in there for safekeeping."

"But the box was buried *after* Joe died."

"But what if Joe buried the box earlier, right after he discovered his mysterious evidence, and what Mrs. Savage saw that night was actually someone digging it back up? Someone who guessed where the evidence was hidden?"

"If that's the case, Henry, there wouldn't be anything there anymore. Besides, it doesn't fit with the rhyming clue he told Mrs. Savage. 'Pull the cord, and you've scored the location of my keys. Unlock the quotes to find my notes, and the evidence you'll see.'"

Henry frowned. "True, but maybe the box is locked, and the clue just refers to finding the keys to it."

"So, you think he wanted her to find the keys and then just guess what they were for? And if she did guess, to go digging in the Rutherford yard? An old lady?"

"All right, smarty-pants. Maybe there is a dead dog in that box. But there's no way to know unless…"

"Unless we dig it up."

"I've been thinking about that, too, and the best time to dig would be early tomorrow morning before the sun comes up. Less chance of anyone seeing us. Why don't we meet in the upstairs hall around five?"

"You are full of surprises, Mr. Finch."

"Is that a yes?"

"Absolutely. I'd like to know for certain, one way or the other. Five in the morning, I'll be there in my new blue jeans, flannel shirt, and work shoes."

"Aren't they still awfully dirty from your excursion to the garage earlier?"

"Yes, but I tried to brush them off as best I could, and I don't want to ruin my good clothes."

"Okay."

"The sun comes up about six thirty, I believe. But Miss Grant will be in the kitchen around six."

"Perfect. I'll grab the flashlight from the car, and we can get a shovel from the garage after we get outside. I doubt he buried it too deep, so it shouldn't take long."

"Excellent. And on that note, I think I should get to bed. It's almost ten."

"Same here, let's go up." The two of them left the blue drawing room behind and climbed the stairs to the second floor, pausing at the top.

"See you in the very early morning, Mr. Finch," Skip said, as he gave him a quick kiss good night.

"Sleep tight," he said, kissing him back. "Do you want some company?"

"I do, but it's late, and we have to be up and ready by five. I think we should wait."

"It wouldn't take all that long, and it would probably help both of us sleep better."

"You, sir, are impossible," Skip said.

"Nothing's impossible," he said with a grin.

"Incorrigible, then," Skip said. "It's tempting, believe me, but we'll be home tomorrow and can canoodle all night without worrying about anyone hearing us or your uncle finding out. If he knew for sure about us, he'd find a way to make certain you were disinherited, and we're already pushing our luck."

"Okay, I guess you're right." Henry wrapped him in a warm hug. "Good night, then."

CHAPTER FIFTEEN

Late Saturday night, October 7, 1950
The Rutherford house

Skip entered his room, closing the door as he switched on the bedside light. Once he had used the bathroom, undressed, and packed away his clothes, he slipped into bed and picked up his book. He read several chapters but found he had difficulty concentrating. There was a decided chill, and he wished he'd packed heavier pajamas. He drew the quilt higher up and snuggled down under the covers with a shiver, setting the book on the nightstand. His eyes were feeling heavy, and he was about to turn out the light when a soft rap at the door brought them fully open. A glance at the clock told him it was six minutes to eleven. It had to be Henry, Skip thought, definitely incorrigible.

The rap came again, slightly louder and longer this time, and he realized it wasn't coming from the connecting door but rather the hall, so he threw back the covers and got out of bed, the wood floor feeling like ice against his bare feet as he stepped off the area rug. He cursed not bringing along slippers, but at least he had the robe, which he quickly put on and wrapped around himself. He fully expected to see Henry standing in the hall, perhaps holding glasses and a bottle of purloined champagne from Mr. Rutherford's private stock, but instead, it was Mr. Rutherford himself, still fully dressed and looking sheepish.

"I'm sorry to disturb you at this late hour, Mr. Valentine, but I saw your light on under the door and assumed you must still be awake."

"A valid assumption, Mr. Rutherford, though I was just about to turn the lamp off. Did you need something?"

"It's my mother, I'm afraid. She's having trouble sleeping, and she's in a state. I went to check on her before I retired for the evening and found her quite distressed. She had calmed down earlier, but something's riled her up again."

Skip drew his robe closer about him and crossed his arms. "I'm sorry to hear that, but isn't Sister Barnabas's job to quiet and calm her? To take care of her?"

"Yes, of course. But she's gone to bed already, and well, to be honest, Mother doesn't seem to care for the sister very much. She does, however, seem to like you, so I wondered if perhaps you would be kind enough to sit with her until she feels drowsy. I gave her a glass of milk a short while ago with a sleeping draught in it."

"Well, I'm not certain I'll be of any help, but I can try, I suppose," Skip said doubtfully. "And I wouldn't exactly say she likes me."

"Oh, she spoke highly of you to me just this afternoon."

"I'm sincerely surprised to hear that, Mr. Rutherford. *You* certainly don't seem to care for me."

Mr. Rutherford looked sheepish. "Oh, yes, about that. I apologize. My behavior was uncalled for, and I was out of line. Sister Barnabas chastised me when I told her about our discussion. I'm sure you're a fine young man, and it's not for me to judge what you may or may not be."

"Hmm." Skip studied him, trying to decide if he was sincere or just wanted his assistance, but he couldn't tell. Still, he figured, it might help Henry if he and Ambrose got along. "Well, all right, I guess I can visit with her for a few moments."

Mr. Rutherford smiled. "Thank you, you are too kind. Her room is opposite yours."

"Yes, I know," Skip said. He followed Mr. Rutherford across the wide hall. When they reached her door, Mr. Rutherford knocked gently and turned the knob. "Oh dear, she's locked it. It was unlocked before." He knocked again.

"Perhaps she's fallen asleep after all," Skip said drowsily, wishing he could do the same.

"Yes, maybe so," Mr. Rutherford said. "I guess I'll check on her in the morning. I'm sorry to have disturbed you."

"It's all right, I understand. Have a good night."

"Thank you. I'll see you and Henry at breakfast. Sleep well."

As Mr. Rutherford spoke, a loud crash and the sound of breaking glass came from behind his mother's door, and the two men looked at each other, both alarmed and startled.

Mr. Rutherford futilely jiggled the door handle. "Mother! Mother, what's happened? Are you all right?" He looked at Skip. "I can access her room through the connecting door in mine. Stay here." Before Skip could respond, he had hurried into his own bedroom. Shortly after that, the locked hall door of his mother's room opened. "Come in," he said, standing aside. Skip entered, noticing at once the broken window, the cold night wind billowing the lace curtains. Mrs. Rutherford was standing unsteadily next to her bed, looking dazed and confused.

Mr. Rutherford went to her. "Mother, what happened? Why did you break the window?"

She stared up at him, her arms limp at her sides. "I was asleep. I heard a noise. *I* didn't break the window."

"Then who did? The hall door was locked, and there was no one in my room just now." He strode over to the connecting door to Sister Barnabas's room. "And this is locked, too. Unless there's someone hiding in here…" He made a show of checking her closet, beneath her bed, and behind the dressing screen. "No, no one here, my dear."

"Someone threw a rock from the yard, perhaps," Mrs. Rutherford said, shivering. "Someone wanted to hurt me. It's so cold in here."

He walked to the window overlooking the carriage house, pulling his coat closed against the chill night air. "I can see the broken glass on the lawn below, and there's none in here, and no rock." He leaned carefully out. "And it appears one of your brass bookends from your dresser is down there, too. *Someone* must have thrown it from inside your room."

"Who?" she said, her voice full of suspicion as she glanced about. "Did you do it?" she said, her voice rising. "Or you?" She pointed a crooked finger at Skip.

Mr. Rutherford walked back to her side. "Honestly, Mother. It had to be you, there's no one else. I checked everywhere. Why did you break your window?"

"No! It was the ghost, Bitters. He's here now, I saw him before, his shadow. He's angry. I'm afraid of him." She looked wildly about the room.

"There's nothing to be afraid of, Mother. There's no ghost here."

She scowled, her voice shrill. "You would say that. You never believe me. You don't believe in spirits, but they're real, they are! I've talked to them."

"Whatever you say," he said, surprisingly calm.

"Arthur believed in spirits. *He* believed me."

"Arthur was five years old when he died. He probably still believed in the tooth fairy, Santa Claus, and the Easter bunny, too," Mr. Rutherford said, less calmly this time, and Skip felt a pang of guilt at knowing the truth about Arthur.

"Go away, leave me alone. Joe Bitters's ghost broke my window. I saw him."

"What did he look like, Mrs. Rutherford?" Skip said.

"It was dark, I couldn't see very well. I tried to turn my light on, but it wouldn't work."

"The light on your nightstand?" Skip said.

"I was in bed. I tried to turn it on, but I couldn't. Joe wouldn't let me."

"Mother, it's too late for this codswallop."

Skip walked over and tried turning on the lamp. "She's right, it doesn't work."

"What did you do to the light, Mother?"

"It was Joe! He broke the window and the lamp."

"Actually," Skip said, bending down, "it's just unplugged."

"The ghost did it, playing tricks on me."

"Okay, Mother. Joe broke your window and unplugged your lamp. I'm glad you drank your milk, because you need to calm down and get some sleep. But you can't stay in here with the window broken, it's too cold. You can sleep in my bed tonight until we can make at least a temporary repair tomorrow. I'll sleep on the sofa in the library."

"Joe's gone now, but he'll be back."

"Then let's go next door to my room where you'll be safe." He took her in his arms, almost carrying her through the connecting door, where he tucked her into his bed like a little child. Surprisingly, Mrs. Rutherford resisted very little. Skip followed behind them, turning out the overhead light in Mrs. Rutherford's room.

"There, now you can sleep more comfortably. I'll be right downstairs if you need me," Mr. Rutherford said. He walked over to the bureau and extracted a pair of pajamas.

"Why are you taking my things?"

"These are *my* pajamas, Mother, and this is *my* room. I'm going to sleep on the sofa in the yellow drawing room so you can stay here."

"Isn't that nice of him?" Skip said.

"Who are you? Do I know you?" Mrs. Rutherford said, staring at Skip.

"I'm Skip Valentine. We met before. I'm here from Chicago with Henry Finch," Skip said gently.

"Oh," Mrs. Rutherford said, softer this time. "Oh, that's right. The well-mannered one. You're a handsome young man. You remind me of Arthur. He had red hair, too. I was pretty once, you know."

"You still are," Skip said softly.

"Thank you," the old woman said, and she gave Skip a toothless smile. "Will you stay with me for a bit?"

Mr. Rutherford looked over at Skip. "Would you mind, Mr. Valentine?" he said. "She'll fall asleep soon, and then you can go back to bed."

"Certainly, for a little while…"

"Splendid, thank you. I shall see you in the morning."

"All right, good night," Skip said.

When Mr. Rutherford had gone, Skip walked over to the oversized bed, taking a chair next to it.

"I'm tired," the old woman said softly.

"It's late, go to sleep," Skip said. He switched out the light, feeling rather silly sitting there with this woman he barely knew, in a strange man's room in the dark, late at night, barefoot and wearing nothing but his robe and pajamas.

"Yes, yes," Mrs. Rutherford said, cooing. She gurgled once or twice, and then stilled. But just when Skip thought she was finally asleep, she called out, "It's so dark. I don't like the dark, not when I'm afraid."

Skip reached over and raised the window shade over the bed, the full moon outside illuminating the room and shining soft light onto the old woman's face. "There, is that better?"

"Yes, that's better, much better." Mrs. Rutherford settled back into the goose down pillow and closed her eyes. In a few minutes, she was snoring softly, and Skip snuck out the hall door and across to his room. He glanced at the clock before turning out the light and noted it was almost midnight. He yawned, his eyelids heavy, as he snuggled once more beneath the quilt and fell quickly asleep.

A couple of hours later, Skip awoke with a start and sat up, his heart racing as he fumbled with the light next to his bed. "The ghostly barking and pounding again," he said to himself. He stumbled to his feet, rubbing his eyes and squinting at the clock, which told him it was two thirty in the morning. Rather than bother Henry, he went directly out into the hall, but the noises stopped as quickly as they had started. Tentatively he took a few steps toward the stairs, but it was dark, he was cold, and he didn't know where exactly the noises had come from, so he retreated to his bedroom once more, where he could hear three knocks coming from the connecting door to Henry's room. He walked over and knocked twice in reply.

"Well, it's about time. Did you hear the barking and pounding again?" Henry said.

"Yes, I did. They woke me from a rather lovely dream about Cary Grant. All quiet now, though."

"Yeah. Ugh, it's practically morning already. Let's try to get a little more sleep."

"Sounds good to me, Henry."

CHAPTER SIXTEEN

Early Sunday morning, October 8, 1950
The Rutherford House

Skip's alarm went off at four thirty, and for the third time since he crawled into it the previous night, he forced himself out of the comfort of his bed. He turned on the lamp and got dressed, putting on his new blue jeans, flannel shirt, and work shoes, still spotted with soot and ash from his garage expedition. He pulled his raincoat on over the dirty clothes, not bothering to shave or even wash his face. True to his word, Henry was waiting in the hall at five, dressed but also unshaven, and looking slightly grumpy.

"Morning," Skip whispered. "You look exhausted."

"Didn't sleep well, thinking about getting up early and all," he whispered back.

"I know. It didn't help getting woken up again at two thirty in the morning by more ghostly noises. And besides *that* rude awakening, your uncle came knocking on my door around eleven."

Henry's eyebrows shot up in surprise and he almost forgot to whisper. "What for?"

"He was having trouble with his mother, she was in a state, and he wanted me to try to comfort her. So, we went to her room, but she'd locked the door, then there was a crash, and apparently, she threw a brass bookend through her window, breaking it. So, Mr. Rutherford put her to bed in his room, and he said he was going to sleep downstairs. I sat with the old girl until she fell asleep and then went back to my bed at nearly midnight, only to be woken up again by that barking and pounding."

"Jeepers. Where was Sister Barnabas during all this?"

"Asleep, presumably."

"She slept through a window breaking and all that commotion in the room that connects with hers?"

"Those without sin sleep divinely, my grandmother used to say," Skip said.

"And soundly. Well, no wonder you're tired."

"Hopefully, we can both nap later. Ready?"

"As I'll ever be. Let's go," Henry said, turning out the bedroom light and closing the door. As silently as they could, they went down the main staircase and around to the door under the landing. From there they proceeded out to the side yard, where the broken window glass and brass bookend still lay, shimmering with dew in the moonlight. They walked carefully around this and then over to the front of the garage, where Henry retrieved the flashlight, which fortunately still worked, from the glove box of the car. They used it to find a shovel inside the garage and then went around to the back of the building. Skip held the light while Henry dug beneath the remains of the wooden stairs next to the fence.

"It's freezing out here," Skip said, his teeth chattering. "I wish I'd packed a heavier coat."

"I know, me too. Hold that thing steady, you're waving it all over the place. And stand with your back to the house so the light isn't as visible."

"Right, sorry," Skip said, moving around to the other side. "My hands are like ice."

"Would you prefer to dig?"

"No, just hurry."

The ground was harder than it had been earlier, but it gave easily enough under the steel blade of the shovel. Skip alternated the flashlight from one hand to the other, sticking the empty hand in the pocket of his raincoat until the other one got cold again. In a few minutes, Henry struck a hard object.

"There's definitely something buried here. I think I got it," he said in a whisper, "unless it's a rock. Shine the light closer." Henry set the shovel aside and bent down, using his hands to scrape some loose dirt away. "It's a box all right. Hang on, almost there." He picked up the shovel once more and dug around the sides as best he could, then brushed off the remaining dirt as Skip knelt beside him.

The flashlight revealed an old wooden crate, about twenty-four inches by eighteen inches, with a flat lid on top. Henry ran his fingers along the edges of the lid, prying up here and there as best as he could.

"Son of a motherless goat!" he exclaimed, yanking his hand back.

"Shh, be quiet. You'll wake the dead."

"Sorry, but that hurt," Henry whispered loudly, glaring at him.

"What happened?"

"Splinter. I hate those things."

"I'll get it out with a needle later. Can you get the lid off?"

"Yeah, I think so. It's not nailed shut. Give me a hand or two."

"Okay," Skip said as he tucked the flashlight under his arm and reached into the dirt. Together they got the lid off and Henry set it aside. "I can't look. If it's Gipper, I just can't look. You tell me what's in there."

"Well, I can't look either if you don't shine the flashlight down here," Henry said, annoyed.

"Oh, right, sorry." Skip reluctantly shone the light inside the box, revealing absolutely nothing.

"It's empty!" he cried out in surprise.

"Shh! Now who's making enough noise to wake the dead, if you'll pardon the expression," Henry whispered. "But you're right. No evidence and no dead dog. So, Gipper did run away. But if Joe buried his notes and someone got here before we did, they took them and buried the box again for some reason. But why? Or is it something else entirely?"

Skip got to his feet, brushing off some of the dirt from his hands and blue jeans. "If we knew for sure who Mrs. Savage saw from her window that night, we might have an answer. Let's get back inside and upstairs before everyone gets up."

"Should we rebury it?" Henry said, getting to his feet also and picking up the shovel once more.

"I suppose so, though if anyone looks closely enough, they'll know someone was out here again anyway. Better hurry, Miss Grant will be up soon."

Henry put the lid on and shoveled the dirt back into the hole, tamping it down with the back of the shovel as best he could as Skip held the flashlight, shivering.

"That will have to do, Come on. I'll put the shovel away if you put the flashlight back in the car," Henry said.

"Deal."

When they had finished, the two of them went back inside and quietly up the stairs as the clock struck five forty-five.

"Do you remember seeing any Mercurochrome in the bathroom?" Skip said softly, stopping outside Henry's door.

"Gosh, I don't know, I never paid any attention. Why?"

"Because I want to get that sliver out of your finger. Go look while I retrieve a needle from my suitcase. And leave your door open."

"Okay. You travel with a needle?"

"And thread. My mother taught me to sew at an early age, and you never know when you might split your trousers and need an emergency repair. Hurry up, I'll be back in a flash."

When Skip returned, needle in hand, Henry proudly displayed the bottle of Mercurochrome. "It was on a shelf in the bathroom next to the spare toilet paper and the aspirin."

"Excellent," Skip said, closing the hall door. "And at least you had the foresight to wash your hands with soap and water. Turn your bedside light on and let me have a look."

Skip dug about Henry's finger, jabbing and pulling at the skin here and there while Henry winced and groaned until Skip had removed the offending piece of wood. He dabbed at it with the antiseptic, turning the tip of Henry's finger an orangish red. "There you go, big baby, all better." He gave Henry a kiss on the lips, and Henry willingly kissed him back.

"Definitely all better," Henry said with a grin.

"Good. Well, I'd better get cleaned up and out of these clothes, and you should, too."

"And better and better!"

Skip gave him a playful shove on his chest. "Out of these clothes and into some clean ones, goof. It's just ten after six now. I'll meet you in the hall at seven."

He slipped out of Henry's room and into the bathroom, thankful no one had seen him. After putting the bottle of Mercurochrome back, he washed up and returned to his room where he changed clothes, choosing one of his favorite sweaters, a black and red harlequin, over a simple dress shirt and black trousers. This time he beat Henry out, and he paced up and down the hall as he waited, pondering everything that had happened since they had arrived. Five minutes after seven, Henry appeared, freshly shaved and groomed but still looking fatigued.

"Sorry to keep you waiting," he said with half a smile. "It was all I could do not to crawl back into bed after I'd undressed."

"I'm tired, too, but coffee will help."

"Lots of it," Henry said. "Come on, let's go down."

CHAPTER SEVENTEEN

Sunday morning, October 8, 1950
The Rutherford house

They descended the broad stairs and entered the dining room, where Mr. Rutherford and Sister Barnabas were already seated, enjoying their breakfast. Mr. Rutherford glanced up at them as they entered. He was wearing the same clothes he had on the night before and was unshaven. "Good morning. You boys are up early."

"Good morning," Skip said. "Yes, I guess we are. So are the two of you."

"I awoke at six fifteen and was in here at a quarter to seven. Sister was right behind me. Miss Grant had everything set already. I'm afraid I didn't sleep well on the sofa. My back is sore."

"That's unfortunate, Uncle."

"Couldn't be helped. Excuse my appearance, by the way, I didn't want to disturb my mother by going into my room this morning to clean up and get fresh clothes."

"As I said a few minutes ago, you should have woken me immediately when you first had trouble with her, Mr. Rutherford," the sister said.

"Yes, I know, but I hated to bother you. I had no idea things would get so out of hand. Anyway, I'm glad *you* got a good night's sleep so *you* can deal with her today."

"Certainly. Since you said you're letting her sleep in, I'll attend to her sometime later this morning."

"Don't forget she's still in my bedroom."

"Yes, you mentioned that earlier," she said, finishing her coffee.

"I'll have Jake board up her window, and I'll call to get it replaced tomorrow. Once it's boarded up, she should be able to move back to her own room."

"Of course."

"And once that's done, I'll go up and wash my face, shave, and put on clean clothes." He looked back at Skip and Henry. "Get some plates and help yourselves."

They once more filled up plates with eggs and sausages, along with a doughnut each, and two mugs of coffee, and took their usual spots at the table.

"Everything looks delicious," Skip said, to no one in particular.

"What happened to your finger, Henry? It's orange," Mr. Rutherford said.

"Oh, uh, I just got a sliver in it, is all. It's fine. How's your ankle?"

"Hardly hurts at all anymore."

"I'm glad to hear it," Henry said. "By the way, did either of you hear that barking and pounding noise again last night? Or rather, very early this morning?"

"Not that again," Mr. Rutherford said. "No, I didn't, but I take it you did."

"We both did," Skip said. "Around two thirty in the morning. It woke us up."

"I'm sorry to hear that," Mr. Rutherford said.

"It's all right. We're heading back to Chicago later this morning or this afternoon anyway," Henry said.

"What about you, Sister? Did you hear anything?" Skip said.

She shook her head as she swallowed the last of the eggs on her plate. "No, I'm afraid I didn't. I took a sleeping draught, you see. I never heard any barking or pounding, and not a thing from Mrs. Rutherford's room. Such a commotion."

"Well, I hope Mrs. Rutherford slept well after I left her," Skip said.

"Most likely she slept like a baby," Sister said. "By the way, the clasp on my cross is loose. Do you happen to have a pair of pliers about, Mr. Rutherford?"

"There should be one on the workbench in the basement. Ask Jake to get it for you. He's probably in the kitchen with Jane. When he's finished helping you, ask him to board up Mother's window."

"All right," Sister Barnabas said. "My work here is about done, so I will be returning to the convent tomorrow after your mother and her sister leave for Forest Glen."

"Of course. I want to thank you for your time and efforts. I will write the Mother Superior a nice letter about you."

She blushed ever so slightly. "Thank you, but I am only doing God's work. After I find Jake and get my cross repaired, I think I'll go up and check on your mother and then see about putting my affairs in order for leaving," she said, getting to her feet. "And of course it's Sunday, so I'll be off to church services in a bit."

"Which church do you attend, Sister?" Skip said.

"Saint Thomas the Apostle on Elizabeth Street," Mr. Rutherford said, standing up. "The same one my mother used to attend. Did you want me to drive you, Sister?" Mr. Rutherford asked, standing up.

"Thank you, but I know your company will be leaving soon, so I can ride the bus. I'll check in with you before I go. Good day."

Skip and Henry got to their feet as well. "Good day, Sister." When she had gone, Mr. Rutherford helped himself to seconds and then sat back down, Henry and Skip doing the same.

"You don't go to services, Uncle?"

"I'm afraid I've fallen out of the habit, especially since Mother no longer attends. How about you boys?"

"Oh, well, Skip goes sometimes. His father was an usher, you know, and his mother was the church organist and member of the choir, so he was raised that way. My family never went, at least not often."

"Ah, I see. Well, I suppose you'll be able to get on the road sooner that way. What route do you plan to take back to Chicago, Henry?"

The three men chatted amicably about good places to stop and rest along the way, the weather forecast, and other things for the next hour or so, until Mr. Rutherford got up from his chair, looking slightly uncomfortable.

"Goodness," Mr. Rutherford said, "I'm afraid the coffee goes right through me lately. Will you excuse me? I'll be back momentarily."

When he had gone, Henry helped himself to another doughnut. "Well, maybe all's well that ends well," he said.

"What do you mean?"

"Just that Mrs. Rutherford will be going to the home tomorrow, Sister Barnabas will be heading back to the convent, and we can go back to Chicago today."

Skip frowned ever so slightly. "I suppose so. Still, I can't shake the feeling something's not right. I keep thinking about that empty box, for one thing."

"I've been thinking about it, too, but I think we're done here. There's nothing left to investigate. We know Gipper wasn't in it, so he probably did run away. And if the so-called notes or evidence Bitters supposedly found were in that box, they're gone now. Who knows? He may have been a crazy lunatic and made the whole thing up. Let's eat and head home. Have a doughnut."

Skip took one and put it on his plate but just stared at it. "Thanks. Gipper liked doughnuts, remember?"

"Yes, Mrs. Rutherford told us that. I'm glad he wasn't in that box."

"Me too. As you said before, *nothing* was in it. So why did someone bury it? I have a theory. What if…"

Mr. Rutherford entered again, looking flushed.

"Is everything all right, Uncle?"

"Oh yes, just a nuisance, you know, this running to the bathroom day and night."

"You should have that checked by your doctor," Skip said.

"Eh, doctors. It's God's will, and God's will be done."

Miss Grant knocked at the hall door and poked her head in. "I'm sorry to bother you sir, but there's a young lady to see you at the back door."

"A young lady?" Mr. Rutherford said, clearly surprised.

"Yes, sir. I was taking some paper to the lavatory, and there she was on the porch as I passed the back door. It's Miss Banning, sir."

"Ah, I see. Well, this is a surprise," he said, looking at Henry. "Marjorie Banning is the young woman I was telling you about. The lady friend I'm seeing." He turned back to Jane. "Tell her I'll be right out."

"Oh, I should truly like to meet her, Uncle. Why don't you have her come in?"

"She's probably in a hurry."

"Well, we're all finished here anyway. We could come out and say hello."

Mr. Rutherford looked back at Henry, then at Jane again. "Very well, show her in, I suppose. Let her know Henry and Mr. Valentine would like to meet her."

"Yes sir." Jane went out into the hall, leaving the door open.

Shortly she returned, followed by Miss Banning, who swung into the room confident and poised. Henry, Skip, and Mr. Rutherford got to their feet as she swept over to Ambrose and gave him a peck on the cheek. Jane was still standing in the doorway, watching.

"Bonjour, Ambrose. I'm so sorry to burst in, but I hadn't heard or seen from you in some time, and I wanted to say hello," Miss Banning said in a thick French accent.

Mr. Rutherford returned the kiss. "It's all right, Marjorie. I'm just surprised, that's all. I wasn't expecting you this morning."

"I hope you don't mind, dear." She looked him up and down with a swift glance. "My, you look unkempt, if you don't mind my saying so."

"I spent the night on the sofa and haven't shaved yet. It's a long story," he said, gesturing toward Skip and Henry. "May I introduce Mr. Finch, and this is Mr. Valentine. Gentlemen, this is Miss Banning."

"How do you do, Monsieur Finch?" Marjorie said, extending her hand. Her wrist was covered in bracelets, and the long nails on her fingers were painted a daring red.

"How do you do?" Henry said, taking her hand in his lightly.

She smiled, parting her ruby-red lips. "Oh my, but you're trés beau."

"Trés beau?" Henry repeated, puzzled.

"It means very handsome," Skip said. "I took French all through high school."

"Trés bien, Mr. Valentine," she said to Skip. "Aren't you charming and clever? That sweater you're wearing is divine."

"Thank you," Skip said. "A bit more modest than your attire."

Miss Banning laughed. "Oh, you Americans are so conservative. There's nothing wrong with showing a little flesh, monsieur."

"A *little* flesh, yes." Skip looked Miss Banning up and down closely. He had to admit she was stunning, with a large bosom, tiny waist, shapely hips, and bobbed platinum blond hair done in ringlets plastered to her head. She wore too much makeup, including a painted-on beauty spot on her upper lip, and her rouged cheeks looked like plump, juicy peaches. Her dress had a plunging neckline, and the hem was a tad on the short side, revealing shapely legs. Her black eyebrows were painted in dramatic arches, and green emeralds bedazzled her earlobes. Over her shoulder was a beaded bag hanging by a gold chain.

"Some people say a little goes a long way. *I say*, a lot goes further," Marjorie said.

"Obviously, Miss Banning. Your name doesn't sound very French, by the way," Skip said.

"Oh, oui, I know, but I am. Well, fifty percent. My father was English. But I was raised in Paris, le capital of France."

"Are you sure it's le capital, Miss Banning?" Skip said.

"Of course I'm sure, silly one, everyone knows that," Miss Banning said, laughing gaily.

"What brought you to the United States?" Henry said, staring at her with his mouth slightly open.

"Opportunity. I want to be on the stage."

"Miss Banning is an actress," Mr. Rutherford said.

"Yes, I came a few years before the war, and a good thing. Europe was not a safe place to be then. And here I met Ambrose, so beau, also."

Mr. Rutherford blushed as he noticed Miss Grant still standing in the doorway. "Have you taken up Mother's tray yet, Jane?"

"No sir. You said to let her sleep awhile since she had a rough night."

"Yes, I know, but I think she should be awake by now."

"I'll get it prepared, then."

"Thank you," he said.

"I think we should go up and finish packing," Skip said, looking at Henry.

"Hmm? Oh, yes, I suppose so," Henry said. "It was nice meeting you, Miss Banning."

She smiled, revealing perfect white teeth. "Merci and likewise. You are too kind."

"Well, goodbye now."

"Never goodbye, just au revoir."

"Okay, au revoir."

"Come back down when you're set, boys, but leave your bags in your rooms. Jake will bring them to the front hall," Mr. Rutherford said.

"All right," Henry said, as he and Skip went out.

CHAPTER EIGHTEEN

After breakfast, Sunday, October 8, 1950
The Rutherford house

"She sure was something," Henry said as they stopped at the base of the staircase.

"She was something all right. A little too forward."

"Aw, that's just how the French people are. Real friendly. I spent a bit of time there in the war, remember? Her accent brought back a lot of memories."

"Yes, I remember you telling me you were stationed there. And yet you learned surprisingly little of the French language. And speaking of…"

"Some people communicate in different ways."

"I do remember you're good with your hands in the dark," Skip said. "Say, if your uncle and Miss Banning get married, does that mean you're out as the heir?"

"No, that was one of the terms. If he marries and has no male children and precedes her in death, I still inherit, but I have to agree to provide for her as long as she lives."

"And it doesn't seem likely they'd have children, male or female. Not at their ages."

"No, it doesn't."

"So, you're set regardless. Just how much money is there, by the way?"

"What do you mean?"

"I mean, there doesn't seem to be enough to repair the garage or fix up the house or anything else. Everything outside is run down and everything inside is ancient. And he couldn't even give you a small loan. I know he said most of the money is tied up in stocks, bonds, and investments, but still…"

"I know what you mean, but the lawyers assured me there's over ten thousand dollars in the bank, held jointly by Mrs. Rutherford and my uncle."

Skip whistled. "Wow, that's three times as much as most people's annual incomes, not counting the stocks and bonds."

"I guess he's just being frugal because he doesn't know how much his mother's care is going to cost or how long she'll live."

"I suppose so. Well, ready to go up?"

"Yes, you?"

"I'm ready, but I think I'd prefer to go up, up," Skip said.

"Up, up?" Henry shot him a puzzled look.

"To the attic. I want to see where Jake sleeps."

"Whatever for?"

"Because I've been thinking. Unless I'm daffy, that barking we've been hearing isn't the ghost of Joe Bitters's dog, but Gipper."

"Huh?"

"I bet Jake has Gipper hidden in his room upstairs in the attic. And I suspect Gipper, probably missing Mrs. Rutherford or maybe wanting to get out of cramped quarters and roam around, occasionally starts barking in the middle of the night, and that's what we've been hearing. I'm guessing it *was* Jake who buried that empty box."

"Why?"

"Maybe someone told him to kill and bury Gipper. Maybe someone wanted the dog dead, and they told Jake to do the dirty work, but he couldn't go through with it. So, he buried the box to make it *look* like he did and hid Gipper in his room in the attic."

"Okay, so what about the pounding?"

"I've been thinking about that, too. It's doubtful Miss Grant would not know about Jake hiding the dog. When the barking starts, I bet she pounds on the ceiling to get Jake to quiet Gipper down before they're discovered. Remember her reaction when we asked her after our first night if she'd heard any noises around three?"

"Yes, she said she didn't, and then you asked her if Jake had, and she said he didn't say anything to her about any barking."

"Exactly. She knows Gipper is alive. I could kick myself for not thinking of that before."

"Okay, Detective. Sounds like you're on a roll, but answer me this. Who would want Gipper killed and why?"

"I don't know for certain. Maybe your uncle felt it would be easier for his mother to agree to go to the nursing home if she didn't have to leave Gipper behind because she thinks the dog ran away. Or maybe Miss Grant's behind it to get back at Mrs. Rutherford."

"But you just said she knows the dog is alive."

"True. When she discovered that, she may have allowed Jake to keep Gipper, knowing how he felt, and that Mrs. Rutherford wouldn't get him back. Or maybe it's something or someone else. At this point, only Jake probably knows for sure, but I think the dog is up in the attic, alive. Come on."

Skip bounded up the steps to the second landing and then went through the door into the small square hall where the bathroom was. He pushed on through another door on the opposite side into the servants' hallway. It was narrow and long, with a window on the right over the stairs from the kitchen, and another at the far end where more stairs climbed to the attic. With Henry following behind, he crept along the passage to the end, past the servants' bathroom, Miss Grant's room, and the empty bedroom that had belonged to Jake's mother. From the stairway, he could hear a radio floating up from the kitchen below.

"Tread lightly," Skip said quietly as they began their ascent.

"How are we going to explain this if we're caught?" Henry said.

"Better to ask forgiveness, remember? What's the worst that could happen? They throw us out? We're leaving today anyway. Besides, your uncle never said to stay out of the attic."

"True," Henry said, "he only mentioned the cellar. Okay, I'm with you, for better or worse."

"Thanks, I appreciate that, truly."

At the top of the stairs, they found themselves in a dark, chilly, low-ceilinged loft area.

"Gee, this is bleak," Skip said, looking about.

"Flat and colorless," Henry said.

"Watch your head. Nails are sticking through from the roof, and you're just tall enough to run into them," Skip said as he moved farther into the space. Boxes, steamer trunks, and luggage lined the walls under the eaves, some decorated with steamship and railroad labels along with delicate cobwebs, and all with a coating of dust.

Henry opened a door and peered in at a cavernous, empty room. "This space must be over the main house."

"Yeah. Might have been intended as a ballroom but never finished," Skip said as Henry closed the door again, and they both turned toward the back of the house. "Looks like there's a partitioned-off area in the rear."

"That's probably where Jake sleeps," Henry said.

"Makes sense."

They walked across the dirty plank floor, grimacing each time a floorboard squeaked, until they reached the simple plain door in the partition. Skip knocked lightly and then tried the knob and opened it, revealing a basic rectangle of a space, with steeply sloped ceilings and exposed rafters. A solitary window was in the center of the back wall beneath the peak, overlooking the yard and the Savage house beyond.

"This is even drearier," Skip said. "A single bedstead, one lamp, and a chest of drawers that looks like it was left on the curb by someone. But see that? Next to Jake's bed?"

"Yes, an old crate filled with blankets. And a water bowl next to it."

"Just right for a small dog," Skip said.

"Like Gipper, if your theory is correct and he's alive," Henry said. "But if he is, where is he?"

"Jake's probably in the kitchen, but the dog should be here unless Jake takes him down in the morning to keep him quiet."

"Maybe, but that seems risky." Henry walked about the space, bumping his head occasionally on the low ceilings but fortunately avoiding the protruding nails, until he made his way over to the unmade bed, which was not much more than a cot, and the simple orange crate nightstand next to it that held a clock and the only lamp in the room. "There's a note, Skip, in plain block letters."

"What's it say? Is it from Jake?"

"It is. It says, 'Dear Aunt Jane. I'm sorry for everything I did.

Gipper and I is going away. You will be happy now; I didn't mean to hurt no one. Love, Jake.'"

"Huh, I wonder what that means?" Skip said.

"It gets stranger and stranger," Henry said.

"I agree."

"Poor kid, where's he going to go?"

"Good question. As much as I hate to, I think we need to let the authorities know so they can look for him."

"But he's eighteen, Skip, they aren't going to do anything. Besides, maybe his leaving is for the best."

"Possibly, but I'm not so sure. He's all alone, how will he take care of himself?"

"That's for his aunt to worry about."

"And she will worry about it when she finds this note."

"So, let her find it, Skip, and then she can contact the authorities if she so chooses. Look, I can't make sense out of anything that's happened here since we first arrived, but I will say again none of it is our business. We've hit nothing but dead ends, and it's time to give up."

"I suppose you're right, but I can't help wondering and worrying."

"I know, and I understand."

"Thanks, Henry."

The two of them left Jake's room and went down to the second floor out into the main hall, where they noticed Miss Grant going into Mr. Rutherford's room with a breakfast tray for his mother.

"Listen," Henry said, "I'm with you, Skip. I'll stand beside you, but I do think we should just finish packing and head back to Chicago."

Skip nodded. "Okay. I'm sorry for being such a pest about all this."

"It's all right. You're a curious person, and I admit I was curious, too, but I think we're done here."

"I *am* curious, but I stand beside you, too, and I don't want to put your chances of an inheritance in jeopardy, so let's gather up our things and go home like you said. Whatever is going on in this spooky old house will just have to remain a puzzle, a—"

"*Help!*" a woman screamed.

"That sounded like it came from Mr. Rutherford's room," Skip said with alarm.

"Yes, I remember you and Uncle saying Mrs. Rutherford slept in there last night. I imagine she's having another fit, probably imagining Miss Grant is some kind of a ghost. All the more reason for us to get out of this nuthouse. Come on, let Sister Barnabas attend to her this time."

"Right," Skip said, but he went across the hall to Mr. Rutherford's door and knocked.

"Skip," Henry said, following him. "Leave it alone. You just said…"

"Oh my God, she's dead! Help, *please!*" came that same shrill voice again.

More alarmed now, the hairs on the back of his neck standing up, Skip opened the door and rushed in, Henry right behind him. Skip stopped in his tracks, Henry ran into him, and they both stared. Mrs. Rutherford was on her back in her son's bed, a red bandana wound tightly about her neck. She had been strangled, her face blue and contorted, frozen into a gruesome expression. Jane Grant was standing off to the side and appeared to be in shock, still clutching the breakfast tray, her knuckles white.

Skip quickly took hold of the situation and began barking orders. "Henry, telephone the police. Use the phone in the library so we don't disturb anything. Miss Grant, go alert Mr. Rutherford. He's probably still in the dining room if he didn't hear your cries." He walked to the lifeless little body and checked for a pulse, just to be sure, but there was none.

Henry left quickly and bounded down the stairs, but Miss Grant just stood there clutching the tray, staring at Mrs. Rutherford.

"Miss Grant, are you okay?" Skip walked over to the woman and touched her arm.

Finally, Jane spoke, haltingly. "The bandana around her neck is Jake's, I'm sure of it."

Skip pried the breakfast tray from her hands and set it down carefully. "When did you last see Jake, Miss Grant?" he asked quietly, staring into her eyes and blocking her view of Mrs. Rutherford.

Jane blinked multiple times and then seemed to focus on Skip's face. "What? Jake? I saw him earlier, in the kitchen. He was helping me. Then Sister Barnabas came in looking for a pair of pliers, I think it was. Jake told her there was one in the basement, and the two of them left."

"She went down to the basement with him?"

"What? Oh, yes, I think so. She said it would save time if they needed some other tool besides the pliers."

"I see. Well, I think you should know he's gone, run away," Skip said, still staring at her.

"Jake's run away?" She looked faint.

"Yes, Miss Grant," Skip said. "And he took Gipper with him, I think."

"You know about Gipper?" Her face drained of color.

"Yes, it's all right. You've had a shock. Why don't you go to your room and lie down? Have some water, too. Henry went to telephone the police."

"The police? Oh, dear. Yes, perhaps I should lie down."

Skip took Miss Grant's arm gingerly. "Come on," he said gently, guiding her to the hall.

Skip closed the door behind them. Once Miss Grant had disappeared from view through the door to the servants' quarters, Skip raced down the main stairs to the first floor, where he found Henry just hanging up the telephone receiver in the library.

"The police are on their way," he said. "How's Miss Grant?"

"I sent her to her room to lie down."

"Good idea. She didn't look well."

"Understandable, I suppose. Go upstairs and guard the door to Mr. Rutherford's bedroom. Don't let anyone in."

"Okay. What are you going to do?"

"I'm going to give your uncle the bad news, I guess. Unless you want to."

"Er, no, thanks. You're better with words than I am."

"All right, see you in a bit," Skip said, crossing the hall as Henry went up the stairs.

Mr. Rutherford and Miss Banning were still in the dining room chatting away intimately as Skip came in through the closed door, his face flushed.

Mr. Rutherford got to his feet, scowling. "What is it, Mr. Valentine?" he said. "Do you always make a habit of bursting in on people without knocking?"

"I'm sorry, but I'm afraid something's happened."

Mr. Rutherford's expression changed to one of alarm. "Is Henry all right?"

"He's fine. It's your mother, sir. I hate to be blunt, but I'm afraid she's dead."

"Dead? Oh no. The poor thing. I knew it was coming, but I didn't expect it so soon." Mr. Rutherford put a hand on the back of his chair to steady himself.

"I'm so sorry, Ambrose," Marjorie said, touching his arm and gazing up at him as she got to her feet, too.

Ambrose put his hand on top of hers. "Thank you. At least she died peacefully, in her sleep."

"Actually, Mr. Rutherford, she didn't. The police are on their way. I take it neither of you heard Jane calling for help a few minutes ago?"

"Jane was calling for help? The police are coming? Whatever for? What do you mean?"

"I mean, sir, that your mother was strangled."

Chapter Nineteen

Late morning, Sunday, October 8, 1950
The Rutherford house

Detective Jacobs paced about the dining room where Mr. Rutherford, Miss Banning, Skip, Henry, and Miss Grant were seated around the table. He glanced at his notebook and then over at Mr. Rutherford. "So, the deceased was your mother?"

"That's correct, Gabria Isabella Peacock Rutherford. I'm her only living child."

The detective made a note of that. "And who's this?"

"This is my lady friend, Marjorie Banning. She stopped by this morning, not much more than an hour ago. She should be free to leave."

The detective stared at Miss Banning, taking her in appreciatively. "Well, she's not."

"I don't mind," she purred.

"Glad to hear it." He pointed his pencil at Henry next. "And you are?"

"Henry Finch. And this is my friend, Horace Valentine. We're visiting from Chicago. We arrived Friday afternoon and are leaving today."

"Not just yet you aren't," the detective said. "What about you?" He looked now at Jane, who didn't appear at all well.

"I'm Miss Jane Grant, the housekeeper," she said, her voice a hoarse whisper.

"Worked here long?"

"Over sixteen years, long enough," she said.

"Right. Is that everyone, then? Everyone here who was in the house last night and this morning?"

"Well," Mr. Rutherford said, "there is Sister Barnabas, my mother's nurse. She seems to be missing."

"Missing?"

"Yes, I'm not sure where she is. I checked her room just before you arrived, but she wasn't there. She might have gone to church, but she said she'd check with me before leaving, and she was going to look in on my mother first, too. The last time I saw her was right here."

"Great, so a dead old lady and a missing nun," he said, jotting down something else into his notebook as a policeman stood nearby the hall door, observing. "Anybody else?"

"Jake, Miss Grant's nephew. He helps out around here, doing odd jobs and whatnot," Mr. Rutherford said. "He always had a red bandana in his pocket or around his neck, just like the one used to strangle my mother."

Miss Grant stifled a cry, and Detective Jacobs raised his eyebrows in surprise. "Now, isn't that an interesting little detail? So, where is he now?"

"I haven't seen him yet today," Mr. Rutherford said.

"I can tell you," Miss Grant said. She looked sicker than Mr. Rutherford did. "Or rather I can tell you where he isn't. He's missing, too. He ran away, taking Mrs. Rutherford's dog with him."

"Mrs. Rutherford's dog?" Detective Jacobs said.

"That's right. A little white terrier named Gipper," Miss Grant said.

"What do you mean?" Mr. Rutherford said.

"Jake told me he was afraid someone was going to harm the dog. I imagine he meant Mrs. Rutherford. He took him and told everyone Gipper ran away."

The detective made another entry in his notebook and looked at Ambrose. "I see. He thought the dog was in danger from your mother?"

"I wasn't aware of that. I honestly thought it had run away," Mr. Rutherford said.

"Right. So, one dead lady, two missing persons, and a dog that supposedly ran away a while ago but didn't and is now also missing."

Another policeman appeared at the hall door and poked his head in. "Bates and I finished checking the interior doors and windows of the house as well as the perimeter, sir. There's no sign of forced entry, but there is a broken window in one of the front bedrooms, next to the one where the body is. The window was smashed from the inside, though. There's broken glass on the lawn below, along with what appears to be some kind of heavy brass object."

The detective jotted that down, too. "That's strange."

"My mother broke it last night, Detective. She threw a bookend through it. She wasn't well, mentally. We were going to transfer her to a nursing home tomorrow morning."

"I see. Which explains why this Jake thought she might harm her dog, I suppose." Jacobs looked over at the officer. "Any chance someone could have climbed in that window after it was broken, Crawley?"

"I considered that, but it's doubtful without cutting themselves on the jagged glass, sir. And they would have needed a tall ladder to get up there. There's no ladder imprints in the ground outside, and the area around the window inside is clean. No footprints, blood, or scuffs beneath the sill that would indicate someone entered that way."

"Okay, thanks. Go outside and wait for the lab crew to arrive. I want photos of the crime scene, and everything dusted for fingerprints once they get here, along with the fingerprints of everyone present. And keep the damned press out of my hair."

Officer Crawley touched the brim of his cap. "Yes sir."

"Oh," Mr. Rutherford said. "There is one other person who was here last night, but I took her back to her hotel, and I saw my mother alive after I returned, so clearly she had nothing to do with any of this."

Detective Jacobs turned to him. "What's this lady's name?"

"Lillian Waters. She's my aunt, my mother's older sister."

"We'll need to talk to her, too, I suppose. Where is she staying?"

"The Allenel Hotel," Mr. Rutherford said. "But she's eighty-seven, and as I said, my mother was still alive when I took her back."

"Doesn't mean she couldn't have returned," the detective said.

"I highly doubt that."

"I don't. I've seen too many strange things over the years. So, your mother was strangled in her sleep, you said."

"Apparently, yes. I left Mr. Valentine with her around eleven thirty, and I went to bed. I was exhausted."

"Why was he with her?"

"She was upset. She liked him and seemed to quiet down in his presence. He agreed to stay with her for a while."

"And what time did you leave her, Mr. Valentine?"

"At eleven forty-five, fifteen minutes to midnight. She wasn't quite asleep, but I knew she would be soon. I went straight to my room and was asleep myself before the hall clock struck twelve."

The detective jotted furiously in his notebook. "So, you were the last person to see the old lady alive."

"No, whoever killed her was the last person to see her alive. And that wasn't me. I barely knew her."

"And you, Miss Grant, found the body just after nine this morning?"

"That's right. I went in to give her the breakfast tray in Mr. Rutherford's room. At first, I thought she was still asleep, but as I got closer, I could tell she was dead, and I screamed."

"So, she would have been killed sometime between midnight and nine," the detective said. "Why was she sleeping in your room, Mr. Rutherford?"

"Because of the broken window in her room. It was too cold to leave her there, so I put her in my bed, and I slept on the sofa in the yellow drawing room."

"Who knew she was sleeping in your room?" the detective asked, chewing on the end of his pencil.

"Just myself and Mr. Valentine until this morning. Everyone else was asleep. Why?"

"Hmm. Because it's possible *you* were the intended victim, not your mother," the detective said.

Mr. Rutherford's eyes grew large. "You mean they thought they were strangling *me?* If that's true, those accidents the last two days weren't accidents at all."

"Ambrose, from what you've told me this morning, they definitely were *not* accidents," Marjorie said, her voice tender and soft.

"What accidents are you referring to?" The detective said.

"The hall chandelier fell on me Friday night, and then I tripped over something on the stairs the next morning. I thought they were accidents, but perhaps not."

"They did seem suspicious," Henry said. "Skip, I mean Horace, even found a screw and a piece of fishing line on the stairs afterward."

"Interesting. Anyone have a grudge against you, Mr. Rutherford?" Jacobs said.

"Just Jake, the missing fellow with the bandana. He seems to blame me for his mother's death many years ago, though I had nothing to do with it. She died in a doctor's care."

Miss Grant's head shot up, and she stared at Mr. Rutherford. "Jake would never! He'd never try to kill you or anyone. I know that was his bandana, but there has to be some other explanation."

"Please, ma'am," the detective said, "no one can say what someone else may or may not do."

"He did leave a cryptic note," Henry said. "Something about being sorry for everything and that he didn't mean to hurt anyone. We found it in the attic, where he sleeps."

"What were you doing in the attic?" Mr. Rutherford said. "Never mind, I don't want to know."

The detective glanced about at everyone. "Interesting. Given that piece of information, it sounds like an open-and-shut case."

"It does?" Skip said, surprised.

"With no signs of forced entry," the detective said, "it leads me to believe it was someone in this house or someone who was in the house last night. And it sounds like this Jake is our number one suspect. That note, the bandana, and the fact that he's missing are as good as a confession."

"He's an angry, mentally unstable man," Mr. Rutherford said, "but I just can't believe he'd want to kill me."

"Your mother was in your bed, the room was dark, and he slipped in and strangled her, thinking he was strangling you. When he realized his mistake, he fled the house in a panic, leaving the note and the red bandana you said he was never without still wound tightly about her neck."

"Good God," Mr. Rutherford said, his face white. "That makes sense, I must admit."

"Where was he last seen?" the detective asked.

"He was with Sister Barnabas in the kitchen. They were going to go down to the basement for a pair of pliers or a wrench or something to fix the sister's cross," Jane said, still looking as though she might vomit, tears welling up in her eyes.

"Did you see them come up again?"

"No, but I was busy starting to get the breakfast things washed and put away."

Detective Jacobs raised his eyebrows. "The two missing persons were last seen together." He nodded to the officer in the doorway. "Adams, did Crawley and Bates check the cellar?"

"Er, no, I don't believe so, just the first and second floors."

"Idiots. Go check the basement, pronto." He looked back at Jane. "The stairs are off the kitchen, I assume?"

"Just before the kitchen," Miss Grant said. "Through the door under the landing, past the side door to the yard."

"I'll check it out, Detective," Adams said, heading into the hall and through the door under the second landing.

"Anyone have a current picture of this Jake? And what's his last name?" he said, looking at the group still seated at the table.

"Bartlett. Jake Bartlett. He was my sister Annabelle's child. I can't believe he'd hurt anyone, I just can't," Miss Grant said, the tears now streaming down her face. Henry handed her his handkerchief, which she took gratefully.

"Do you have a photo of him, miss?"

"Yes, Joe Bitters took one of him and me not long ago."

"Who's Joe Bitters?" the detective said, flipping over to a new page.

"He was the handyman here," Mr. Rutherford said. "He was killed in the garage fire a couple of months ago."

"Right, I remember that fire. So, he took a photo of you and this Jake?" Detective Jacobs said to Miss Grant.

"His hobby was photography, among other things," she said, her voice a whisper that everyone had to strain to hear.

"Okay, well, would you be so kind as to get that photograph, Miss Grant?"

She stared at him a moment before answering as she got slowly to her feet. "All right, it's in my room. Excuse me, please." She went into the pantry, still clutching Henry's handkerchief, as Adams came in from the hall, looking grim.

"Find anything, Adams?" the detective said, looking over at him.

"As a matter of fact, sir, I did. You may want to have a look."

"What is it?"

"Rather *who* is it, sir. I think it may be the missing nun. There's a woman's body down there in the workshop, strangled to death with a thick gold chain that has a cross hanging from it. And she's naked, her face beaten badly. A pair of eyeglasses and a habit were next to her in a heap, along with another red bandana."

Gasps were heard throughout the room, even from the hardened detective, who shoved the notebook and pencil back into his pocket. "As soon as Miss Grant gets back with that photograph, get an APB out for Jake Bartlett's arrest. He may possibly be with a small white dog. Be sure copies of the picture are circulated everywhere. He should be considered dangerous."

"APB?" Mr. Rutherford said.

"All points bulletin. We'll check the bus depot, train station, and major roads out of town, as well as areas in town. We'll search the property here, too, top to bottom. Don't worry, we'll find him."

Chapter Twenty

Afternoon, Sunday, October 8, 1950
The Rutherford house

After everyone had been fingerprinted and photographs of the crime scene taken, the two bodies were removed to the morgue while the police searched the property for Jake to no avail. When they had left, Miss Grant inexplicably decided to bake a pie, perhaps to keep herself busy, and Mr. Rutherford, having shaved and changed his clothes, retired to the yellow drawing room with Miss Banning. Skip and Henry found themselves once more in the blue drawing room, Skip nursing a cup of coffee Henry had brought him.

Skip rolled his head about his neck, which was stiff and sore, and rubbed his bloodshot eyes. "Thanks for the coffee, Henry."

"Sure, my pleasure. Are you sure you don't want to eat something? It's afternoon."

"I'm just not hungry right now. I'm still full from breakfast. In fact, I feel a bit nauseous."

"I guess that's understandable with all that's happened. And you've barely slept. Neither of us got much rest."

"I know, and yet I don't feel tired at the moment."

"You can nap in the car on the way back to Chicago. That detective said we're free to leave, though we may need to come back at some point, depending."

"Yeah, but if we do, let's get a room at the Allenel Hotel."

"Fine by me. I agree with Great-Aunt Lillian—this house gives me the heebie-jeebies."

"Me too."

"We should get on the road soon, though. I don't want to be driving after dark, and we still haven't finished packing."

"Yeah. I suppose we should do that. Ugh, none of this makes any sense."

"You keep saying that."

"Because it's true. I simply can't believe Jake would murder Mrs. Rutherford and Sister Barnabas."

"Why not? You barely knew him and only spoke to him once."

"But to murder a defenseless old lady? Why would he do that? Especially when she was going to be put in a nursing home tomorrow anyway."

"Because he hated her. And the police believe Jake thought he was killing my uncle."

"Okay, he did seem to have a grudge against Ambrose, but why Sister Barnabas?" Skip asked, taking a sip of his coffee.

"Maybe when they were alone in the basement, he attacked her sexually, you know? It's sick, but it happens sometimes."

"So, he murdered Mrs. Rutherford, leaving his bandana around her neck, then came downstairs as if nothing had happened to help his aunt in the kitchen? And then, when the sister came in looking for a pair of pliers, he took her to the basement to rape and kill her and just happened to drop another of his bandanas?"

"Maybe. I know it's horrible, but you have to remember Jake's not all there mentally. And he ran off with Gipper, leaving that note saying he was sorry for what he did. If he wasn't guilty, why would he write that and then take off?"

Skip shook his head. "I don't know. I wish I did. I wonder if somehow Miss Grant is involved. She despised Mrs. Rutherford and held a grudge against Mr. Rutherford for the death of Annabelle."

"So you've said," Henry said.

"But Jake's bandana doesn't fit with that theory. I find it hard to believe she'd try and frame him, and I don't see how she'd be physically strong enough to kill Sister Barnabas."

"I don't either, and I can't figure out why she would want to. I just don't think she's a murderess."

"I don't either, but I have so many questions. Could there be two murderers? One who killed Mrs. Rutherford and the other who killed the sister?"

"I suppose, but it seems unlikely to me."

"True, but it could be. I keep thinking about that shiny liquid in the medicine cabinet, too. The makeup and stuff I can understand they wanted to keep away from Mrs. Rutherford, but why mercury, if that's what it is? Why would they have that at all?"

"Who knows? As I told you before, an Army doc I worked with when I was a medic told me that besides syphilis, it was sometimes used as an antiseptic and diuretic. I imagine lots of folks kept it on hand. Maybe they just never got rid of it."

Skip groaned. "All right, so maybe there's a logical explanation for it, but then there's the fire, and Bitters and his dog Bullseye, and what Mrs. Savage said about the notes he left behind."

"Most likely burned if they ever existed."

"But if they did exist, why would Bitters leave them in his room? Or anywhere in the carriage house, for that matter? He said he wanted Mrs. Savage to find them if something happened to him."

"But Joe didn't know there was going to be a fire. He might have felt his notes were safe tucked away in his quarters."

"Maybe, but it seems more likely he'd hide them someplace she could find them easily if he died or something happened to him. It doesn't make sense he'd bury them in a box behind the carriage house, either."

"Okay, I agree, but then where did he hide them? Mrs. Savage said she's looked everywhere she could think of."

"I know." Skip felt defeated, exhausted, and sick as he finished his coffee.

"And there's still the matter of the buried empty box, too."

"Yes. Who buried it in the middle of the night, and why was it empty?"

"Maybe you were right when you said it was Jake, and he stole the dog and then buried the empty box."

"Maybe. But if he was protecting Gipper from Mrs. Rutherford, and told people the dog ran away, why bury the box?"

"That's a good question. We keep going round and round."

"Yes, it's all so puzzling, like that weird rhyming clue he left."

Skip set the cup and saucer down, got up from the gray-blue sofa, and walked about the room, thinking. Slowly he examined the vases and crockery atop the fireplace mantel and studied the gray-toned picture above it, a landscape of gray trees in a gray forest, with more trees beyond it, seemingly to infinity. From there he moved to the old upright piano standing against the wall. He trailed his fingers across the ivory and black keys, plunking out a song absent-mindedly from memory.

"I don't recognize the song, but the tune is familiar," Henry said.

"Hmm? Oh, it's 'Greensleeves,'" Skip said. "One of the first songs I learned to play. I had piano lessons twice a week for many years."

Henry laughed. "My mom wanted me to take piano lessons, and I did for about two months, but then I gave it up. Why pound keys when I could pound a baseball instead?"

"I tried baseball once but quit when I got beaned on the head. That's why I prefer the piano, it's much safer. Same with the marching band. If I drop my baton, no one gets seriously hurt, including me."

"Yeah, you're right there. A baseball can do some damage."

"It knocked me out cold and gave me a lump on my noggin."

"Ouch. So, I guess playing ball with you some time is out of the question."

"I wouldn't object to a gentle game of catch, but maybe you should take up music again, Henry. I could give you a few lessons, and we could play together."

"I like the idea of playing with you," Henry said with a mischievous grin.

"Hush, they'll hear you, and you know what I mean."

"Ah, I know, but I wasn't much good at piano. All those notes, scales, and keys are Greek to me," Henry said. "I tried but I couldn't figure out an A-sharp from an A-major, and don't get me started on all those chords." Henry stopped and snapped his fingers. "Hey, maybe that's it."

"What?"

"Notes, scales, chords, and keys. I wonder if that's what Joe Bitters meant."

"What do you mean?" Skip said.

"The puzzling rhyme. Maybe I'm good at puzzles after all."

"Oh, I get it. You think he was talking about music. But what about it?"

Henry frowned. "Hmm, I don't know, exactly, but that's got to be it."

"A musical clue?"

"Well, Mrs. Savage did say he played the piano for her sometimes. What was the exact rhyme again?"

"Uh, 'A sharp mind will find a major clue in these. Pull the cord, and you've scored the location of my keys. Unlock the quotes to find my notes, and the evidence you'll see.'"

"Right, good memory. What if 'a sharp mind' is actually referring to A-sharp? And 'a major clue' is A-major? 'Pull the cord' could be a piano chord, and the keys refer to piano keys. 'Unlock the quotes to find my notes,' meaning musical notes. What else could he mean?"

"I suppose so. Maybe he wrote her some special song or something, and the words will indicate where whatever it is he found is located."

"You're on the right track, but maybe you're overthinking it. What if he left a note or notes inside her piano for her to find? What better hiding place? They'd be safe there."

"Too safe. If that's where he's hidden them, she hasn't found them."

"But that's why he left the puzzle clue about notes, chords, and keys."

"Trying to be clever," Skip said.

"But it's too clever, she couldn't decipher it."

"Let's go pay her a visit, and I'll have a look inside her piano while you distract her with your charms and manly ways. If there's something there, I can slip it beneath my sweater before she notices."

"Why do I have to distract her? Can't we just say we think Joe Bitters left his notes in her piano?"

"What if she refuses to let us in? She *seems* like a sweet old lady, but all we know about Augusta Savage is pretty much what she herself has told us. Better to err on the side of caution. I recall Sister Barnabas saying your uncle wanted to buy the Savage house, and Mrs. Savage was none too happy about it. Like it or not, she's a suspect, too. She may even have a key to the Rutherford house, finagled from Mrs. Rutherford at some point."

Henry sighed. "You're usually right about everything, but this time I must object."

Skip cocked his head. "You don't think she's a suspect?"

"No, I agree with you on that. But I object to distracting her so you can sneak something out."

"Why?"

"Because *if* we find something, we can't just take it from her home without her knowledge. It doesn't belong to us, regardless of what it is or how involved she is or isn't. There are laws against that."

"But what if she won't let us have it?"

"That's a chance we'll have to take, Valentine. Deal?"

Skip pursed his lips and squinted at him. "All right, Finch, let's go."

"I'll get our hats," Henry said, glancing out the windows. "And you'd better take your umbrella, it looks like rain."

CHAPTER TWENTY-ONE

Sunday, October 8, 1950
Mrs. Savage's house

They exited the house quickly, slamming the front door and dashing down the walk. They went right this time, taking the shortest route to the other side of the block and Mrs. Savage's place.

"Think she'll be home?" Henry asked as they turned the corner. The skies above were gray and ominous, and the wind whirled the autumn leaves about their feet.

"What time is it?"

"Just after two."

"It's well after church, so I should think so." Once more Skip unlatched the white picket gate and strode up the walkway onto the porch, Henry trailing behind. He rang the bell and waited as they took off their hats.

The door opened wide this time, and Mrs. Savage, wearing a blue and red dress, covered from the waist down by a white apron with yellow embroidered flowers upon it, beamed at them.

"Well, what a pleasant surprise. I wasn't expecting you two back so soon. I'm baking a cake, come in." She stepped aside as the two of them entered. "I just have to put it in the oven, won't be but a moment. Please, put your hats on the table there and go sit down. May I bring you some coffee or tea?"

"Ah, no, thank you, Mrs. Savage," Henry said, putting his hat down as Skip did the same. "I'm afraid we can't stay long."

"Oh? Well, you must tell me all about it. You both look troubled. I'll be right back. Sit, sit."

Skip put his umbrella in the corner by the door, and he and Henry sat on the sofa once more, in the same spots they had sat in yesterday. Both of them found themselves staring at the upright piano next to the fireplace. True to her word, Mrs. Savage was back in a few minutes, wiping her hands on her apron as she took her usual seat in one of the chairs.

"Now," she said, "What's all this about?"

"It's about the notes you mentioned the other day, the ones Joe Bitters supposedly left," Skip said.

"And the keys," Henry said.

"Yes, I remember. Don't tell me you found them?"

"No, not yet, but we think we may know where they are. You see, an unimaginable number of things have happened since we last saw you," Skip said.

"Good things, I hope," Mrs. Savage said, moving forward in her chair so she was perched on the edge of the seat.

"No, I'm afraid not. I'm sorry to have to tell you this, but Mrs. Rutherford has been murdered."

"What?" Mrs. Savage said as if she hadn't heard correctly.

"It's true," Henry said. "They found her this morning, strangled during the night."

Mrs. Savage's mouth dropped open. "That's horrible. I can't believe it. Who would do such a thing? A burglar?"

"We don't think so, ma'am, and neither do the police. There was no sign of forced entry. It appears Mr. Rutherford was actually the intended victim, but they killed his mother by mistake because she was in his bed," Skip said.

"She was in his bed? I'm afraid I don't understand," Mrs. Savage said, looking from Skip to Henry and then back to Skip.

"It's a long story. The police have a suspect in mind and are searching for him now."

"I don't know what to say. It's unbelievable. Poor Gabria. I wish now I hadn't stopped calling on her." She pulled a handkerchief from a pocket and wrung it about her hands as she looked at the young men before her. "You know, I was just thinking about her this morning."

"Oh?" Henry said.

"Yes, because I was first thinking about my grandfather. I haven't thought of him in many a year, not *really* thought of him. He was a hat maker by trade and worked in a small factory in England. When he became ill, my mother and I cared for him in our home. He died when I was in my teens."

"I'm sorry to hear that," Skip said.

"Thank you, dear. Afterward my parents, brothers, and I came here to America."

"Okay, but I'm afraid I don't understand the connection," Skip said.

"You see, because I thought of him this morning, I thought of Gabria. I never realized it at the time, but when she first became sick, her symptoms were similar to those he experienced. In the early stages, I seem to remember feelings of anxiety or nervousness. And Grandfather got moody and irritable, too. That was followed by difficulty breathing, lack of coordination, insomnia, confusion, and terrible headaches similar to what Gabria went through."

"What exactly did kill your grandfather, Mrs. Savage?" Henry said.

"Why, mercury poisoning. The mad hatter disease. So called because they used mercury in the making of hats up until not that long ago. But of course, Gabria most likely had something else, as I'm sure she wasn't exposed to mercury. Probably early onset dementia, as the sister said. Still, it made me think."

Skip and Henry exchanged glances. "Perhaps you're more right than you realize. But there's something else you should know, too," Skip said.

"Oh dear, what?"

"I don't want to shock you further, but Sister Barnabas has also been killed. They found her strangled body in the cellar this morning."

Mrs. Savage's mouth dropped further, her face now completely white. She clutched at her breast, handkerchief in hand, and gasped for breath.

"Henry, get her a glass of water," Skip said.

"Right." He sprang to his feet and headed off where he figured the kitchen would be.

"I just can't believe it, I just can't," Mrs. Savage said, taking in gulps of air, her eyes wide. "Oh, my."

"It's all a shock, I know, and we completely understand. There is one more thing you should be aware of, though. Jake is missing."

"Jake? The housekeeper's nephew? Oh dear, my heart is racing a mile a minute. You don't think he had anything to do with the murders?"

"The police do, I'm afraid. He's the suspect they're looking for. That's why we want to find the notes Joe Bitters left behind and hopefully discover whatever it is he found."

Henry returned with a glass of water and handed it to Mrs. Savage, who took it in her trembling hand and forced down a couple of swallows.

"I don't know where they are," she said at last, slowly, before taking another sip of water and wiping her mouth with the handkerchief.

"We think we may have an idea, ma'am," Skip said.

"It's the rhyme he told you," Henry said. "A sharp mind will find a major clue in these. Pull the cord, and you've scored the location of my keys. Unlock the quotes to find my notes, and the evidence you'll see.' He may have been talking about musical notes, chords, and keys, do you understand?"

She set the water glass down on the side table, put the handkerchief back in her pocket absentmindedly, and leaned on the arm of the chair, still breathing heavily. "No, I'm afraid I don't understand any of this. I can't believe this. You said the police think Jake murdered Gabria and that nun woman? And that they're looking for him? Oh dear, I just remembered my back door is unlocked."

Skip sighed. Time was of the essence, and he wished he had done this his way, but he supposed Henry was right. "I don't think you need to worry, Mrs. Savage, though you should keep your door locked regardless. They are looking for him, but he may be innocent. We need to find the notes Mr. Bitters left. You told us he played the piano for you sometimes, isn't that right? I think Joe Bitters may have hidden his notes in your piano, hoping you'd find them if the need arose, but he didn't want you to locate them unless absolutely necessary, which is why he gave you only a puzzle clue. May we search your piano?" Skip said.

"He gave me a clue? What clue was that?" Mrs. Savage looked more bewildered now.

"About the notes, the chords, and the keys," Henry said, also getting impatient. "The poem. May we please search your piano?"

"I don't know what you're both talking about, but it's right there, so help yourselves, I suppose. I never touch it."

"Thank you," Skip said, jumping to his feet to join Henry at the old upright.

Henry opened the lid on top and peered in at the various wires and felt hammers within but could see nothing out of the ordinary. "Another dead end," Henry said. "I don't see anything in here."

Skip got on tiptoe and peered in, too. "I don't either, but it's dark," he said. "Do you have a flashlight, Mrs. Savage?"

"A flashlight?" She got to her feet, though she still looked pale and shaken. "Yes, there's one on the shelf near the back door. That front panel on the piano drops down, too, you know. It used to have a knob but it broke off years ago, so just pull that piece of twine. It's where the music rolls go. It's a player piano, also, as I believe I mentioned the other day."

"A piece of twine? Hey, that could be a cord." Skip tugged on the string above the keys, and the panel came down with a thud.

"Careful, my dear," Mrs. Savage said.

But they weren't listening, for taped to the inside of the panel was a manila envelope.

Skip was so excited he was practically hopping up and down. "It wasn't a chord with an 'h,' it was an actual cord!"

"A cord with an 'h'?" Mrs. Savage said.

"Yes, but I was right about the rest of it," Henry said.

"You were! So, is that it? Is the envelope from Joe Bitters?"

"I don't know yet, hang on," Henry said. He carefully removed the envelope and held it gingerly in his hands. "It's addressed to Mrs. Savage, which makes sense, I suppose, since it is in your piano in your house."

The old woman came closer, staring at it as if it might explode. "I've never seen that before," she said.

"No doubt Joe placed it there when you were out of the room, hoping you would only find it if something happened to him. May I open this?" Henry said.

"Yes, yes, don't keep us in suspense," she said. "I'm too nervous to do it."

Henry undid the clasp and slid out two white pages, upon which were written, in a sloppy hand, *Taken August 22nd, 1950, in the Ambrose Booth Rutherford cellar.*

"Hmm, only a week before the fire happened," Skip said.

Slowly Henry tuned the pages over, revealing the black-and-white photographs. As he did so, he recoiled in shock, almost dropping the photos as Skip took them from his hands.

"What? What is it? Pictures? Of what?" Mrs. Savage said, trying to see what was in Skip's hand.

"Mrs. Savage, I think you've had enough shocks for one day. Perhaps you shouldn't look," Skip said.

"What? No, they were addressed to me, weren't they? I want to see."

"They're photos of a naked dead woman, her body stuffed in Mr. Rutherford's vodka freezer, if I'm not mistaken. She appears to have met with a violent end. There's a newspaper with the body, too, probably put there by Joe to verify the date."

Mrs. Savage took several steps back until she bumped into the arm of her chair, falling into it sideways and landing with a thump on the cushion, her legs in the air.

"Mrs. Savage," Henry said, alarmed. "Are you all right?" He hurried over to her to offer his hand, but she swung her legs about and righted herself with surprising agility.

"I'm fine. But you're right, I don't want to see those pictures." She was shaking from head to toe. "What's it all about?"

"Based on these photos, I think Mr. Bitters was blackmailing the Rutherfords because he found this woman's body. If all went as he had hoped, once he got his money, he probably planned to come back here for another visit, collect his evidence, and skedaddle out of town," Skip said.

"Oh, I think I see now," Mrs. Savage said, her voice a mixture of quiet excitement and nervousness. "But it didn't go as planned and they murdered him, just as I said. Who is the dead woman in the pictures?"

"I'm not sure," Skip said, "but I'm willing to bet it's Sister Barnabas."

"Sister Barnabas?" Henry said. "But that's impossible. These photos were taken almost two months ago. She wasn't killed until after breakfast this morning. She was alive and well earlier today."

"I think someone *pretending* to be Sister Barnabas was alive and well this morning, and still is," Skip said.

"Who?" Mrs. Savage said.

"If I had to put money on it, I'd say Marjorie Banning," Skip said.

"Miss Banning? Why her?" Henry said.

"Because she's an actress. Who better to portray the role of a nun, and quite well, I must admit, though hardly flawlessly. It just occurred to me, Catholics aren't supposed to eat or drink anything from midnight until they receive communion at church. Yet she was eating breakfast this morning."

"Who's Marjorie Banning?" Mrs. Savage said.

"Why would she pretend to be a nun?" Henry said, ignoring Mrs. Savage for the time being.

"Because I don't think your uncle was the intended victim, and there never were any attempts on his life. I think it was all an act."

"I don't understand what you're saying," Mrs. Savage said, still trembling. "Attempts on his life?"

"I think the intended victim was Mrs. Rutherford all along, Henry. The chandelier and trip wire were just to throw us off and make it seem like *Jake* wanted to kill him."

"But if that's true, my uncle must have been in on it. He had to know Sister Barnabas was not Sister Barnabas. He picked her up from the convent himself."

"Exactly. I'm not sure yet why they killed the real sister and had Marjorie assume her identity."

"How will you prove it, though? Neither of us recognized Miss Banning out of the habit."

"Fingerprints. She picked up my pocket watch and fob while I was taking a bath. I bet the fingerprints on it are hers, and if they are, it proves she was portraying Sister Barnabas. I think you'd better phone that detective. What was his name again?"

"Jacobs. I'll get right on it. May I use your phone, Mrs. Savage?"

"Yes, it's in the hall. I must admit, I'm completely flummoxed."

"No time to explain right now," Henry said. "Be right back."

While Henry was using the telephone, Skip got Mrs. Savage another drink of water, which she drank in sips, a little color returning to her face.

Henry returned in just a few minutes. "The desk sergeant said he'd have Detective Jacobs and a patrol car meet us at the house."

"Good. Hopefully, Miss Banning and Mr. Rutherford are still there," Skip said.

"He also told me they picked up Jake and Gipper just outside of town a short while ago," Henry said.

Skip turned once more to Mrs. Savage. "We have to get these photos to the detective right now, I'm afraid."

"Yes, go, go."

"And maybe you should lie down. Take a nap," Henry said.

"I'm too excited to nap. Besides, I've my cake in the oven. Keep me posted on what happens. I don't understand much of any of this or what's going on, but clearly, it's important."

"We'll explain later, I promise," Skip said, grabbing his hat and bolting toward the door, the envelope firmly in hand.

"Be careful, you two," she said as Henry zoomed out behind him, picking up his own hat along with Skip's umbrella from the corner.

"Bye, now," he called out over his shoulder. Skip was already at the gate. It had started raining ever so lightly, and the wind was gusting, but Skip seemed barely to notice as Henry caught up to him.

"Want to put up your umbrella?" Henry said, handing it to Skip while hanging on to his hat.

"Thanks, but I think the wind is too strong. Besides, it's a short distance back and it's only a sprinkle," Skip said, but the thunder boomed and the rain began coming down in torrents as they went around the corner. Skip tucked the envelope beneath his sweater and picked up the pace. Once back at the Rutherford place, they dashed up onto the porch and shook themselves out.

"We should have waited at Mrs. Savage's," Skip said.

"But the detective is on his way here. It wouldn't do for him to beat us."

"Then we should have met him at her house. What are we supposed to do now?"

"Wait. Hopefully, he won't be too long." They both glanced up at the roof of the porch, which was leaking in several places.

"It's not much drier up here on the porch than it was on the sidewalk," Skip said. "But at least there's some protection from the wind. Maybe I should put my umbrella up after all."

Chapter Twenty-Two

Sunday, October 8, 1950
Back at the Rutherford house

The front door opened with a creak, and Mr. Rutherford peered out. "Where did you two run off to in such a hurry earlier, slamming the front door and making a commotion? And what on earth are you doing standing out there now?"

"Oh, hello, Uncle," Henry said. "We, uh, went for a quick walk and got caught in the rain. We, uh, thought we'd wait out here until we dried off so we don't track water on the floor."

"Don't be ridiculous. Jane will mop up any mess you make. Come in, both of you, before you catch your death." He stepped back and held the door open as Henry and Skip looked at each other, Skip nodding imperceptibly.

"Sure, sure," Henry said, removing his hat and stepping through the door into the entry and then into the hall beyond as Skip did the same.

"Bonjours," Marjorie Banning said. She was standing in the doorway of the yellow drawing room, smoking a cigarette, her elaborately beaded bag hanging from its gold chain off her shoulder.

"Hello," Skip said warily.

"You two left so quickly before, scurrying away like scared little mice," she said. "I saw you from the window. It didn't seem to me like you were going for a walk."

"Well, we did," Henry said, crossing his arms.

"Where to?"

"Just around the block."

"Not to see Mrs. Savage again?" Ambrose said.

"Why not? She's a nice lady," Skip said.

"What are you two up to?" Ambrose said. "You're acting nervous and suspicious. And Miss Grant told me you were asking all kinds of questions earlier."

"Where is Miss Grant?" Henry said.

"The police called and said they found Jake and are holding him. She set her pie out to cool and went downtown to the station to see if she could bring Gipper back."

"You didn't drive her?" Henry said.

"I offered, but she preferred to take the bus," Mr. Rutherford said. "She said something about wanting to stop by the Anderson house first to see a friend. She left shortly after you two did, before it started raining."

"Oh," Skip said. "By the way, Miss Banning, I've been racking my brain trying to remember something you said. You told us you were raised in Paris, didn't you? And that Paris is the county seat of France?"

"Oui, I was raised in Paris, but Paris is le capital, not the county seat, whatever that is."

"That's what I thought you'd said. It's been a few years since high school, but I seem to remember my teacher, Madame Hoffman, telling us Paris is la capitale, and le capital is money, if I remember correctly."

Miss Banning stared at him, narrowing her eyes. "That is what I said. La capitale."

"No, you didn't." He sneezed, causing the manila envelope beneath his sweater to shift.

"What's under your sweater, Mr. Valentine?" Ambrose said.

"What? Oh, nothing. I suppose we should go up and bring our bags down, Henry. Perhaps I did mishear you, Miss Banning."

Marjorie stepped closer to Skip. "Mon chéri, what do you have under your sweater, hmm? Something for me? Or is it something you don't want us to see?" She slid a hand expertly up under his sweater and extracted the envelope before Skip knew what was happening.

"Hey! Give that back, that's private property," Skip said.

"I'll say it is. It's addressed to Mrs. Savage," Ambrose said, coming over to Marjorie's side. "What's this about?"

"It's nothing. And everything. Give it back, please," Henry said.

Marjorie ignored him as she opened the envelope and handed the contents to Ambrose, who perused them quickly, his brow furrowed.

"Where did you get this?" he said, staring at Skip and Henry.

"At Mrs. Savage's. Joe Bitters hid it there for safekeeping. Photos of the real Sister Barnabas," Henry said.

"Clever," Ambrose said. "I didn't think Joe was that smart."

"The man you killed, you mean, along with his dog," Skip said.

"His dog had died earlier that day from the cancer, and its body was just lying there next to his bed. Joe was morose over it, drunk by the time I showed up to discuss his blackmail terms. It wasn't long before he was comatose. I didn't kill him, I just lit the fire and left."

"I think that qualifies as killing him," Skip said. "And you killed your mother and the real Sister Barnabas, too."

"Only the nun," Mr. Rutherford said. "Marjorie took care of Mother."

"Shut up, Ambrose," Marjorie said, her French accent completely gone.

"What happened to 'mon chéri'?" Skip said. "Have you ever even been to France, Miss Banning?"

"No, but I played a French prostitute once in a play in Des Moines, and a nun in the Detroit production of *Angels of Sin*, based on the movie. I need another cigarette," Marjorie said, grinding out the one she'd been smoking in an ashtray on the center table. She opened her bag, but instead of a cigarette withdrew a small caliber pistol, which she pointed at Skip and Henry. "So, if they know what they know, we must eliminate them now, before Jane gets back."

"What? No, Marjorie, no. He's my nephew, or at least I've always considered him to be. Besides, how would we ever explain it?"

"No need to explain it," she said. "We shoot them both dead and bury their bodies in the cellar."

"What about their car?"

She considered that briefly. "Oh, yes. That is a problem. Somewhat more difficult to dispose of. But we could drive it to Canada and sell it up there. No one would be the wiser. In the meantime, we hide it in the garage. When questioned about the boys, we say they drove off happily on their way back to Chicago, and that's the last we saw of them."

"You'll never get away with it," Henry said.

"We won't get away with everything else if we don't get rid of you two," Marjorie said. "You never should have come here to this dreadful house. I hate it here, and you've only made things worse."

"We're not the only ones who know," Skip said.

"Mrs. Savage?" Ambrose said.

"No, she wasn't home. Her back door was unlocked, and we went in and found those photos hidden in her piano. She doesn't know anything about them," Henry said.

"You're a terrible liar, Henry. I suspect you're just trying to protect that old bat."

"No, he's right," Skip said, "She doesn't know anything, but that police detective is on his way here now."

"I don't believe it," Miss Banning said. "You're bluffing."

"I'm not. Henry telephoned the police from Mrs. Savage's house."

"I see," Ambrose said.

"It doesn't matter. If he's telling the truth, the only proof they have is here in this envelope, which we will soon destroy along with both of them. I didn't spend all that time waddling around in that ridiculous penguin outfit, wearing those Coke bottle glasses and those ill-fitting false teeth, and putting up with your awful mother's abuse, just to have these two fools ruin it," Marjorie said, glancing at Ambrose. "I hate this house, and I hate Ann Arbor. I want to live in New York, and I intend to see we do."

"Is that why you never fixed up the house or repaired the garage, Uncle? Once your mother was dead, you planned to sell this place as is, is that it? You and Marjorie would close your accounts, sell the stocks, and move to New York City so Miss Banning could be on the stage."

"That's our plan, more or less," Mr. Rutherford said. "Though I thought I'd keep this house for the summers. I didn't want to do the repairs right now because I needed capital to buy a place in New York and get Miss Banning started. Houses there are over ten thousand dollars, and even decent apartments are expensive. A shame you two had to stick your noses in where they don't belong."

"Not to worry, Ambrose. When the police arrive, *if* they arrive, we'll tell them our little Skip and Henry must have been playing a joke on them before they drove off for Chicago. They'll never be seen or heard from again. But they're stalling for time. Let's get it over with now."

"All right, I suppose. I hadn't counted on this." Ambrose looked shaken and slightly ill.

"You're the one who wanted them here. You thought they'd be the perfect witnesses to the accidents we staged and would back you up on your claim that Jake was out to kill you but accidentally killed that old witch of a mother of yours instead."

"I know. I just never dreamed we'd have to kill them."

"I don't see any other way. If we don't, we probably go to jail for life. Is that what you want?"

"No, of course not, but they're so young," Ambrose said, looking at Skip and Henry.

"God, you're weak sometimes. Fine, I'll kill them if you can't do it, but we probably should take them down to the basement first. Bullet holes and blood here in the hall would be suspicious and hard to explain."

"I...I suppose. I mean, if there's no other option..."

"There isn't," Miss Banning said, glancing at Ambrose.

Skip was watching Marjorie carefully, still clutching his umbrella. As soon as she looked sideways at Mr. Rutherford, he expertly flipped the umbrella across the hall, using his baton training. It struck Marjorie hard in the face, and she dropped the gun, which skidded sideways across the floor. Henry leaped for it as Skip tackled Mr. Rutherford, wrestling the envelope away from him and socking him in the jaw.

Henry was on his feet in a flash, holding the gun aimed at Marjorie, whose nose was bleeding profusely. Skip got up quickly and came to his side, just as the front doorbell rang.

"And that would be the detective," Skip said, breathing heavily and shaking out the hand he'd used to strike Mr. Rutherford.

CHAPTER TWENTY-THREE

Late Monday morning, October 9, 1950
The Savage house

"Did either of you want coffee?" Mrs. Savage said.

"No, thank you, ma'am," Skip and Henry both said.

"All right. I'll get the cake and then you can tell me what's happened. I've been so anxious." She disappeared into the kitchen, returning shortly with three generous servings. "Here we are," she said, setting the plates down on the dining room table where they had gathered. "Now, tell me everything."

"Well," Skip said, "presented with the evidence, the detective arrested Mr. Rutherford and Miss Banning."

"Who's this Miss Banning? You never did tell me. And what evidence? Those awful photos you found inside my piano? Start at the beginning, please, gentlemen."

"It is a bit involved," Henry said, taking a generous forkful of layer cake, "but we'll try to explain it as best we can."

"Right," Skip said. "You see, Mr. Rutherford's been dating Miss Banning, whom his mother despised. I think Mr. Rutherford came up with the idea to kill his mother several months ago. He couldn't stand that she had partial control of the family fortune, and he probably resented her constant comparisons to Arthur, and her frequent criticisms of him, as well as the fact that she was trying to keep him and Miss Banning apart. Of course, he realized his mother was a bit dotty, but certainly still mentally competent, and could live for years. That's most likely what gave him the idea to hurry things along by slowly poisoning her with mercury, driving her mad and eventually to her death over a matter of a few months."

"The mad hatter syndrome, just like I said earlier," Mrs. Savage said.

"Yes," Henry said. "I spent a bit of time with a doctor in the Army when I was a medic, and he told me that over time inhaling mercury vapors can cause damage to lungs and kidneys, and it can induce kidney failure if ingested."

"It's unlikely an autopsy would be performed if it wasn't a suspicious death," Skip said. "But he needed it to appear to the outside world he was doing everything he could to care for his mother, so he enlisted his girlfriend, a trained actress, to portray Sister Barnabas. Miss Banning was probably only too happy to help. I'm sure she knew with the mother out of the way, she could marry Ambrose and be set for life, keeping the old house for summer use, but setting up permanent residence in New York City."

"So, the original plan was that when Mrs. Rutherford died," Henry said, "a few days later, the nun would turn up dead, or rather the real Sister Barnabas's body would be found with a red bandana about her neck, and they would claim Jake killed her. And then sometime later Marjorie Banning could safely return."

"Yes, that's right. But to pull it all off, Mr. Rutherford needed a nun's habit, and he needed a real nun. Therefore, he contacted the Reverend Mother and most likely drove to the convent on the excuse of wanting to interview potential caregivers himself," Skip said.

"Whatever for?" Mrs. Savage said.

"Because he wanted to select a nun who was similar in age and height to Miss Banning. Of course, Sister Barnabas was heavier, so they used stuffing to fill out the clothing. Encased in the wimple and tunic, free of any makeup, her eyebrows bushy, her bosom strapped down, wearing Sister Barnabas's glasses, clothing, and a set of false teeth, she was transformed. When she reappeared later as Marjorie Banning, we didn't recognize her. And of course, the phony French accent helped, too."

"How fiendishly clever," Mrs. Savage said.

"Yes. He chose Sister Barnabas and arranged for her to come on a day when Miss Grant, Jake, and Joe Bitters were all out. He picked her up from the convent, but upon their arrival at the house, Joe Bitters showed up unexpectedly and carried her bag. I'm sure Mr. Rutherford sent him on his way, then made sure Miss Grant and Jake were still out and his mother was asleep in her room. Then he most likely lured the sister to the basement where he strangled her, stripped her naked, and put her body in his walk-in freezer, locking it securely. After that, Marjorie Banning donned the nun's habit and her glasses. Remember how she was always peering over the top of them?" Skip said. "It's because she couldn't see through the lenses."

"That's horrible," Mrs. Savage said, though she was eating up every word, her cake almost forgotten on the plate in front of her. "But wouldn't anyone who had met the fake sister, like the two of you, for instance, or Miss Grant, recognize the woman in the freezer was a different person when she was eventually discovered?"

"That, I think, is why he beat her face when the body had warmed up. He wanted the bruises to be fresh, and for her face to be altered in case we saw the body," Henry said.

Mrs. Savage pushed her cake away. "I just lost my appetite, but do go on."

"All right. Mr. Rutherford introduced the fake Sister Barnabas to his mother, and she began giving her increased doses of mercury, saying it was medicine. Breathing in the mercury fumes along with wearing someone else's glasses probably contributed to Marjorie's headaches. But they figured his mother would die soon enough, especially with higher doses."

"Diabolical," Mrs. Savage said.

"Most certainly. But then Bitters decided to nip into some of Mr. Rutherford's vodka stash in the basement freezer. He went down and picked the lock easily, but instead of booze, he found the body. It must have been a shock, but since he had met the real Sister Barnabas, he recognized her and figured out at least some of what was going on. I recall you saying, Mrs. Savage, that Joe told you the second time he'd run into the sister she was cold and rather rude, keeping her distance. That was deliberate, of course, so he couldn't get a good look at her and realize she was an imposter."

"It makes sense," Henry said.

"The day after he found the body, he came back with his camera and the morning newspaper to prove the date, and took photographs as evidence," Skip said. "When the photos were developed, he put some of them in an envelope with a note and hid the envelope in your piano, because you're one of the few people he trusted."

"And he confronted Mr. Rutherford," Skip said, "with copies of the photos and a demand for blackmail."

"I'm afraid so," Henry said. "My uncle was at the point of no return, having already killed the real nun, so he arranged to kill Joe, too. He visited Joe in his quarters late one night on the premise of discussing the terms of the blackmail. According to my uncle, Bullseye had died earlier that day, and Joe, heartbroken, was quite intoxicated by the time he arrived. When Joe passed out, my uncle lit a fire and escaped under cover of darkness. He assumed the photographs and negatives were burned up, too."

"But Bitters made a point of telling you before that, Mrs. Savage, that he had found something out, and gave you the puzzle clue," Skip said.

"Except I couldn't figure it out," she said.

"You may have eventually," Henry said. "Anyway, with Bitters out of the way, my uncle and Miss Banning could continue their plan."

"Yes, but then dear Aunt Lillian got into the act," Skip said, "insisting her sister be put into a nursing home and making arrangements for her to be admitted to Forest Glen. Ambrose knew if that happened, a doctor would most likely examine his mother and discover the mercury poisoning. And even if he didn't, Mr. Rutherford knew she could linger for years in a nursing facility, eating away at the family fortune until there was virtually none left."

"That would be a problem for him," Henry said.

"Yes. Even if she'd been declared mentally incompetent, he'd still have to pay for her care, not to mention I think he truly did despise her, so Ambrose decided to up the game and kill her outright the night before she was to be taken to the nursing home. He needed a scapegoat, though, and Jake was the most likely suspect, especially since he'd already planned on pinning the real Sister Barnabas's murder on him eventually. And then, of course, we entered the picture, which Miss Banning saw as a problem, but your uncle saw as an opportunity."

"What do you mean?" Mrs. Savage said.

"Marjorie was upset that we had come, thinking we would spoil their plans. But it seems my uncle told Marjorie we would make perfect patsies. They would stage a few accidents, the chandelier, and the trip wire, making it look like Jake was out to murder him, and we would be the witnesses. Each of them, in turn, told us how angry and unstable Jake was and how he seemed to have a vendetta against my uncle. I think we both fell for it hook, line, and sinker. I know I did, anyway. If necessary, I would have sworn to all that in court," Henry said. "Scary to think about."

"I admit they were convincing," Skip said, "though I did have my doubts."

"And I should never have doubted you," Henry said.

"It's okay, I sometimes wondered if I wasn't just imagining things, to be honest."

"But how did they kill poor Gabria?" Mrs. Savage said.

"I think Mr. Rutherford stole a couple of Jake's bandanas and gave them to Marjorie. Then Saturday night he came home from dropping off Mrs. Waters and went upstairs, where Marjorie was waiting at the connecting door between her room and Mrs. Rutherford's. Mr. Rutherford knocked on my door and pleaded with me to come to his mother's room."

"But why?" Mrs. Savage said.

"Because he wanted it to appear *he* was the intended victim, not his mother, and for that to happen she had to be in his bed, and he felt it better if he had a witness. So, with me in tow, he knocked on his mother's door. That was the signal for Marjorie to slip into Mrs. Rutherford's room, unplug the bedside lamp, and smash the window using one of the brass bookends."

"Why did she unplug the lamp?" Mrs. Savage said.

"Because she was afraid that even with a sleeping draught, Mrs. Rutherford might wake up at the sound of the breaking glass and turn on her bedside lamp, exposing Marjorie," Henry said.

Skip nodded. "Yes, you're right. After the window had been broken, Marjorie went back into her own room in the dark. I think Mrs. Rutherford awoke and probably saw her from the rear, assuming it was a ghost. Meanwhile, Mr. Rutherford, claiming the hall door was locked, went through his room into his mother's, turning on the overhead light and letting me in so I could witness everything."

"And then he put her to bed in his room because of the broken window, and he went to sleep in the drawing room," Henry said.

"Sometime during the night, Marjorie slipped into Mr. Rutherford's room, probably via his mother's. Using one of the stolen bandanas, she strangled Mrs. Rutherford, making it appear *Jake* was out to kill *Mr.* Rutherford in his sleep."

"From there they just had to wait for Miss Grant to discover the body the next morning," Henry said.

"But how did they get Jake to run away? And why?" Mrs. Savage said.

"I think their plan would have worked if he'd stayed, but running away certainly made him seem more guilty. So, Marjorie, still pretending to be Sister Barnabas, asked Jake to help her fix the clasp on her cross, which she had deliberately broken. The two of them went to the basement, where he fixed it, getting his fingerprints on it. Then, and I'm just guessing here again, I'm willing to bet the sister told Jake that Mr. Rutherford was angry about Gipper and was going to fire Jake's aunt and have the dog put down. She probably suggested to him he run away with the dog. That scared Jake into action, no doubt, and he ran upstairs, gathered up the dog, and took off."

"And I'm willing to bet that note he supposedly left was actually written by Mr. Rutherford, who placed it up there after Jake had fled," Henry said.

"Why?" Skip said.

"It should have dawned on me earlier, but it was written in plain block letters, with bad grammar, making it appear it was penned by a poorly educated person. But it had a semicolon in it, not a punctuation mark a fairly illiterate person would use."

"Sure, that makes sense. Your uncle wrote it to make it appear Jake felt bad for killing Mrs. Rutherford."

"I think so," Henry said.

"And after he left the note, Mr. Rutherford went down to the cellar, got the body out, dropped the other bandana on the floor, and wrapped the gold cross about the dead nun's naked neck, careful not to disturb Jake's fingerprints."

"That's logical, but I remember my mom defrosting a big piece of meat once," Henry said. "If he just took her body out then, it would have still been mostly frozen by the time the police discovered it."

"True, but I believe Mr. Rutherford unplugged the freezer days earlier. When I explored the basement and the ice room the other night, it was eerily silent. I *should* have heard the freezer motor running. I didn't think much of it at the time."

"Ah, so he unplugged it ahead of time, allowing the body to thaw out slowly."

"Correct. After he removed the corpse to let it warm up to room temperature, he went back upstairs to have breakfast, and Marjorie went up to her room to transform herself back into Marjorie Banning. At some point, maybe when he supposedly used the bathroom, he went back down to the cellar, beat Sister Barnabas's face, and dragged the body to the workroom."

"I remember when he came back to the dining room, he looked flushed," Henry said.

"Yes, he did."

"But what about Gipper?"

"I think Mr. Rutherford wanted the dog dead because Gipper only liked Jake and Mrs. Rutherford, and for good reason, I'd say. Probably he barked or growled anytime Mr. Rutherford or Marjorie came anywhere near Mrs. Rutherford. So, Mr. Rutherford, probably hating the dog anyway, instructed Jake to kill it and bury him behind the garage. They couldn't risk having the dog barking while Mrs. Rutherford was being strangled."

"But Jake couldn't do it, so he hid Gipper in the attic and buried an empty box, probably with Mr. Rutherford watching from his window to make sure," Henry said.

"Yes, and when the dog started barking during the night, locked up in Jake's bedroom, Miss Grant pounded on the ceiling. It wasn't long before Mr. Rutherford realized he'd been duped, and he threatened Jake if he didn't get rid of the dog once and for all."

"But what if Jake had told someone Uncle wanted him to kill Gipper?" Henry said.

"I'm guessing your uncle told him he'd fire his aunt and put them both out on the street if he did tell anyone. Remember Miss Grant said Jake told her he took the dog because he thought someone wanted to harm it. Jake didn't say who."

"But how did you two fit all the pieces together? How did you figure it out?" Mrs. Savage said.

"The idea that Jake thought he was strangling Mr. Rutherford rather than his mother made sense, but when I was in her room that night, I raised the shade because she didn't want to be in the dark. When I did, her face was illuminated in the moonlight. Surely, he would have been able to tell once he got close to the bed that it was Mrs. Rutherford sleeping and not Ambrose. That made me suspicious that the intended victim was, in fact, Mrs. Rutherford, not her son, and Jake wouldn't have known she was in his bed," Skip said. "But that wasn't proof enough."

"But then we found the hidden photos of the real Sister Barnabas's body," Henry said.

"Yes, thanks to you figuring out the mysterious puzzle clue. Finding those pictures proved she died over a month earlier than they wanted us to believe, her body frozen until they needed it. But I had to ask myself, who would have killed her and why? And then I remembered the actress, Marjorie Banning, and how she happened to appear at the back entry just after Sister Barnabas was last seen. I think Miss Banning was attempting to slip out of the house unseen."

"Of course," Henry said. "My uncle planned for her to change into her regular clothes and makeup after breakfast, using the items she had locked in the closet and medicine cabinet, ditch the habit and glasses in the basement next to the body, and slip out of the house and away, free of suspicion. But Miss Grant noticed her on the back porch and naturally assumed she was coming *to* the house, rather than away from it. Uncle never planned for us to meet Miss Banning, as it would have been too big a risk that we'd recognize her, even though we didn't."

"That's right, Henry."

"Therefore, Marjorie had to pretend she was just dropping by, and told Miss Grant she came to the back door because she was hoping to slip in without Mrs. Rutherford seeing her."

"It must have been a shock to your uncle when Miss Grant said she was at the back door," Skip said.

"I bet, but they covered well enough."

"They did. If it hadn't been for Joe Bitters's photos, they might have gotten away with it," Skip said.

"Yeah, good thing he hid them in a safe place."

"But a bad thing he didn't report it to the police, preferring instead to be greedy and try to blackmail your uncle. If he hadn't done that, he and Mrs. Rutherford would both probably still be alive today."

"Gosh. But you were suspicious of the nun all along," Henry said.

"Yes, I was, but they were both fiendishly clever. Nothing seemed to fit together. I found the makeup and clothes, but Mr. Rutherford had a logical explanation that made sense. I questioned the Reverend Mother, but she assured me there really was a Sister Barnabas at the Rutherford house, which there was. We investigated the fallen chandelier and the trip wire, heck, we even dug up an empty box in the early morning hours. The fire seemed legitimate, we believed the story of little Arthur hook, line, and sinker, and I was starting to believe Bitters and his dog actually were haunting the house."

"Who knows? Maybe they were."

Nothing would surprise me anymore," Skip said. "The poor French Miss Banning used was a clue, too, but mine is so rusty I wasn't entirely sure I was correct. It was all so puzzling."

"Puzzles can be deadly."

"Most definitely," Skip said.

"What was the story about little Arthur?" Mrs. Savage said.

"Oh, Mrs. Rutherford made him up. He never existed," Henry said.

"What? What do you mean? Why would she do a thing like that?"

"Only she knew for certain," Skip said.

"But my friend Velma talked to Arthur's spirit in a séance."

"Maybe she was just trying to comfort Mrs. Rutherford," Henry said.

"But it seemed so real. I was there. Perhaps it was a different boy's spirit she talked to."

"Perhaps. It's an ancient house. By the way, your cake was delicious, Mrs. Savage, thank you."

"You're welcome, but what will happen now?"

"Now Skip and I go home, I suppose," Henry said.

"But what about the house?" she said. "The Rutherford house?"

"I'm not sure. There will be a trial, and Skip and I may have to give testimony and all. If that's the case, we'll have to come back. In the meantime, I think we can leave it in Jane and Jake's care, and Gipper's."

"That's a good idea," Skip said. "I'm more than ready to get back to Chicago and Purrvis. I had to place a long-distance call to my neighbor to let her know we'd been delayed."

"And I had to drive Great-Aunt Lillian to the train station this morning. Poor woman, I think the shock of everything nearly killed her, too."

"I'm glad it didn't. You know, Henry, you may end up owning the place when Mr. Rutherford is convicted," Skip said.

"Hard to say. Michigan doesn't have the death penalty, so he'll end up with life in prison. I would think he'd still have a legal right to the property."

"Not if he is convicted of killing his mother, the rightful owner," Skip said.

"But Miss Banning killed her. Uncle killed Sister Barnabas."

"But they were both complicit in each killing, *and* he killed Joe Bitters. I think the courts will declare you the rightful heir and owner," Skip said.

"Could be. If they do, I think I'll use whatever money there is to fix the place up and sell it. With the proceeds from that, I can get back on my feet financially, enroll in school, and help out my mom and siblings. Of course, I'll give a generous amount to Jane and Jake, too. They've been through so much."

"You're a good man, Mr. Finch," Skip said.

"Thanks and likewise, Mr. Valentine," Henry said, leaning in close to him.

"I'd say you're both good men," Mrs. Savage said sagely. "I'm glad Miss Grant and Jake will be okay. I've often wondered about her."

"What do you mean?" Henry said.

"She's a lovely woman, smart, too, but she's never married, and in all the many years I've known her, she's never dated or shown any interest in men. I tried to be a matchmaker once with her and the grocer, among others, but she wasn't interested."

"Maybe she had her hands full raising Jake, and no time for men," Henry said.

"Or no interest. She was devoted to her sister Annabelle and was devastated when she died. Of course, they looked nothing alike and had different last names. It was strange."

"It sounds like you're implying something, Mrs. Savage," Henry said.

"Oh, I don't mean to imply. I am happy, though, that Miss Grant has Edna."

"Edna?" Skip said.

"The new housekeeper for the Andersons over on Brooklyn Avenue. A nice woman, dark-skinned, with a kind face and bright brown eyes. She's a bit older than Jane, but also a spinster, and they seem to have become close friends. The two of them were spotted in the park, at the movies, and they took a trip to Chicago together last summer. It's raised a few eyebrows in the neighborhood and has been the fodder for some nasty gossip, but I'm glad they have each other. And I'm glad you two have each other."

"Er, yes, Skip's a good friend," Henry said.

"I may be old but I'm not foolish, Mr. Finch. I know love when I see it."

"I don't know what you mean," Skip said, his cheeks flushing a brilliant pink.

"Oh, I think you do, always choosing to sit next to each other on the sofa, exchanging warm glances, almost touching. Don't you worry, I can keep a secret, yours *and* Miss Grant's. I don't judge. You're welcome here anytime, with open arms, and I hope to see you again."

"I think you can count on it," Skip said with a grin as he took Henry's hand in his.

MYSTERY HISTORY

- Television, though still rather new and expensive, was growing fast in popularity. By 1950 approximately 9 percent of Americans owned a television set. *I Love Lucy* debuted in October of 1951. By 1959, over 85 percent of households owned TVs.
- Party lines were common in the 1940s, 50s, and 60s. A party line was shared by multiple subscribers, and anyone on the party line could pick up their telephone and listen in to someone else's conversation. Most party lines ended between 1988 and 2000. The author's grandparents had one.
- Mercury was used to treat syphilis until 1943. It was used in the manufacturing of hats up until 1941, leading to the term "mad as a hatter."
- Gabria, Mrs. Rutherford's first name, was discovered by the author while riding in his car and staring at the word "airbag" on the dash. He thought it made a perfect name spelled backward.
- Daley's restaurant at 6257 S. Cottage Grove in Chicago is the city's oldest, opened in 1892, and known for its twenty-four-hour breakfast.
- The Convent of the Immaculate Heart of Mary is fictional but inspired by convents of the 1940s and 50s.
- Cary Grant and Van Johnson were successful, handsome movie stars who were at the height of their popularity in the 1930s, 40s, and 50s. They were both rumored to be gay.
- The Allenel Hotel opened in 1911 and boasted telephones in every room and an electric elevator. Former president Gerald Ford and

his wife Betty spent their wedding night at the Allenel. It was demolished in 1964.

- Alcoholics Anonymous, or AA, was founded in 1935 in Akron, Ohio. However, in the 1940s, 50s, and 60s, people with alcohol addictions were often shunned, made fun of, and scorned. It wasn't until 1956 that the American Medical Association recognized alcoholism as a disease.
- *Angels of Sin* was a 1943 movie starring Renée Faure. To the best of the author's knowledge, it was never made into a stage play.
- The story of how Skip and Henry met, and how Henry asked Skip to dinner and Skip agreed, though he'd just eaten, was inspired by a real-life meeting that took place in Seattle many years ago between the author and a handsome radio DJ named Terry.
- Tuberculosis was the leading cause of death in the United States in 1908, which is when Giles Rutherford would have died, Ambrose being just a year old.
- Saint Thomas the Apostle Church on Elizabeth Street was built in 1842 and still exists.
- Drake's Sandwich Shop was an Ann Arbor institution for many years, lasting through the Depression and into the early 1990s. It was known for specialty sandwiches such as bacon and peanut butter, chopped green olive nut, and orange marmalade.
- On October 7 the Michigan Wolverines defeated Dartmouth 27–7. A crowd of 75,000 was in attendance, and anywhere from 20,000 to 25,000 automobiles were in the city from out of town.
- The United States entered the Korean War on June 27, 1950. The war lasted until July 27, 1953.
- Flat feet stopped being a reason for military exemption around the time of the Vietnam War.
- The first nine holes of the Barton Hills Country Club in Ann Arbor were completed in 1919. The country club remains to this day.

About the Author

David S. Pederson (http://www.davidspederson.com) has written seven Heath Barrington and three Mason Adler mysteries highlighting the difficulty of being gay in the 1940s and has been a finalist twice for Lambda Literary Awards. His second book, *Death Goes Overboard*, was selected by the GLBT Round Table of the American Library Association for the 2018 Over the Rainbow book list. He's passionate about mysteries, old movies, ocean liners, and reading.

He, his husband, and their sweet rescue cats reside in the sunny Southwest.

Books Available From Bold Strokes Books

Puzzles Can Be Deadly by David S. Pederson. Skip loves a good puzzle. Little does he know that a simple phone call will lead him and his boyfriend Henry to the deadliest puzzle he's ever encountered. (978-1-63679-615-4)

Triad Magic by 'Nathan Burgoine. Face-to-face against forces set in motion hundreds of years ago, Luc, Anders, and Curtis—vampire, demon, and wizard—must draw on the power of blood, soul, and magic to stop a killer. (978-1-63679-505-8)

Head Over Heelflip by Sander Santiago. To secure the biggest prizes at the Colorado Amateur Street Sports Tour, Thomas Jefferson will do almost anything, even marrying his best friend and crush—Arturo "Uno" Ortiz. (978-1-63679-489-1)

Mississippi River Mischief by Greg Herren. When a politician turns up dead and Scotty's client is the most obvious suspect, Scotty and his friends set out to prove his client's innocence. (978-1-63679-353-5)

Murder at the Oasis by David S. Pederson. Palm trees, sunshine, and murder await Mason Adler and his friend Walter as they travel from Phoenix to Palm Springs for what was supposed to be a relaxing vacation but ends up being a trip of mystery and intrigue. (978-1-63679-416-7)

The Speed of Slow Changes by Sander Santiago. As Al and Lucas navigate the ups and downs of their polyamorous relationship, only one thing is certain: romance has never been so crowded. (978-1-63679-329-0)

Manny Porter and The Yuletide Murder by D.C. Robeline. Manny only has the holiday season to discover who killed prominent research scientist Phillip Nikolaidis before the judicial system condemns an innocent man to lethal injection. (978-1-63679-313-9)

Murder at Union Station by David S. Pederson. Private Detective Mason Adler struggles to determine who killed a woman found in a trunk without getting himself killed in the process. (978-1-63679-269-9)

Corpus Calvin by David Swatling. Cloverkist Inn may be haunted, but a ghost materializes from Jason Dekker's past and Calvin's canine instinct kicks in to protect a young boy from mortal danger. (978-1-62639-428-5)

A Champion for Tinker Creek by D.C. Robeline. Lyle James has rescued his dad's auto repair business, but when city hall condemns his neighborhood, Lyle learns only trusting will save his life and help him find love. (978-1-63679-213-2)

Heckin' Lewd: Trans and Nonbinary Erotica, edited by Mx. Nillin Lore. If you want smutty, fearless, gender diverse erotica written by affirming own-voices folks who get it, then this is the book you've been looking for! (978-1-63679-240-8)

Inherit the Lightning by Bud Gundy. Darcy O'Brien and his sisters learn they are about to inherit an immense fortune, but a family mystery about to unravel after seventy years threatens to destroy everything. (978-1-63679-199-9)

Pursued: Lillian's Story by Felice Picano. Fleeing a disastrous marriage to the Lord Exchequer of England, Lillian of Ravenglass reveals an incident-filled, often bizarre, tale of great wealth and power, perfidy, and betrayal. (978-1-63679-197-5)

Murder on Monte Vista by David S. Pederson. Private Detective Mason Adler's angst at turning fifty is forgotten when his "birthday present," the handsome, young Henry Bowtrickle, turns up dead, and it's up to Mason to figure out who did it, and why. (978-1-63679-124-1)

Three Left Turns to Nowhere by Jeffrey Ricker, J. Marshall Freeman & 'Nathan Burgoine. Three strangers heading to a convention in Toronto are stranded in rural Ontario, where a small town with a subtle kind of magic leads each to discover what he's been searching for. (978-1-63679-050-3)

One Verse Multi by Sander Santiago. Life was good: promotion, friends, falling in love, discovering that the multi-verse is on a fast track to collision—wait, what? Good thing Martin King works for a company that can fix the problem, right…um…right? (978-1-63679-069-5)

Fresh Grave in Grand Canyon by Lee Patton. The age-old Grand Canyon becomes more and more ominous as a group of volunteers fight to survive alone in nature and uncover a murderer among them. (978-1-63679-047-3)